PRAISE FOR

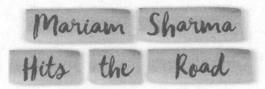

"A warm, witty, generous book, written with an enlivening
dose of what the world needs now (and always): an open heart
and mind. It was a joy keeping company with the unforgettable
Mariam, unstoppable Ghaz, and pure-of-heart Umar. *Mariam
Sharma Hits the Road*, and what a journey it is: one that plunges
the characters into unknown territory, all the while returning
them to themselves and each other, again and again . . . and
ever closer to finding home, often in unexpected places, along
the way. Absorbing, engaging—and, as Mariam's mother hopes
for her, 'a rollicking good time.'"

—TANUJA DESAI HIDIER,

author of *Born Confused* and sequel *Bombay Blues*

"Sheba Karim has done it again! Funny, heartwarming, and
achingly real, *Mariam Sharma Hits the Road* is the road trip
novel everyone needs to be reading right now."

—SANDHYA MENON,

New York Times bestselling author of *When Dimple Met Rishi*
and *From Twinkle, with Love*

"*Mariam Sharma Hits the Road*, like all great road trip stories, is about finding adventure, finding surprises, and finding yourself. It's also so much fun that it's not until the journey is over that you realize the depth of what you've just read."

—Abdi Nazemian,
author of *The Authentics*

"*Mariam Sharma Hits the Road* is hilarious and heartfelt, powerful, tender, and so much fun. Karim's writing is like a jolt of electricity on the page, leaping with truth and a perfectly dark humor. I loved these characters from page one and laughed out loud countless times. This is a beautiful book that's destined to become a road trip classic."

—Margo Rabb,
author of *Kissing in America*

Mariam Sharma Hits the Road

Sheba Karim

HARPER TEEN
An Imprint of HarperCollinsPublishers

ALSO BY SHEBA KARIM

Skunk Girl

That Thing We Call a Heart

HarperTeen is an imprint of HarperCollins Publishers.

Mariam Sharma Hits the Road
Text copyright © 2018 by Sheba Karim
For information address HarperCollins Children's Books, a division of HarperCollins Publishers, 195 Broadway, New York, NY 10007.
www.epicreads.com
Library of Congress Control Number: 2017949926
ISBN 978-0-06-244573-5
Typography by Erin Fitzsimmons
18 19 20 21 22 PC/LSCH 10 9 8 7 6 5 4 3 2 1

First Edition

To my fellow members of the Sunday Night Drive Club,
Rahim Rahemtulla and Taniya Kapoor. This one's for you.

Mariam Sharma Hits the Road

One

"YOUR BROTHER HAS just the right amount of chest hair," Umar observed. "Nice spread on top, thick line down the middle."

My brother, Shoaib, was half-naked and lunging across the living room, heavy weights in each hand. A mere year ago, Shoaib had been an annoying, scrawny, pimply fifteen-year-old. Now he was sixteen and even more annoying, but also chiseled, broad-shouldered, smooth-complexioned, and, apparently, perfectly hirsute.

"When he's watching TV and thinks no one's looking he digs at his nose with his middle finger and flicks it behind the couch," I said.

"Mmmm," Umar said.

"Did you even hear me?"

"What?"

My phone began to vibrate.

"It's Ghaz," I said, answering it on speaker. "Ghaz! Are you back home from NYU yet? And did Umar tell you he got off the waitlist at Cornell? Hurry up and join us so I don't have to drink to him alone."

"Listen," Ghaz said. "Something major happened."

"What?" Umar asked, his gaze still fixed on Shoaib. "CVS sold out of Jolen? Your favorite fro-yo place ran out of cake batter?"

"No, no. You guys, this is *serious*."

This got Umar's attention. For Ghaz not to joke back, something really had to be wrong.

"What happened?" he said.

She took an audible breath. "So remember when Brooklyn Attire came to campus and I tried out to be in one of their ads?"

"Yeah, and you got picked," Umar recalled. "They wanted you to wear a thong but in a rare moment of caution you insisted on boy shorts. Did you end up in their catalog?"

"No," she said.

Ah. That explained her distress.

"I'm sorry," I consoled her. "They obviously have no taste."

"But maybe it's better," Umar offered. "Someone in the community might have seen the catalog—I mean, what would you have done if your parents found out?"

"I didn't say they didn't *use* me," she said, bristling.

"Then what?" I asked.

"I'm not in the *catalog*. I'm on a *billboard*. In *Times Square*."

"Are you serious?" I said.

"Why would I joke about something like this?"

"Are they allowed to put your photo on a billboard like that?" Umar asked.

"The contract basically says they have the right to use my image however and wherever they want," she said.

"Really? And you were okay with signing a contract like that?" I said.

"I didn't read it very carefully before I signed," she admitted.

This was typical Ghaz, plunging in headfirst without first checking the depth of the water.

"Is it big?" Umar asked.

"It's a *billboard*!" Ghaz cried.

"Can't you ask them to take it down?" he said.

"I tried. No dice. They even told me I should be proud, because plenty of women would kill to be on a billboard in Times Square. My parents are going to flip when they find out. They're on their way to pick me up as we speak."

Ghaz's parents were conservative, and she and her mother already had a fraught and contentious relationship. There was no doubt they would react badly. Very badly.

"Maybe they won't find out," Umar suggested. "I mean, how many people go to Times Square? Besides tourists."

"Whatever happens, Ghaz, we're here for you," I assured her. "We love you and it's all going to be okay."

"Hold on. I think I'm going to throw up." A few retching sounds later: "Nope, not happening. Argh, my mom's calling me. I gotta go."

Umar and I frowned at each other across the table. Though Umar's response to almost everything was to turn it into a joke, even he was at a loss.

The prayer app on his phone went off, a sonorous male voice singing out the call to prayer.

Allahu akbar Allahu akbar . . .

"I gotta pray namaz," Umar said. "Can I use your room?"

"How can you pray at a time like this?" I asked.

"Ummm . . . times like this are when you need to pray the most," he replied. "BRB."

After he left, I scanned the wine rack, selecting what was hopefully one of my mother's less expensive bottles of red. As I poured myself a glass, Shoaib walked into the dining room.

"Whassup?" he said, removing one earbud from his ear.

"What?" I replied. "Am I not worthy of both your ears?"

He made a face but took out the other one. "Why are you drinking wine at, like, three in the afternoon?"

"None of your business, Sho," I said. Shoaib went by Sho because non-desi people couldn't say his name, which was pronounced kind of like "Shoe-abe," correctly.

"Umar is ITCWHDO, isn't he?" he asked, sitting where

4

Umar had been but taking up twice as much space.

"English, please," I said. Among Shoaib's annoying habits was his fondness for inventing acronyms.

"In the Closet with His Dick Out."

I hadn't told Shoaib Umar was gay; I worried his response would require me to actually start hating him. Plus, Umar wasn't out, so it wasn't my place to tell.

"He's not," I said.

"Then why was he staring at me like he was about to jizz his shorts?"

I had no good answer to this besides the truth. "He rarely wears shorts," I dodged.

"I have good gaydar. I knew this guy in school was gay before he even came out, and he's a jock, not your typical gay dude."

"There's no such thing as a typical gay dude."

He snorted, wiping down his sweaty pits with a dinner napkin embroidered by our deceased grandmother and tossing it back onto the table.

"Most of the gay guys in my school are all the same, theater geeks who travel in a pack and hit on the straight guys and tease us if we act uncomfortable, like we exist for their entertainment. But if we say anything back, then it's like, we're homophobic."

"I can't talk about this with you," I admonished, "because each word coming out of your mouth makes me want to stuff your face in the mountain of boogers you leave behind the couch. Which, by the way, you really need to vacuum."

"Anyway, isn't he religious?" Shoaib continued. "I mean, his phone is singing *Allahu akbar*. Can you be Muslim and gay, isn't that, like . . . what's the word . . ."

"Dissonant?" I offered.

It was true that Umar's life embodied dissonance. He tried to pray at least once a day, if not more, he didn't drink alcohol or eat pork, he believed in Allah and the Prophet and that the Quran was the holy book, and he had always been attracted to guys. His humor sensibility ranged from corny and juvenile to shameless and lewd. He'd blow 150 bucks on a cashmere scarf and then drive ten minutes out of his way to save three cents a gallon on gas.

"Hey," Umar said, appearing in the doorway. I tensed, wondering how much of our conversation he'd heard.

"Whassup, Omes," Shoaib replied, raising his hand for a fist bump, to which Umar complied.

"Would you mind leaving us alone?" I asked Shoaib. "We have something important to discuss."

"What? Is HBBC up to no good?"

"The bank?" Umar asked.

"Ignore him," I insisted. HBBC was Shoaib's obnoxious acronym for Ghaz. Hot but Batshit Crazy. She was the former, but certainly not the latter, at least not in the way he meant it. "Can you get lost, please?"

He shrugged. "I have to take a shower anyway. Hot date. Some of us have a life."

We waited until he'd gone upstairs before speaking.

"Well, I just said *du'a* for Ghaz, that everything will turn out okay," Umar said.

In many ways, Ghaz was the strongest of the three of us, and the most stubborn. But some of her strength was rooted in denial, which also made her more vulnerable. We all had our unique versions of dissonance.

"How much trouble do you think Ghaz will be in over this billboard?" I asked.

"I don't know," he replied. "How soon can we get to Times Square?"

Two

WE TOOK NEW JERSEY TRANSIT to Penn Station and the 1 train up to Times Square, resurfacing at Forty-Second Street and Seventh Avenue. Instead of asking Ghazala where the billboard was, Umar suggested we try to find it ourselves; if we couldn't find it, then maybe no one else would. We began by walking up Seventh Avenue to Fiftieth Street, and, seeing no sign of Ghaz, headed back down Broadway.

As we walked along Broadway, I became increasingly hopeful. We'd seen ads for LG watches, Broadway musicals, the Mormon church, and Coach sunglasses, video billboards for Dunkin' Donuts and a Samsung phone, but no Ghazala in sight. Maybe she was inconspicuous, tucked away on a side street, visible only if you stood directly across from her. Maybe they'd heeded her complaint and decided to take the billboard down.

We reached Forty-Sixth Street, at the small pedestrian square dividing Seventh Avenue from Broadway. At one end of the square was the TKTS booth, over which they'd built a series of red steps for people to lounge upon.

"If we go all the way to the top of those steps, we'll get a good view," Umar said.

As we crossed the square, Umar stopped so suddenly that a huffing man in a purple pinstriped suit rammed into him. His scuffed gray briefcase fell open, a stack of handwritten papers torn from a composition notebook spilling out.

"Goddamn tourists!" the man snapped. I bent down and helped him collect his papers. When I glanced up, I saw Umar hadn't moved. He was craning his neck, mouth ajar, the ends of his scarf wound, boxer-like, around his hands.

He'd found her.

Ghaz was perched above a souvenir shop, ten feet long and on her knees, Photoshopped to be even skinnier than she already was. She was wearing hot-pink boy-short underwear and a low-cut black tank top, one strap slipping off her shoulder. The thin fabric of her tank top revealed a silhouette of nipple. Her right hand cupped the back of her neck, her left hand cinched her waist, and her thumb was tucked into her underwear's waistband like she might be enticed to pull it down. Mussed tendrils framed her long, lovely face; one of them rested artfully across her collarbone. She'd been ethnically accessorized, a floral, diagonal henna pattern decorating the backs of her hands, gold bangles circling one wrist, a small bindi on her forehead. Her chin was angled down slightly, her lips seductively parted. Her deep brown eyes gazed straight ahead, sultry and inviting while maintaining a youthful innocence. She encapsulated the quintessential Brooklyn Attire girl; the young, beautiful virgin yearning to be ravished, this one with a touch of the exotic.

She looked amazing, and very sexualized.

It was quite the end to her freshman year.

A Japanese tourist, noticing our rapt expressions, paused to snap a photo of the billboard.

"Her parents are going to flip the F out," Umar breathed. "Oh, man. When she said she was going to audition, I should have told her not to do it."

"You know Ghaz. Once she's made up her mind, that's it," I reminded him. "What we have to do now is help her deal with the fallout."

Umar freed his hands from his black-and-white giraffe print scarf, the ends falling in an X over his chest. He was almost as vain about his scarves as he was about his hair, and wore them nearly every day, even in the thick heat of summer.

"This makes me nervous," he confessed.

I hooked my finger around a belt loop in his jeans, pulling

him close. "It's Ghaz. We're there for her. She'll get through this. She always does."

I said this to reassure him, but I wasn't quite sure I believed it myself.

Three

THERE WAS NO HIDING a billboard in Times Square. All it took was one member of the community to see it, and boom, Pakistani WikiLeaks. Umar relayed the community gossip to me. *Such a respectable family, father attends every Friday prayer at the masjid, how ashamed they must be. Their eldest daughter always seemed rebellious; it was their fault for allowing her to go to school in New York. Parents should keep their daughters close because once a girl's reputation is ruined it can never be restored. Look at her, naked like a prostitute and wearing a bindi on her forehead like a Hindu, who will marry her now?* No matter how piously Ghaz's brother and sister behaved, Umar said, her family would always be marked as the one whose eldest daughter posed on a billboard in her underwear. The community had a long memory, and it especially savored scandal.

The last we'd heard from Ghaz was a text that she'd reached home. Since then, silence. No response to our calls, texts, emails. I contacted one of her cousins and two of her college friends. No one else had heard anything, either.

"We have to go to her house," I told Umar. "Tomorrow, after you get out of school."

"I can't," he said.

"Why not?"

"What if it gets back to my parents that I went to her house? How am I going to explain why I ended up at the front door of the community's most *besharam*, *badnaam* girl? My parents don't even know that we're friends."

When I first befriended Ghaz and Umar, I was astonished at the number of secrets they kept from their parents, and they were equally astonished that I had such an open relationship with my mother. When I told her I'd tried pot senior year of high school, she said not to make a habit of it. When I'd started dating my high school boyfriend, she made me promise that I'd go on the pill before having sex—both conversations neither of them could even imagine having with their parents.

"Come with me, please," I pleaded.

"All right," he agreed. "But I'm staying in the car."

That evening, as my mother sipped her nightly half glass of red wine, I showed her an article that a friend from Swarthmore, where I was a rising sophomore, had forwarded me. It was from a hipster desi arts and culture online magazine called *The Sub-Continental*. The headline read "Brooklyn Attire Ad Features South Asian Female Model: Progress or Commodification?" The author wrote that though she was glad to see Brooklyn Attire use a diverse model, its ad campaign of sexualizing young women was a form of misogynistic objectification and the use of mehndi and the bindi amounted to Orientalism in the service of selling hot pants. A photo of the billboard was attached.

"Oh," my mother said. "The ad is quite provocative. Ghaz looks beautiful, but, yes, I can understand the argument that she's being objectified. How are her parents handling it? How is she doing?"

"I don't know. She's not picking up her phone. Umar and I are going to go to her house tomorrow. And she didn't know it would be on a billboard," I added. "But she signed the contract without reading it."

"Well, that was foolish. Tell her next time she receives a modeling contract, she should let me read it first," my mother said. "I hope she's okay. Girls have been sent back to Pakistan for less."

"She's eighteen. They can't force her to board a plane against her will." I had a surreal image of Ghaz, mouth gagged, hands and feet bound, in the hull of a ship bound for Karachi. But her parents would never go to such extremes. Were there even ships that went from New York to Karachi?

"You want a little wine?" my mother asked. "You look like you need it."

I nodded. I could have used a hug, too, but that wasn't her style. The stereotype of the desi mother was someone who was both loving and overbearing, who enjoyed feeding people and was adept at using guilt as a means of control. Unlike Ghaz's and Umar's mothers, mine was raised here. She'd never made dal or even baked a cookie in her life and didn't plan to. She could come off as cold and aloof, and had impressive control over her emotions. She'd gone prematurely gray, and instead of dyeing her hair black like most women would have done, she let it be. Her hair was now a striking silver, her eyes steel gray. When my friends first met her, they were often intimidated, and occasionally fascinated.

My mother sipped her wine, eyeing me over the etched rim of her glass.

"And you, Mariam?" she said. "Have you made your peace with how you treated Doug?"

Doug was my amazing college boyfriend whom I'd ghosted on this spring. "I still feel terrible about it."

"Everyone makes mistakes. Only fools don't learn from them. And you're not a fool."

"Thanks, Mom."

She waved me away. "Now get lost. I need some alone time, and then I have work to do."

Four

GHAZ LIVED IN A DEVELOPMENT of cookie-cutter redbrick colonials with small, grassy lawns. Unlike the other houses, every curtain in the front of Ghaz's house was tightly drawn. It felt ominous.

"There's no car in the driveway," I noted.

"Could be in the garage," Umar said.

"You don't think they would hurt her, do you?"

"There goes her modeling career."

"Not funny."

"I know." We'd been parked for five minutes, but Umar was still gripping the steering wheel. He was wearing his lucky scarf, soft white cotton printed with tiny navy butterflies.

"All right," I said. "Here goes."

Umar closed his eyes and began to recite a prayer. As I walked up to the house, I observed the curtains, wondering if someone was peeking from behind, noting my hesitant approach. I rang the doorbell. No one answered. None of the curtains moved.

I glanced back at the car. Umar had sunk down in his seat, but I knew he was watching.

I rang the bell again.

This time, Ghaz's mother opened the door halfway. I'd only met Uzma Auntie once. Though she'd been civil, there was a definite sharpness to her, an air of discontent. But the woman at the door seemed overwhelmed by exhaustion, pale-faced, sunken-cheeked, dark circles framing her red, weary eyes. I was actually relieved by her appearance, because the weaker she was, the less likely it was she'd beaten Ghaz.

"Salaam, Auntie," I said, trying to sound casual, unconcerned. "I'm Mariam, Ghazala's friend. Is she home?"

Uzma Auntie shook her head. "She's not here."

"Oh. Where did she go?"

"She's visiting relatives."

"Okay. She's not answering her phone."

Uzma Auntie frowned. "Why do you want to see her?"

"Uh . . . because she's my friend."

"Your friend," she repeated slowly. "Your full name is Mariam Sharma, *hai na?*"

"Yes."

"You're Hindu?"

17

"My father was—" I bit my lip. "My father is Hindu."

"Did you give her the bindi?"

I was confused for a moment, and then realized she was talking about the bindi Ghaz wore in the ad.

"No. I don't even own a bindi."

This was true, but it felt like the wrong answer, like I was playing into her prejudice against Hindus.

"Did you know she was going to do this?" she demanded. "If you're her *friend*, why didn't you stop her?"

"I didn't know about it," I answered. And I *hadn't* known about the billboard, though she had told me about winning the audition. It may have been a half lie, but to someone accustomed to telling the truth, it tasted bitter on my tongue.

"Of course she wouldn't tell anyone, so no one could tell her no," Uzma Auntie said, switching to Urdu. "She's been stubborn since the beginning, and now she's destroyed her reputation. She's a stupid girl. Better for her, and you, if you stay away."

"But—"

"Good-bye." Uzma Auntie shut the door in my face.

She may have been exhausted, but she'd still managed to commandeer the conversation.

"What happened?" Umar exclaimed when I returned.

"She said Ghaz is away visiting relatives—total lie, I think. She was upset that I hadn't prevented Ghaz from ruining her reputation. She didn't give me a chance to stick up for Ghaz, and now she might have the impression that I also think what Ghaz did was wrong. Man. People think my mother's intimidating, but Ghaz's mother . . . she's intimidating and *unkind*."

"Do you think it's wrong?" he asked.

"What Ghaz did? Unwise, maybe, given her circumstance, but not wrong. Why—do you?"

He didn't respond.

"Umar? Come on, you don't, do you?"

"No . . . I mean, I think she should live her life the way she wants, but why would she try out for a Brooklyn Attire ad campaign? It's not like she wants a modeling career, she was only doing it for kicks, and she knew it could devastate her family. But then, who am I to judge? One day, I'm going to devastate mine."

Umar rested his head against the steering wheel with one of his trademark deep sighs, his shoulders rising and collapsing with his breath. I reached over and toyed with his mass of ebony hair, so thick that when you ran your hand through it your fingers disappeared. It was the longest I'd seen it, past his ears, curling cutely at the tips.

"So what do we do now?" he asked.

"I don't know. I suppose we wait, and hope her father isn't beating her. My guess is that her mother is only lashing her with her tongue."

"Her father is shorter than her," Umar pointed out. "Though I guess that doesn't matter, if you have a baseball bat."

"Umar! Why do you have to go there?"

"Because she could possibly *be* there," he replied.

"Should we call the police?" I said.

He sat up, an indent on his cheek from the leather steering wheel. "I don't think her dad would beat her, but . . . what do you think?"

"I think if we don't hear from her by Friday, we go back to her house. If her mother doesn't let us see her then, we go to the police," I said.

"Okay," Umar agreed.

"I am a firm believer in nonviolence," I told him, "but if comes to it, we're bringing our own damn baseball bat."

Five

UMAR GOT A CALL from Ghaz at three thirty a.m. that night. She had managed to convince her somewhat sympathetic younger brother to sneak her his phone for five minutes. She assured Umar that she was okay, but her parents had taken away her phone and laptop and literally locked her in her room, and were trying to convince her to complete her college education in Pakistan and not return to the US until she was married. They knew they couldn't force her or keep her locked up, but they were so angry and freaked out they couldn't think straight. She didn't want to call the police because there'd already been enough drama. She said she'd been biding her time, planning her escape, and she'd finally figured out how.

All she needed was for us to come get her.

"We set the day and time of escape," Umar said, lowering his voice though no one else was home. "Next Thursday night, two a.m."

"That's, like, a week away!" I said. "Why so long from now?"

"Because I have a plan. It's kind of crazy, but I think it'll work."

These were not typical Umar words. Of the three of us, he was the most risk averse, the most intimate with inertia, perfectly content to spend an entire weekend in his bedroom, eating ice cream, jerking off to gay porn, watching reruns of *RuPaul's Drag Race*. The fact that he'd come up with not only a plan, but a crazy one, was a testament to how much he loved Ghaz.

"Do tell," I said.

"Well, my high school graduation is this weekend, and two days later my parents are leaving for three weeks on one of their medical missions to Pakistan and Bangladesh."

Among his many accomplishments, Umar's renowned reconstructive plastic surgeon father had also founded a medical charity. Every few years they'd visit Pakistan and Bangladesh with a team of doctors. His father would perform reconstructive surgery on women who'd had acid thrown in their faces by husbands or relatives or men they'd refused to marry, and his ophthalmologist mother removed poor people's cataracts. Whenever Umar spoke to us of his father, it was with admiration, sadness, and longing. He wanted desperately for his father to be proud of him, but his father was unapologetically homophobic. When gay marriage was legalized, he'd called it an abomination of nature.

"So by next Thursday you'll be parent free," I said. "What then?"

"We rescue Ghaz and go on a road trip," Umar said.

"Really?"

"I'm going to tell my parents I'm driving to New Orleans to attend the annual IANA convention," he explained.

"The what?"

"The Islamic Association of North America convention. It's the biggest Muslim convention in North America."

"And they're doing it in New Orleans?"

"This year, yes."

"Who will you tell them you're driving with?"

"Myself."

"They won't object to you driving alone?"

He shrugged. "I'll tell them it's something I've always wanted to do. They have no reason to suspect anything."

"Wow. I'm impressed," I commended him. "A road trip, blatant subterfuge—this isn't the Umar I know."

"Tell me about it," Umar said, and for a moment I thought he might cry. The only time I'd witnessed him shed actual tears was when we watched *Lion* and the son reunited with his mother after a lifetime apart. "It was her voice, Mars. She sounded scared. . . I'd never heard her that way. And when she said, 'Umar, please, you have to get me the hell out of here,' she didn't just mean down the block."

"Are you sure you're okay with this? Your parents will flip if they find out."

Umar shrugged. "They won't. Find out, I mean. If we're careful."

"All right. I'll call my internship and ask if I can start later."

"You mean your internship at Screw the Children?"

"Funny. It's Save the Children. And my internship isn't there, it's at Safeways."

"The grocery store?"

"That's Safeway! Safeways is an anti–child trafficking group. And I was going to waitress at Olive Garden again. Hopefully they'll let me start later, too."

"Keep the change!" Umar declared.

The Olive Garden I worked at was popular with desi families, many of whom were demanding customers and bad tippers. Last summer, an Indian family got seated in my section, stayed for nearly two hours, spilled a drink, sent back a dish, requested a full basket of breadsticks *after* they'd finished eating and then asked me right away to pack it. At the end, the father paid the check and said, very gallantly, "Keep the change!" He'd given me a one-hundred-dollar bill. The check was for ninety-seven dollars. Since I'd told Umar the story, it had become a catchphrase of his.

"Ooh," Umar said, opening the top drawer of my dresser.

"These jeans are new. I'm trying them on."

"You really need to stop stealing my jeans. I have, like, two pairs left."

"You really need to stop buying jeans that perfectly mold to the contours of my buttocks," he countered.

It was a relief to hear Umar joking again. And in a week, Ghaz would be safe, and we'd be laughing together as the open road stretched ahead, leading us toward infinite possibilities.

I even had an idea as to what one of those possibilities could be: my father had a brother who lived in Virginia. I'd never even corresponded with him, but now that we were heading south, it seemed to be a sign, a green light from fate.

"Hey, do you think we could drive through Virginia?" I asked.

Umar pulled my jeans over his hairy, skinny legs, reaching his hand inside to smooth out his boxers underneath. "Sure. What's in Virginia? Someone gay and cute?"

"Ha. I'll tell you later. Need to figure some things out first."

He walked over to the mirror, fluffed his hair, lifted his shirt, sucked in his stomach, and shifted from side to side, assessing the fit.

"Seriously, why do my jeans always look better on you than me?" I said.

Umar tossed one end of his scarf over his shoulder. "Can I help it if Allah made me sexy?"

Six

THE LAST TIME I'D TALKED to my mother about my father, she was driving me to see a shrink. One day my junior year of high school, my boyfriend, Sasha, a black-clad over-achiever who name-dropped Foucault and Beckett as I acted suitably impressed—though when I'd tried to read *Madness and Civilization* I'd immediately fallen asleep—unceremoniously dumped me.

"We get along well enough," he informed me, "but I need to be with someone who challenges me, who acts as a flint for my intellect. I want my girlfriend to be more dynamic, a defibrillator for my mind."

After nodding in agreement, I hid in the locker room and cried.

My way of processing the painful inanity that is life was to lie down, close my eyes, and breathe deeply until I began to disengage with my surroundings. After a while, I'd experience the sensation of sinking, like I was entering a peaceful, subterranean womb where I could safely allow my thoughts to meander, expand, and intensify and, on a good day, crystallize into some semblance of clarity. The day Sasha broke up with me, I lay on the couch and thought about the devastation humans were causing to the oceans; how islands of plastic trash bigger than Texas were choking the oceans; if it was weird that Sasha had never wanted me to take my bra off; why I'd baked peanut butter cookies, not once, but thrice, for this guy who'd treated me like a doormat. I didn't hear my mother come home, and she let me be, but when she returned two hours later and I was still in corpse pose, she insisted I go see a shrink.

On the drive there, I said, "Can I ask you something?"

"No need to preface a question with a question," my mother replied. "Unnecessary delay."

"Did my father ever do what I do? You know, lie still to think? Do you think I got it from him?"

Her expression was unreadable, but her accidental turning on of the windshield wipers gave away her surprise. "Not that I remember."

"Well, you would remember that, wouldn't you?"

"I believe I would."

I had no memory of my father; he'd left when I was two and

my mother was pregnant with Shoaib, but I'd always been curious, unlike Shoaib, who hated him for abandoning us, or my mother, who preferred to act like he never existed. Maybe it was because I resembled him, the same round face with a slight point to the chin, thin nose, straight across eyebrows, deep-set eyes.

My mother changed the subject, and I met with the shrink. He concluded that since my behavior was not affecting my ability to perform at school or my relationships with friends and family, I did not merit a diagnosis. I was, he said, a sensitive person who needed to occasionally disengage with the world to understand it.

After ghosting on Doug this spring, I wanted more than ever to understand my father, because I was now guilty of bailing on someone like he'd done to us. I'd become haunted by questions of what he was like, which other of his unsavory traits I may have inherited that had yet to surface.

Now, after a lifetime of wondering, this road trip presented an opportunity to seek out answers.

On the night we left to rescue Ghaz, Umar waited outside in his Prius as my mother and I said good-bye. I could count on one hand the number of times I'd lied to my mother, but I hadn't told her about my potential plan to meet my uncle in Virginia. I figured I'd tell her after the fact, if I actually went through with it.

I gingerly pressed my cheek to hers, our version of an embrace. I loved her nighttime scent, almond oil and rose water.

"Don't forget that we can recycle number six plastics now," I reminded her.

"I wouldn't dare," she said. "Drive carefully."

"We will."

"Try to have some fresh fruits and veggies every day. Encourage Umar to do so as well. I know he likes his junk food."

"We will."

"Ghazala might be going through a lot of different emotions. Sometimes it's hard to know when to listen, and when to offer advice."

"We'll do our best."

"Text me every day."

"I promise."

"And Mariam?"

"Yes?"

My mother took a step back and smiled. "Have a rollicking good time."

Seven

WHEN I OPENED THE TRUNK of Umar's Prius, I had to push his Louis Vuitton suitcase to the side to make room for my small duffel bag that said *No One is Illegal*, a freebie from one of my mother's legal conferences.

"Since when do you have a Louis Vuitton suitcase?" I said.

"Don't knock it, it's vintage," he replied. "And are you seriously bringing that backpack? It's a road trip, not a library excursion."

I'd had this backpack since freshman year of high school. It was a gift from my mother, monogrammed with my initials. Though I didn't consider myself a material person, I did have a few objects I was attached to. One was my canary yellow backpack, the other two were tucked into a pocket inside.

"I don't leave home without it." I looked at him. For his Ghazala-jailbreak outfit, he'd chosen formfitting black pants, a black V-neck T-shirt, and a green kaffiyeh scarf.

"You look like a member of Hamas," I told him.

"Like you, I believe in nonviolence," he declared, gesturing toward an object in the back of the trunk.

"Is that a baseball bat?"

"Softball. My sister used to play."

"Don't you think having a bat in our trunk will make us more likely to engage in violence?" I said. "Studies show that the minute you start keeping a gun in your house, your chance of experiencing gun violence within the home increases by thirty percent."

Umar shrugged. "We could leave it at your house."

"No, it's fine." I pointed to the navy water vessel next to the bat. "Is that a lota?"

"Yup."

In the interest of cleanliness and hygiene, Muslims, and most desis, like to use a lota to rinse their private parts after going to the bathroom. "You're bringing your own lota on the road trip?"

"Why not? There's enough space in the trunk. I don't want to walk around with a dirty stank ass if I don't have to."

"Well, between the softball bat and the lota, I guess we're pretty much ready for anything," I said.

Umar squeezed my arm. "Then what are we waiting for?"

We parked a few doors down from Ghaz's house. Aside from a dog barking plaintively in the distance, all was quiet in suburbia. Fortuitously, the streetlight closest to Ghaz's house had gone out, cloaking the sidewalk in relative darkness. As we crept along, Umar let out a cry.

"Umar!" I hissed.

"I think I stepped in shit," he groaned, lifting his shoe.

"Shhh. We'll deal with it later."

I checked the time: 1:59 a.m. We bent down low and tiptoed along the side of her house, my heart jackhammering my rib cage. The last time it had pounded like this was when Doug and I were on opposite ends of the whispering bench at Swat and he whispered, "Would it be okay if I kissed you?" The second it took him to cross the bench was the longest of my life.

Umar and I simultaneously sighed with relief when we saw Ghaz's bedroom light was on. I glanced at my phone: 2:04 a.m.

We waited for Ghaz to appear.

"Where is she?" Umar said.

"I really hope she's not operating on desi standard time," I said.

"And how is she planning to get down? Jump?"

"Too risky," I said. Except what if the time she'd spent imprisoned had addled her brain, made her so desperate to escape she would forgo common sense? I glanced around for anything that could break her fall. There were a few chairs on the deck to our right, but that might make it worse.

"Look!" Umar exclaimed.

I'd never been so happy to see Ghaz, standing in the bedroom window, greeting us with a wave and a thumbs-up. The window opened slowly, and she dangled a duffel bag outside. As it fell, Umar rushed forward to catch it, swearing as he stumbled backward, clutching the bag to his chest.

"Shhh!" I chastised him, bracing for lights in the house to turn on, for Ghaz's parents to come running into the backyard. Ghaz's mother looked like she'd stopped sleeping long ago.

But the rest of the house remained dark, and I kneeled next to Umar.

"I think I pulled my groin," he moaned.

"You didn't need to catch it," I said. "It's not like she packed her fine crystal."

"Where'd she go?" Umar said.

A moment later, Ghaz reappeared at the window holding a braided rope, which she lowered down until the end dangled several feet above the ground. Dressed in cutoff jean shorts and a tank top, she climbed out the window and, knees bent, the rope between her legs, began shimmying down like she'd spent her childhood retrieving coconuts. We held our arms out, in case, but a minute later, both her feet were on the ground.

"Let's go!" she said, and we ran like hell.

Eight

GHAZ, UMAR, AND I lived in different towns, went to different schools, and may never have become friends, if, during my junior year, I hadn't decided to try cooking Pakistani food and visited the Indian grocery store, where I'd seen an announcement for an Eid Milan party celebrating the end of Ramadan, the Muslim month of fasting, pinned to the bulletin board. Along the bottom it stated, in bold letters, *Musical Entertainment: Hamid Jafri*. Hamid Jafri was an old Pakistani singer that Naani, my mother's mother, used to listen to. After my father left, she moved in, helped take care of us while my mother attended law school. She died of pancreatic cancer when I was seven. During her illness, Hamid Jafri's voice was one of the few things that gave Naani solace.

I asked my mother if we could go to the party. She said no. I said, "Why? I know it's to celebrate Eid, but it's a banquet with music; it doesn't seem that religious."

She said, "It's not the event, it's the community that comes with it."

Because my dad abandoned us, I never knew the Hindu side of my family, and my mom kept her distance from the Muslims. My mother, brother, and I became an island to ourselves, religionless, stateless, living more like white people than anything else. I didn't grow up watching Bollywood, I never had to lie to my parents, I wasn't expected to become a doctor or engineer. If it hadn't been for my grandmother, I would hardly know a word of Urdu.

My mother's last interaction with Naani was an argument in which Naani asked, "What answer will I give Allah when He asks why my daughter isn't a Muslim?" and told my mother that because of her atheism, my mother would be turning circles in her grave as she awaited Judgment Day rather than resting in peace. Naani was the sole person who could cause my normally unflappable mother to lose her cool. Though I was only able to truly understand it later, when my grandmother died I could sense both the immensity of my mother's guilt, and the depth of her relief.

It was the guilt that made her finally say yes to the Eid banquet.

Shoaib didn't want to come, but my mother, who rarely

insisted, gave him no choice. She dragged a suitcase out of her closet and chose saris for herself and me. She hadn't worn one in so long, we watched a YouTube video to learn how to drape it. My mother struck a graceful, elegant figure in hers, but I felt like a poseur, worried that the pleats my mother had folded for me would come apart, the long bolt of silk unraveling before one thousand aunties and uncles, exposing me as a fraud.

The party was held in a Marriott hotel in central New Jersey, and they had set up a photographer to take family portraits near the ballroom entrance. When my mother, Shoaib, and I stepped in front of the white cloth backdrop, the photographer lowered his camera.

"Is your husband coming?" he asked in Urdu.

"Take the photo, please," my mother said coolly, and the photographer knew better than to argue.

The ballroom was a cacophony of guests dressed in brightly colored outfits and heavily ornamented jewelry that shimmered beneath the chandeliers, the women's hands decorated with reddish-orange mehndi. Though the bling factor was too high for my taste, many of the women, and their clothes, were beautiful. By contrast, the uncles were dressed in more sober colors: blacks, whites, browns. Like the aunties, they greeted one another with an enthusiastic "Eid Mubarak," hugging thrice, tossing their heads with each hearty laugh. Shrieking little kids chased one another around the tables, and packs of teenagers roamed the perimeter, pausing to take selfies.

There were dozens of round banquet tables, and no assigned seating. We walked along the farthest row, my mother in front in her lovely teal chiffon sari, giving off her *don't mess with me* vibe; my Bollywood-beautiful brother, in jeans and a baseball cap, glued to his phone; followed by me, wincing because one of the safety pins securing my sari pleats had come undone and was jabbing me in the waist. Some aunties regarded us strangely, like we were a lost tribe trying to assimilate into civilized society. I watched as an elderly woman, deeply wrinkled, heavily stooped, leaning on a cane, regarded my mother with a diamond-sharp stare.

I'd forgotten about the staring. When Naani saw a person who was disabled or deformed or scantily clad, she had no qualms about taking a good look, at least until the person stared back.

"When some of these women die, the last thing to go will be their eyes," I said to my mother, and she laughed.

We chose a half-empty table toward the back. Shoaib didn't look up from his phone. He didn't know Hamid Jafri; he had only a few vague memories of rapidly deteriorating Naani, a slightly loopy, absentminded though still argumentative woman who once put her dentures in his orange juice. He didn't remember the Naani who was cuddly and affectionate with us but harsh with her judgment, unwilling to go one step beyond the boundaries of right and wrong she'd created from her culture and convictions. He didn't remember how once in a while she'd tell us terrifying stories about jinn and witches right before bedtime, how he'd come sleep in my arms afterward.

It was weird, to think that I was the only holder of those memories.

The auntie closest to my mother was wearing a fancy emerald-green *shalwar kameez,* emerald-green eye shadow, emerald-green heels, and paisley-shaped emerald-and-pearl earrings. An emerald-green silk clutch embossed with crystals lay next to her water glass.

She started asking my mother questions, fishing for her status, her husband, her class, her career, her religious sect, markers by which she could judge her. My mother answered tersely, and I began to wonder if Hamid Jafri was worth all this. He was probably going senile by now anyway.

Shoaib nudged me, gesturing at the auntie with his chin. "Someone should tell her it's Eid, not Saint Patrick's Day."

I withheld a laugh.

"Your husband didn't come?" asked Auntie Leprechaun.

"No," my mother said.

"He has night rounds?"

"No."

"Not feeling well?"

"He's dead," my mother replied.

"Oh." She paused, and I thought, *at least that should end her inquisition.* "So sorry. Heart attack?"

I knew I ought to stay and support my mother, but I couldn't bear to hear the two of them speak any further about my father's "death."

"I'm going out for a bit," I told my mother, and ran off before she could protest.

Outside the ballroom, the photographer was taking a photo of a proper family: mother, father, three children, a grandmother. In the hotel lobby, three Pakistani kids were lounging on the couch playing on their devices, too cool for the ballroom social scene. One of them had a shaggy haircut and was wearing Converse with his nicely starched *sherwani*. Already a hipster and not even twelve.

Outside, I fixed the errant safety pin and began to walk, aimlessly, toward the farther end of the parking lot. The cars' windshields reflected the soft light of dusk. In the distance, you could hear the frenetic whir of a New Jersey highway.

Alexey Fyodorovitch Karamazov was the third son of Fyodor Pavlovitch Karamazov, a landowner well known in our district in his own day, and still remembered among us due to his gloomy and tragic death . . .

I had the first page of *The Brothers Karamazov* by Fyodor Dostoyevsky practically memorized. I'd picked it up off our bookshelf years ago, the cover creased, one edge slightly torn. Inside was an inscription written in elegant cursive, each word ending in a flourish. *To my dearest pari Tasneem, Love, Rahul.* Tasneem was my mother's name, Rahul my father's. "Pari" means *fairy*. My mother had highlighted some of the passages in the first three chapters; I could tell it was her from the extremely straight, double underlines, except she'd done it in purple ink. The mother I knew would never use purple ink. I didn't dare show the book to her: she'd get rid of it. So I kept it in my nightstand drawer, and tried several times to read it, but, like my mother's highlighting, I never made it past the beginning chapters. One day, I realized I had no intention of reading it, that the story of the book would remain as much a mystery as the story of my parents. Still, I kept it close, because it was one of the few pieces of my mother, my father, of their shared past, that I could actually touch.

Unlike Fyodor Pavlovitch Karamazov, my father wasn't really dead. My mother would have told us; his family would have contacted us. Though they'd never been in touch in all the years since my father left. But still, if he'd died, surely someone would have let us know.

My sari's fanned pleats had loosened and were beginning to drag along the concrete, so I gathered them with a fist as I walked, wishing I could take the sari off, wishing I'd never come here.

I heard someone cough and turned. A row away, a girl was sitting on the hood of an SUV, smoking. She was statuesque, with long, silken hair and high cheekbones, huge, deep brown eyes, and full pouty lips. Her outfit was stunning, a *lengha* woven in a shimmering spectrum of pale to dark red, hemmed with gold-bordered red brocade, a matching red brocade bodice with a heart-shaped neckline, a filigree gold necklace in a V-shaped leaf pattern, gold bangles circling her slender arms. Naani had once watched a TV drama called *Anarkali*, set in a medieval Mughal court, about a beautiful courtesan who tragically falls in love with a prince, and it almost seemed as though this girl had dropped down from the sky from another era, when all of South Asia was India, and princesses wandered palace harems.

The cigarette, though, killed the effect.

My father, apparently, had been a chain-smoker. My mother hated the smell of tobacco. I did, too.

The girl blew a stream of smoke out the corner of her lips. "Trouble with your sari?"

I looked sheepishly at the swath of silk bunched in my fist. "Never wore one before."

"I couldn't tell," she said, but then smiled. "What brings you out here?"

"It's not really my scene in there," I confessed.

She made a *hmmm* sound while exhaling, and I waved off the smoke from my face before realizing this might be insulting.

"Not a fan?" She put out the cigarette on the side of the hood, and I tried not to look too relieved.

"Big Tobacco is evil," I told her.

"They're American Spirit. Got anything against Native Americans?" she asked.

"Uh, no. Though I think American Spirit is actually corporate."

"You're one of those do-gooders, aren't you?"

I shrugged. "Kinda."

"It's okay, I think cigs smell worse than an unwashed ass-hole after a Taco Bell dump," she said. "I don't even know why I'm smoking one, except that it's giving me something else to do besides having a smile plastered on my face for five hours and pretending I'm someone I'm not, you know?"

"Yeah," I said, though whenever I'd pretended to be anyone but myself, it was due to insecurity rather than cultural restraints.

She did a sweep with her eyes, and I hoped she didn't notice my scuffed shoes. "I've never seen you before."

"We don't usually come to these things."

She extended her hand. It was decorated with mehndi, a pea-cock's tail ringed with flowers. "I'm Ghazala. You can call me Ghaz."

"Mariam."

"Mariam, excuse me while I freshen up." She reached into her sparkly gold clutch, popped two Altoids, offered me one. After liberally unleashing a pink bottle of Victoria's Secret body spray into the space between us, she hopped off the car and stepped into the chemically sweetened mist.

"Hey!" she said. "Isn't that Umar?"

I followed her gaze a few cars down, where a teenage guy was leaning against a Jeep, looking intently at his phone. He was cute, dressed in a well-tailored black *sherwani*, a black-and-red scarf loosely wound around his shoulders.

"Who's Umar?" I asked.

"His dad is this famous plastic reconstructive surgeon, a community hero, and his mom is a successful ophthalmologist. I think they donated half the money for their *masjid's* renovation. And his older sister is a doctor who married another Pakistani doctor, every parent's dream, and of course Umar is going to be a doctor, too. In a few years, he'll be the community's most eligible bachelor. Umar is such an *achha bachcha*, so nice, so polite, so smart, so fair, blah blah," she said, mimicking an auntie. "Do you think he saw me smoking? I bet he's a tattletale, the little prick."

"He seems nice," I said.

She gave me a quizzical look. "What's *he* doing out here anyway? Let's investigate."

She bent down and started moving between the rows of cars, her *dupatta* slipping off one shoulder, a diaphanous red snake trailing the asphalt. I bent down and followed her, holding up her *dupatta* so it wouldn't get dirty.

Umar was so riveted to his phone that he didn't notice the two of us comically creeping toward him.

When Ghaz drew close enough to catch a glimpse of the screen, she shrieked, "No way!" and snatched the phone from his hands.

"Hey!" he cried, but Ghaz had ducked behind a neighboring car. The other end of her *dupatta* had fallen off her shoulders, and I gathered it in my hands, smiling awkwardly as Umar looked at me with terrified big brown eyes.

Thankfully, Ghaz reappeared a moment later.

"Here," she said, returning his phone, and then surprising him again with a kiss on the cheek. "Sorry! I didn't mean to frighten you. And I shouldn't have taken your phone. But I *love* that you're watching sexycubs.com outside the Eid Milan party."

"Cubs, like the baseball team?" I asked.

Ghaz laughed. "No, cubs, like bears, but younger, and not as large, and maybe a little less hairy."

It took me a second to figure out she was referring to men. "Oh."

Even in falling darkness I could make out the pink flush of Umar's cheeks. "Please don't tell anyone," he pleaded. "I won't tell anyone you were smoking a cigarette."

"Don't worry!" she declared. "Believe me, we all have secrets, and *wa'Allahi*, yours is safe with us. Right, Mariam?"

"Right," I said.

After regarding us warily, Umar sighed deeply, realizing, I supposed, that whether or not he trusted us wouldn't change the fact that we knew.

"Gay boys are my jam," Ghaz continued. "My ex and I got along *so* much better after he came out."

After a moment of silence, we started laughing. I barely knew Umar and Ghaz, but it gave me pleasure to hear them laugh, to see Ghaz link arms with him like they were already the best of friends.

"You know," she said, "I think this is the beginning of something beautiful. There's a diner across the street. Let's get some crappy coffee and apple pie à la mode?"

Umar hesitated. "I've already been gone awhile."

"This thing is going until midnight at least. Come on, a half hour tops. Trust me, it'll be the best decision you've ever made, and if it's not, at least you got to eat pie!"

He didn't protest as she grabbed his wrist and led him away. How could he? Ghaz's exuberance could wash over you like a tidal wave, sweeping everything, your heart, your laughter, occasionally your better judgment, out to glorious sea.

But she hadn't grabbed my wrist, and so I stayed behind, uncertain, wondering if I should remind her I still had her *dupatta*.

A few cars later, Ghazala spun around, her *lengha* elegantly twirling.

"Mariam!" she cried. "What are you waiting for?"

Hiking my sari to my knees, I dashed forward to join them.

Nine

WE HAD DIFFERENT METHODS of dealing with the adrenaline spike that followed Ghaz's successful jailbreak. Umar drove fast, Ghaz lay in the back seat, kicking her feet against the roof and releasing howls of glee, while I kept my eyes closed and my palms braced against the glove compartment, waiting for Umar to feel we were far enough from danger to slow the hell down.

After a few exits on I-95, when Umar deigned to drive below eighty, and Ghaz had ceased her high-pitched exclamations, I said, "How did you come up with that rope idea?"

"Before Google, there were books," she said, "and I happened to have this one. I got it in high school, for, like, fifty cents at the Strand. I brought it with us because you never know." She unzipped her duffel bag and tossed a worn paperback onto my lap.

"*How to Escape Every Situation*," I read. "The essential guide to breaking free, whether from a banana republic or a Republican boyfriend."

"A lot of it is tongue-in-cheek," she explained. "But they did have a section on how to escape curfew, which said to make a rope from strips of bedsheets, secure it to a bedpost, and climb down."

"How did you know how to make the rope?" I asked.

"Girl Scouts! When they taught us basic knot tying, I used to practice tying knots in my mother's *dupattas* and she'd get so annoyed. I wasn't sure I'd be able to climb down, but I guess my yoga practice paid off."

We stopped at a rest area to refuel. Ghaz got out of the car, unleashed another howl, ran in place for a second, then threw her arms around us, crying, "Darling Umar! Magnificent Mais! Thank you, amigos! I love you!"

Umar grunted his assent. Though deep down he was a hopeless romantic, a sucker for a cheesy rom com, he was uncomfortable verbalizing his own sentimental emotions. His preferred method of expressing he loved you was making fun of you.

"We love you, too," I said. "I'm so glad we're all together."

As she stepped back, I scanned her for bruises but didn't see any, at least not on the outside.

"Why are you dressed like you're a member of Hamas?" Ghaz asked Umar.

"Ha! Great minds think alike," I said.

Umar tugged at the kaffiyeh scarf around his neck and rolled his eyes.

"I'm going to get a coconut water," she announced. "Requests?"

"A Kit Kat," Umar said. "And a Mountain Dew."

As Ghaz walked toward the convenience store, Umar nudged me. The attendant filling our tank was a skinny, mustached Indian uncle. He was checking out Ghaz so intently he didn't hear the click of the fuel nozzle.

"Do you think he recognizes her from the billboard?" Umar said.

"I don't know. A lot of men have that reaction to Ghaz," I replied.

"True. She has, like, the elegance of Waheeda Rehman, and the spark of Kangana Ranaut."

"Who are they?"

"Waheeda Rehman is this beautiful, famous Bollywood actress from the sixties, and Kangana—haven't you seen *Queen?*" Umar said. "*Tanu Weds Manu?*"

"You know the only time I watch Bollywood is when you make me."

He shook his head. "And to think you're the actual Indian among us."

"Half Indian," I reminded him.

Ghaz returned with a bag stuffed with drinks, candy, and chips. This time, when Umar started the car, he was careful to say *bismillah ar-rahman ar-rahim*, which he recited before driving, eating, taking an exam, or embarking on any activity in which he had a stake in the outcome.

"So where are we going?" Ghaz asked.

"New Orleans, baby," Umar said.

"Sweet! I've always wanted to go there. Wait—Napoleon and company is cool with you driving so far alone?"

Napoleon was our nickname for Umar's dad. I'd only ever seen him in photos. He was small in stature and wore impeccably tailored suits. He had been captain of his school's cricket team, class president, chief resident, navigated the world with the confidence of someone accustomed to being both uber-successful and highly respected, and expected his children to follow a similar trajectory. Umar said he became uncharacteristically quiet around him. His father didn't appreciate Umar's penchant for humor. "No one takes a joker seriously," he'd tell Umar.

"Well," Umar said, "they're not thrilled I'm driving alone. They don't get why anyone would want to drive so far by themselves. But since I'm driving to the biggest Islamic convention in the US, they're cool with the destination."

"*Subhan allah!*" Ghaz declared.

"But I have to message them and my sister every day. And none of us are posting anything on social media! They cannot know I'm with you guys."

"Girls," I corrected him.

"Witches," he said.

"Speaking of social media, give me a phone," Ghaz said. "I need to check my email. I'm sure my friends have been going nuts."

"Tell them you're safe, but don't tell anyone where you are," Umar warned her.

"What? Even my friends?"

"No one," he insisted. "I'm serious. We need to be on the DL, like, for real."

"All right, all right. How are we on dough?" Ghaz said. "I've got, like, one hundred dollars in cash."

"I've got my credit card," Umar said. "I can cover gas and our accommodations, though nothing too fancy."

"My mom gave me a couple hundred," I said, "and I've got a couple hundred more in the bank, plus a credit card."

"We're rich!" Ghaz said.

"Keep the change!" Umar cried.

Ghaz leaned forward, planting a fat kiss on Umar's cheek, then mine.

"The Big Easy or bust!" she exclaimed. "Let the road trip begin."

Ten

UMAR AND I BEGAN TO FADE, but Ghaz was wired, singing along to Madonna. When "What It Feels Like for a Girl" came on, she ratcheted it up ten octaves.

"Do you knooooow what it feeeeels like for a girl," she crooned, swaying the length of the back seat. Ghaz's voice was one aspect of her that was decidedly unbeautiful, though unfailingly impassioned. Umar was the talented crooner among us, but he hardly ever sang.

After a minute, Umar turned the volume down, but Ghaz didn't seem to notice.

"Ghaz," Umar said.

Ghaz stuck her head between our seats. "Do you knooooooow—"

"Ghaz!"

"What? You should thank me. I'm keeping you awake."

"And giving me a migraine."

"Tone-deaf people have rights, too."

"Friends, we are a half hour from Philly and we have no idea where we're staying," I reminded them. "Ghaz, maybe you can find us a place on Umar's phone?"

"Is this so I will shut up?" Ghaz objected, but started searching. "What's the budget, Sugar Daddy?"

"Fifty bucks."

A few minutes of peaceful quiet later, Ghaz announced, "Okay, I booked one for one hundred dollars a night right in town."

"One hundred dollars!" Umar exclaimed.

"You can't get cheaper than that in Center City unless we stay in a hostel. Which means sharing a room with strangers. And a bathroom."

"No way," he said. "Unless the strangers are hot guys."

"Like you'd do anything anyway! One hundred bucks a night it is."

We perked up as we crossed the Ben Franklin Bridge and the Philly skyline beckoned. There was only a handful of proper skyscrapers, concentrated in the same area but comfortably spaced apart. Even though Swarthmore was within commuting distance, I'd only visited Philly a few times. I liked it immediately. It was unpretentious, easy to navigate, a city you could breathe in.

The hotel Ghaz had booked faced the back of the convention center, on a narrow street that lacked both charm and adequate lighting. The stringy-haired male receptionist in the cramped lobby was possibly inebriated, and after sneezing into his shirt, failed to notice the huge asparagus-colored gob of phlegm he'd deposited on his sleeve.

"Ghazala?" he said. "That's a pretty name."

"Thanks," she told him.

"What does it mean?"

Umar and I exchanged an exhausted glance. It was a mistake to have Ghaz check in; tasks often took longer with her because you had to account for flirting time. Usually, she played along for a bit, longer if she thought the guy was cute, but even she was too tired to be nice.

"It means *gazelle*," she said. "And, um, there's something on your sleeve."

He raised his arm. "Would you look at that," he declared, yet did nothing about it.

"The key, please?" Ghaz said sweetly.

"I hope Booger Man isn't also in charge of cleaning the rooms," Umar grumbled after the elevator doors had closed.

"Ah, give him a break. He's working the graveyard shift for minimum wage," Ghaz said. "You'd be drunk, too."

Given the conditions down below, we weren't surprised by the sorry state of our room, which smelled like mildew and antiseptic. The toilet lid had marks like some cat had used it as a scratching post, and the shower was tiny and plastic. The sink was in the main room, in a corner next to one of the beds. Even the muddy brown color of the carpet couldn't mask its amoebic-patterned stains.

"One hundred bucks a night for this?" Umar exclaimed.

"Location, location, location," Ghaz said dryly.

"Maybe opening the curtain will help," I said, pulling back the drapes before realizing the room's only window looked out onto the interior hallway.

"Guess not," Umar said.

"Only keep one lamp on," Ghaz suggested. "Mood lighting."

"On the bright side," I offered, "things can only get better from here."

We had just changed into our pj's when the call to dawn prayer sang out from Umar's iPhone.

"Umar!" Ghaz groaned. "You have got to silence that app."

Umar only prayed Fajr when school was out, because then he could go back to bed and sleep in. He'd told me once that the first light of day rose vertically in the sky, but this was called the false dawn, because this light would disappear and the sky would turn dark again. The time for Fajr was the true dawn, which appeared as a horizontal glow, a river of light stretching along the earth's edge. He said in the old days the muezzin would climb to the top of the masjid's minaret while it was still dark, and wait for the true dawn light before singing out the call to prayer. There was something romantic about it, the muezzin in the tower waiting for the river of light.

Umar used his phone to figure out the direction of Mecca, spread out his prayer rug by the door, and started to pray. Next to me, Ghaz was falling asleep, her long lashes fluttering, her full lips slightly parted.

I reached into my backpack. In the inside pocket, tucked inside *The Brothers Karamazov*, was my only other memento of my father. My mother had thrown out his photos a long time ago, but I'd rescued this one and kept it hidden at the bottom of my sock drawer. In it, he has long, hippie hair and is dressed in baggy, light blue jeans and a rose-colored *kurta*. He's standing in front of a carved wooden doorway. Over the doorway it says *Restaurant*, to the left of that, it says *Volga* in large brown letters. This restaurant doesn't seem like it's in India, more like eastern Europe somewhere. I'd always wondered who took this photo. I guessed it was a woman, because as he's lighting the cigarette he's looking up at her, his gaze both playful and intense, his lips set in a coy half smile. We look so much alike, but the attitude of his in the photo—cocky, coquettish with a hint of smoldering—was something I'd never be able to replicate.

"Hey," Umar said, and I hid the photo under my pillow.

"How was your prayer?" I asked.

"Good. I spent most of the *du'a* asking Allah to look out for us, and especially Ghaz."

I sat up, gave Sleeping Beauty's soft cheek a gentle stroke. "She looks so peaceful. You'd never guess her parents had just kept her hostage in her room. But we can't let her pretend everything is okay, not with something as intense as this, right?"

"No," he agreed. "But let's give her some time to decompress. And don't worry so much, Mars. Everything will be better in the morning."

"Darling Umar," I said, "it *is* the morning."

Eleven

I WOKE UP TO GHAZ jumping up and down on our bed, waving a white paper bag and singing, *"Subah ho gayee, Mamu!"* *Morning has come, Uncle.*

She was already dressed, the same jean shorts as yesterday and a different tank top, hair pulled back in a slick ponytail, black eyeliner and pink lip gloss. She looked great, though she was the kind of girl who could wake up crusty-eyed with a head-splitting hangover and still look beautiful.

"What are you singing?" I groaned. "Why are you singing?"

"You've never seen *Munna Bhai MBBS?*" she exclaimed.

"Why do you even bother with the Bollywood references?" I said.

"True. By the way, it's like homeless dude central outside this roach motel." She waved the bag around my face, my nostrils flaring happily at the aroma of butter and sugar. "Chocolate or almond croissant?"

"Chocolate."

"Eat up. We have a busy day ahead. How is Umar sleeping through this?"

"He's that tired," I said.

Umar was sleeping with his mouth wide open, his dream punctuated by the occasional snort. He was still in his clothes from yesterday, his scarf crumpled underneath him. In one graceful bound, Ghaz left our bed and landed on his, straddling him and slapping his face with her ponytail while eating her croissant. It normally took her several hours and a venti skinny latte to achieve this level of acrobatics.

Umar groaned, swatting away Ghaz's hair. "Go away, witch. What's up with you? You're usually Zombie Apocalypse until at least ten a.m."

"Call it . . . the road trip effect," she declared.

"It's either that or there's cocaine in that croissant," I said.

"Mars!" Ghaz cried. "You really are becoming funnier every day. Now get up, both of you! *Chalo, utho!* We have lots to do."

"Like what?" Umar asked.

"Well, first off," she told him, "we have to get you a fake ID."

"I don't have a fake ID either," I said.

"What? You went through freshman year without one?" she said.

"I didn't really need one."

"Wow. Swat sounds like a blast. Correction—we need to get both of you losers fake IDs," she said.

"Fake IDs for what?" Umar asked.

"Uh, to go to bars and clubs, what else? We are planning to have fun on this road trip, yes?"

"Fake IDs are illegal," Umar pointed out.

"So is sodomy, in Louisiana," she shot back.

"I'm not planning on doing that, either."

"That's what you think!" she exclaimed, pushing his hair off his forehead. "Although this dandruff has gotta go."

"I can tell you something else that's gotta go," he protested, somehow managing to flip onto his stomach with Ghaz still on top of him.

She folded her arms. "What is up with you guys? It's the first day of our road trip and you won't even get out of bed! Come on, we need to celebrate!"

"Celebrate what?" I inquired.

Ghaz lay down next to Umar. "Listen, I know you guys think that I should be all traumatized, but it's cool. There are actually positives that came out of the billboard. I'm now free of all expectation. My parents aren't going to pressure me to get married because no decent Pakistani boy would marry me anyway. They aren't going to tell me not to have sex because the whole world's already seen me in my underwear. And I get to go on a road trip with my best friends! So, in short, life is good, and worth celebrating."

"Speaking of your parents, shouldn't you call them and let them know you're safe?" I suggested.

"Yes," Umar agreed, claiming what remained of Ghaz's croissant. "They're probably worried."

"I already sent them an email from Mars's phone. **I'm safe, won't be in contact for a while, peace.** *Now get up! Let's goooooo.*"

My mother texted as I was brushing my teeth.

How is Ghazala?

I wasn't sure how to answer this question. Fine, yet probably not fine? Happy, yet suffering in secret? Acrobatic, yet surely wounded?

I settled for

Okay. I think.

Twelve

TO ME, THE SCENT OF PHILLY was grilled meat and hoppy beer, which, even though I was a vegetarian, was actually kind of nice. The stretch of Spring Garden we were walking along, however, smelled like putrid heat radiating off broken asphalt, with the occasional whiff of Chinese takeout. Ghaz led us into a decrepit Laundromat at the end of a block that boasted two firearms shops and a pistol range. After engaging in hushed conversation with Ghaz, the woman behind the counter opened a back door, yelling down in what seemed to be some kind of code. She gestured for us to descend a dark set of stairs that led to a basement room with a computer and industrial-looking printers. A white guy with a fake tan and dreadlocks was sitting cross-legged on a metal stool, playing a video game on his phone that featured explosions and an occasional high-pitched shriek, which I hoped wasn't a woman dying or being assaulted.

"How many?" he asked.

"Two," Ghaz said. She turned to us. "It's one fifty each, but I bargained for two for two fifty."

"Two hundred and fifty dollars? Are you serious?" Umar said.

"Best IDs money can buy," the guy said. "Cheaper ones can be had, but those won't fool any bouncer worth his hulk."

Ghaz gave us an imploring look, and Umar sighed.

"Fine," he said.

"Cash only," the guy said, hopping off the stool and picking up his camera.

When asked to pick a state, I chose New Mexico, because that's where Doug was from. He made it sound so beautiful. In high school, he and his friends used to drive onto a mesa outside of Santa Fe to watch the monsoon lightning storms. He liked the nocturnal storms best, when the whole sky would go from black to deep purple, and there might be what he called a monotheist—a single lightning bolt—or several bolts intertwined, a radiant web of light. Sometimes it was so intense, he said, you'd feel it in your veins. I'd imagined that we'd drive onto the mesa together one day and watch the lightning dance, hold hands as our bodies turned electric.

As we walked toward the city center, Ghaz said slyly, "So,

the name on your ID, Myra Harper, do tell."

"Myra is close-ish to Mariam."

"And Harper?"

"Is Doug's last name," I admitted.

"What exactly happened between you two?" Umar demanded.

"Yeah," Ghaz said. "You kept saying you'd tell us when we were all together. Well, we're all together."

"And what about the name on Umar's ID?" I deflected. "Omar T. Generous? Why T. Generous?"

Umar blushed.

"Come on, tell us!" Ghaz insisted.

"It stands for Tabitha Generous. It's my drag name; I combined the name of our first cat, Tabitha, with my last name; Karim means generous."

"Tabitha Generous." Ghaz nodded. "I like it."

Umar pointed ahead. "You guys, Chinatown. Should we have dim sum?"

"We're in Philly! We have to eat cheesesteaks," Ghaz insisted.

"But I'm starvation nation," he grumbled. "How much farther?"

With the exception of tennis, Umar's idea of exercise was dancing in his room and traversing the mall weighed down by shopping bags. "Keep walking, Tabitha," I said.

Some friends from Swat thought Sonny's had the best cheesesteaks so that was where we went. It was in Old City, a historic neighborhood with quaint boutiques and restaurants and brick sidewalks planted with trees. When we arrived, the line was out the door.

"Gimme a phone," Ghaz said. "I have to thank my friend Emory for telling us about the ID place."

"You're not supposed to tell anyone where you are!" Umar protested.

"I only asked if she knew a good fake ID place in Philly. I didn't tell her I was *in* Philly. And now I'm going to ask her if she knows any good parties tonight."

The notion of spending the night partying when we'd barely slept was not particularly appealing, but when Ghaz was on a mission, there was little point in protest. Besides, this road trip was for her. Still, I hoped she wouldn't be go, go, go the entire time. When I'd visited her at NYU for the weekend, it had taken me almost a week to recover.

"I should warn you, Cheez Whiz makes me gassy," Umar said as we finally sat down to eat.

"At least you'll fart happy." Ghaz clapped her hands. "Fart happy! That's a great slogan. Eat cheesesteaks. Fart happy. Have anal. Fart happy."

"We're eating," I objected.

"*We're* eating," Umar corrected me, gesturing at my side order of cheese fries. "Are you sure that's going to be enough?"

"It'll do," I said.

"Was Doug a vegetarian, too?" Ghaz asked.

"Pescatarian."

"Is it true that vegetarian semen tastes better?" she inquired.

"Can we not discuss bodily fluids at lunch?" I said.

"Okay, okay. But can you at least tell us what happened?"

"Yeah," Umar agreed. "Was he your boyfriend? Were you in love with him?"

It was true I'd been putting off this conversation because I still carried so much shame over what I'd done. But Ghaz and Umar had been patient, and I owed them the truth. "Yes, and yes. We became friends in the fall, and we started dating spring semester, for almost two months."

Ten weeks and four days, to be exact, from first kiss to last.

"And? Was he a good guy?" Ghaz questioned.

"He was awesome. He was smart, and kind, and silly, and funny, and so easy to be around. I felt so comfortable with him that I even went into one of my meditative states in his presence."

"You mean your vampire trance," Umar corrected me.

"Don't vampires sleep standing up?" I said

"The vampires in *Twilight* don't need to sleep at all," Ghaz said. "But getting back to the story—if everything was so great, what happened?"

"That was the problem!" I said. "Everything was great, and I was starting to fall in love with him, and one day I got totally overwhelmed by the intensity of it all. I freaked out so badly that I left my dorm and ran into Crum Woods in my pajamas, and I sat on a rock and looked up at the moon and all I could think was, *I can't do this, it's too much, I can't do this.* And then I ghosted on him. I stopped answering his calls, his texts, his emails. I avoided him on campus. If I saw him, I'd walk the other way. After a few weeks, he gave up, and that was that."

"Oh, burn," Umar said.

"That's not like you," Ghaz observed.

"I know! But I also knew if I talked to him about it, he'd ask me for a reason. And I didn't have a good reason, at least not any that made sense. I knew he'd ask me to reconsider, and that I probably would, so I thought it was better not to talk to him at all."

"*Bechara* Doug Harper," Ghaz said. "What a way to break a heart."

Having lost my appetite, I slid my cheese fries over to Umar.

"But it's obvious why you did it," she continued. "You have a subconscious fear of commitment because your father abandoned you. Falling in love made you vulnerable to being hurt, so you ran."

Before I could respond, my phone buzzed.

"Hey," Ghaz said, picking up my phone. "You have an email from Sanjeev Sharma."

"Holy shit," I said, sitting up.

"Who's Sanjeev Sharma?" she asked.

"My *chacha.*"

"Your father's brother?" Umar said. "You're in touch?"

"I emailed him. I wasn't sure if he'd respond. Will one of you read it?" I requested. "I'm too nervous."

"Okay . . ." Ghaz cleared her throat. "'Dear Mariam, How nice to hear from you. I hope you are in good health and spirit. I must tell you I am not in contact with your father. But you are most welcome to come and meet us if you are passing near Ashburn. Please to allow us a twenty-four hours' notice. Have a nice day, sincerely, Sanjeev Sharma.'"

"Where's Ashburn?" Umar asked.

"Virginia," I said.

"And this is the first time you've reached out to him?" Ghaz said.

I nodded.

"Why now?" Umar inquired.

"Ever since the thing with Doug, I've been thinking a lot about my father. I mean, I did the exact same thing my father did to us. Half my genes come from him, and aside from a photo and the fact he left us, I have no idea what he's like. My mom doesn't talk about him, so I thought maybe my *chacha* would."

"Wow," Umar said.

Next to me, Ghaz was smiling, and I realized it was directed toward a California surfer dude guy in line who was making eyes at her. She did, however, have the ability to flirt and listen at the same time. "So you're going to ask your *chacha* what your father's like?"

"I guess so. Is that crazy?"

"Nah."

"Your *chacha* says he's not in touch with him, but he might have his contact information," Umar said. "What then? Would you contact your father?"

"Haven't thought that far."

"You don't need to. Baby steps!" Ghaz said, planting a kiss on my shoulder.

"Are you going to tell your mother?" Umar asked.

"I have to. At some point."

"Wow. So I guess our next stop is Ashburn, Virginia," he said.

I shook my head. "I'm totally opening a can of worms, aren't I? What if I find out something terrible? Maybe I shouldn't do this."

"You obviously want to," Ghaz replied. "And we'll be with you, all the way."

"Yeah." I nodded. "The road trip, my *chacha* writing back, it all does seem pretty serendipitous."

"Oh, for sure, the definition of serendipity," Ghaz assured me. "I'm glad you're doing this."

"And I'm glad," Umar said, "that at least someone's got daddy issues worse than mine."

Thirteen

DOUG AND I LOOKED nothing alike. He was a freck-
led redhead, so pale that if you pressed your finger into his skin,
it left a mark that faded slowly. When we first started hooking
up, I was so fascinated by our contrasting bodies that I'd stay up
staring at our legs juxtaposed. Dark, light. Hint of black stubble,
brush of reddish-gold fur.

But, like me, Doug no longer had a father. His died when
Doug was seven, so he had memories of him. Nice memories.
And photos, and cards, and videos, and stories he'd heard from
his mother, and relatives he was close to on his dad's side. He had
a sense of what he'd lost.

All I had was a book, a photo, and a black hole. Now I was
about to stare into the jaws of a great, gaping unknown and hope

whatever emerged didn't cause permanent damage.

We'd returned to the roach motel to nap, but I couldn't sleep. As I was about to leave for a walk, Umar whispered, "Hey— where you going?"

"Not sure yet."

"Can I come with?"

"Of course."

He got up, washed his face in the sink next to his bed, put on a white polo shirt, slim-fit navy pants, a white scarf with a pale pink paisley pattern, and cherry-red sunglasses. "Are these too red?" he asked as we stepped into the elevator.

"I don't know. Are you trying to be mistaken for a fire truck?"

"You're so cute when you're trying to be funny. Let's take a selfie." He took many, deleting all but one.

"I look pretty good in this one, don't I?" he said, as if he didn't know how handsome he was.

"Please. You could be a Bollywood star. You and Ghaz both."

"You're not so bad yourself."

I smiled. I rarely turned heads like my friends, or my mother and Shoaib for that matter, but I had a nice enough face, and a body toned from high school swim team. Unlike 99 percent of girls my age, I wasn't too hung up on my looks, though I did wonder if I'd be as curious about my father if we didn't bear such a strong physical resemblance.

"Where should we go?" I asked. "Do you want to walk to the gay neighborhood?"

"Sure."

Umar took more photos at the intersection of Thirteenth and Locust, where instead of white stripes the crosswalks were huge, painted gay pride rainbows, and then we walked down Quince Street, one of my favorites. Philly had a lot of these small, serene side streets, lined with trees and narrow, centuries-old row houses steeped with a sense of history. After another series of selfies, we headed over to the picturesque row houses of Camac Street. When we passed by a gay bar, I asked, "Should we try our fake IDs here?"

"No," he said.

Ghaz would have pushed it. I didn't. We kept walking, observing a group of three fit young guys, one white, two black, stand outside 12th Street Gym, sipping on smoothies. One of the guys had rainbow shoelaces in his sneakers, another was shirtless, his ripped abs beaded with sweat. They were laughing loudly over a story the third one was telling them.

"Do you wish you had that?" I asked. "I mean, friendships with gay guys?"

"Um, sort of. But I'm never going to be like that," Umar said.

"Be like what?"

"You know, standing on the sidewalk without a shirt on, showing off my six-pack abs, sipping on a protein shake."

"You're thinking of it the wrong way. Maybe you don't have to fit in with them, maybe you have to make space for yourself."

"But how do you do that?"

"I don't know. Figure out what it is you want, and the person you want to be, and go from there?"

He made a face. "That sounds exhausting. The only thing I know right now is that I want to be with a Muslim because I need to be with a guy who washes his ass after shit comes out."

"What about a white guy with a bidet?" I suggested.

"You really are getting funny!" Umar exclaimed, clapping my back.

"God, you two act like I was the Grim Reaper before I met you."

"You mean the Grim Sleeper, like when you go into your vampire trance."

"Ha-ha. Should we go check on Ghaz? We forgot to leave a phone for her."

"I'm impressed she hasn't insisted on getting her own phone yet. This is the girl who gets annoyed if her Instagram photo only gets one hundred likes."

"Hey, Umar?" I broached as we headed back. "Do you think it's okay I'm making us go meet my uncle? This is supposed to be a road trip for her, and I feel like I'm making it about me."

"Don't worry. It's not like she has any agenda, except having fun," he assured me.

"Well, whatever she wants to do tonight, we should do it."

"What if it's illegal?" he said.

"Especially if it's illegal."

"Dude, I can't end up in jail."

"I was kidding."

"Oh," he said. "Yeah, okay. I'm down to go crazy town."

A fashionable older gentleman in a stylish pinstriped suit and carrying an embossed leather man purse nodded at Umar as he walked past. "Nice scarf," he told him.

Judging by Umar's expression of utter delight, this road trip was already worth it.

Fourteen

WHEN WE RETURNED to our dingy room both beds were empty.

"Where is she?" Umar said.

"Down yonder."

I turned on the lamp. Ghaz was on the floor between the bed and the wall, lying in *Shavasana*.

"Why are you doing yoga over there?" Umar asked.

"This is the part of the carpet with the least stains." Ghaz sat up and bowed her head, pressing her palms together before her heart. *"Nah-maas-tey,"* she said in an American accent, to make us laugh.

"I went to take a piss and there was an actual roach in the shower!" she informed us. "I killed it with Umar's shoe."

"Why my shoe?" Umar cried. "Why not one of your shoes?"

"Would you have rather I saved the roach for you to kill?"

"No," he conceded, and stretched out on the carpet, resting his head in Ghaz's lap. She started to give him a scalp massage, her knuckles bobbing in and out of his thicket of hair. Umar closed his eyes, released a dreamy exhale.

It was nice we could have this kind of comfort level with a guy. Umar had no interest in women beyond friendship. Once we offered him the hypothetical choice of sticking his finger into a pile of feces or a vagina, and he actually paused for a moment before answering. He'd seen Ghaz's loveliest of bosoms and was neither intrigued nor interested. He appreciated female beauty, but he had no sexual interest in female bodies. Around him, we could be hairy and loose and unkempt.

"You're getting flakes again," Ghaz told Umar.

"I need to shower."

"You better do it today, because we have a party to go to tonight."

The lamp flickered and went out.

"Oh, for Chrissake," I said, pulling back the curtain to let in some of the hallway's fluorescent light.

"What party?" Umar asked.

"So my friend Emory is away for the weekend, but she said her older brother goes to Penn and is having a party at his off-campus house tonight."

"It's not a frat party, is it?" I'd only applied to schools where

Greek life played a minimal role. I didn't want to have to suck up to a bunch of cliquey girls to get into some sorority in order to have a social life; it sounded like four more years of high school.

"I don't think so. Her brother's a theater arts major— I bet it'll be a blast. And get this—the theme is Knights and Queens!"

"Like Arthur and Guinevere?" Umar said.

A naughty smile lit up Ghaz's face. "Sort of. It's a cross-dressing party. And is it not uncanny that only today were we introduced to a certain someone, who up to now had been in hiding?"

"Who?" Umar asked.

Understanding what she meant, I hooted.

"What?" he said, and then stretched his scarf over his face. "Noooo!"

Ghaz yanked it back. "You say no, but what does Tabitha say?"

"Yes!" I said.

"No way, witches," he protested.

"Come on," Ghaz pleaded. "Please please please."

"Umar," I said sternly, "you promised to be down for crazy town."

He groaned. "I am not shaving my legs."

"You don't have to," Ghaz said. "I brought my Epilady."

"Hell no!" Umar cried, pulling his knees to his chest.

"You know," I told him, "you're lucky that you have the privilege not to shave. If I walked around with my legs even half as hairy as they really are, people would be, like, 'gross.'"

"That's because it is gross," he said.

"At least shave your legs, Umar. That doesn't hurt. Come on, hairy-legged queens are the worst," Ghaz said. "What would RuPaul say?"

"I shudder to think. But I'm still not shaving. It'll be too much of a production."

"God, Tabitha is already being difficult," she said. "But you have to do your pits. I've got a sparkly tank top I want you to try."

"I'll do my pits. But no high heels."

"No heels?" Ghaz pouted.

"I'm still traumatized from my last experience," Umar said.

"Which was?" I asked.

"When I was little, I liked to go into my parents' closet and try on my mom's heels. I was walking in them and somehow I fell and hurt my ankle, and it was my dad who heard me cry out in pain. His face when he saw me, lying there with my mother's fake leopard skin stilettos half on my feet and one of my mother's *dupattas* around my head. It was the same expression he had when he came to a parents' day at kindergarten and someone offered him a slice of pizza with pepperoni."

Ghaz clucked her tongue in sympathy.

"We always ate pork growing up," I said. "Well, not when Naani was living with us."

Ghaz shook her head. "Your upbringing astounds me. Okay, so what did your dad say when he saw you like that?"

"Nothing. He left and sent up my mother. And then I got signed up for karate lessons."

"You learned karate?"

"I kept making myself puke before class until my mom convinced my dad to let me withdraw. But I've never worn high heels since."

"So Tabitha is going to be, like, a hairy-legged Birkenstock queen?" Ghaz said.

"Birkenstocks! No way. More like gold strappy gladiators. Wide width, please."

Ghaz snapped her fingers. "Rise, ladies! It's time to go shopping! Tabitha Generous is stepping out tonight!"

Fifteen

TABITHA GENEROUS WAS a good-looking broad, from the waist up. She was dressed in one of my black bras stuffed with socks, my black cotton skirt, Ghaz's sparkly gold tank top, a long gold-and-black beaded necklace, and gold gladiator sandals purchased from a discount shoe store on Chestnut Street. Her head was crowned with a cheap wig of long, straight black hair we'd found in a beauty supply store tucked inside a subway concourse.

Ghaz had done Umar's makeup to accentuate his lovely bone structure. She concealed his five o'clock shadow with foundation, shaded his cheekbones a dusky rose, emphasized his chocolate eyes with eyeliner, mascara, and glittery eye shadow, and dabbed his pulse points with Chanel.

"Well, bitches," he said, shaking his hair and thrusting out his hip. "Am I glamazon for the runway?"

"If glamazons can be hairy with back fat, then yes," Ghaz replied.

"Oh, she threw so much shade the lights went out!" Umar exclaimed in a falsetto.

"I'm not a she," Ghaz corrected him. "I'm Sukhinder Singh."

For her drag outfit, Ghaz had traversed the city. She'd bought a men's *shalwar kurta* and a dark yellow turban for her head from an Indian store, a long black beard from a costume store, added an eyeliner mustache, and voilà! A Sikh uncle.

"Hopefully no one will mistake you for a Muslim and try to kill you," Umar said.

"Ha-ha."

"By the way, Mars's mustache is lopsided," he pointed out.

As usual, I'd put the least effort into my clothes. I was wearing my own jeans and one of Umar's shirts and a baseball hat I'd found that had a photo of the Liberty Bell and said *Come to Philly for the Crack!*

"I should just hold a photo of me from sixth grade in front of my face," I said. "I had a great mustache then."

Ghaz evened out my mustache with blunt black pencil eyeliner. "Much better," she said, squinting at my upper lip. "Okay, let's take pics!"

After making us swear that these photos would stay between the three of us, Umar held up his phone. "Everyone say, the family that drags together stays together!" he exclaimed.

Our photos began tastefully and quickly deteriorated, like one with each of us holding one of Umar's boobs, which then turned into five minutes of readjusting the socks until they were more or less even.

It took forever to walk the few blocks to the Market Street SEPTA stop because we kept posing for pictures, even taking photos inside random stores we passed. We went into a store called Asia Supermarket and Ghaz posed lewdly with long, packaged strips of seasoned squid that said *Big Squid* in large letters. We went into Burlington Coat Factory and made Umar strike serious poses dressed in faux furs and trenches. We went into CVS and Ghaz bought a bag of lollipops, which she handed out to people on the street, to their great amusement and confusion, welcoming them to the City of Brotherly Love.

It was Umar, though, who got the most attention—catcalls and "hey, babys" and comments about his breasts and hairy legs and his ass, which, yet again, looked really good in my clothes.

As they descended into the subway station, Ghaz linked arms with him and started to sing in a desi accent, "Do you knoooow what it feels like for a girl."

"Your singing voice sounds better in Indian," I told her.

Umar's phone rang.

"Shit," he said, stopping in the middle of the stairway. "It's my parents."

"Ignore."

"They're calling from Pakistan; I have to get it."

"Hello?" he answered, running back up the steps. "*Salaam alaikum.* I'm fine. Yes, I'm in Philly. You guys okay? *Achha.* Don't worry. I like driving by myself. Huh? I listen to audio-books. Which ones am I listening to?" He frowned, brushing his wig from his eyes and picking at a clump in his mascara. "Uh, all the Harry Potters. Tonight? Nothing, I might go see a movie. I told you why, I've always wanted to do a road trip alone. So, I have to time to think, and see our great country. No, it's not weird. Listen, I'm stopped at a red light. I will. I will. *Allah hafiz.*"

Umar returned his phone to the back pocket of his skirt, took a deep breath, wiped the sweat off his upper lip.

"Are your parents okay?" I asked.

"Yeah, they're fine. They still don't get why I'm on a road trip alone. My mother told me not to talk to strangers, like I'm twelve years old."

"You'll always be her darling Umar," Ghaz said. "At least they're worried about you. My mother wrote me two lines: *'Please don't do anything stupid, and don't think you can come home if you get into trouble.'*"

"What?" I gasped. "You didn't tell us that."

Ghaz shrugged. "My mother's been wanting to write me off completely, and now she finally can."

I didn't understand how she could say something so unnerving with such nonchalance.

Umar had barely opened his mouth when Ghaz put her hand up. "Seriously, guys, it's cool. What I need to do now is to not talk about it. What I really need to do now is dance. *Capiche?*"

I didn't see how it could be cool, but I knew any attempt to force Ghaz to talk when she was desperate to dance would probably result in her storming off into the Philly night. "Okay," I said. "Let's go dance."

We got off at 40th Street Station. As we approached the Penn campus, the fried chicken and cheap Chinese joints and ramshackle storefronts began to give way to recently constructed buildings adorned with glass, trendy eateries with floor-to-ceiling windows, with the occasional odd juxtaposition that happens during gentrification, like a fancy fresh grocer across from an old, slightly decrepit McDonald's.

The party was at a house a few blocks west of campus, on a residential street lined with tall brick row houses that may once have been stately but had been subject to years of student neglect. It was easy to tell which house: a guy wearing a blond beehive wig, pink prom dress, gold lamé sneakers, and a sash that said *Queer Every Day* stood at the top of the steps.

"Hi," Ghaz said. "We're here for the party."

"And here I was hoping you always dressed this way," he joked. "You guys got five bucks for the punch fund?"

"Anything for punch," Ghaz said. "What's your name?"

"Constance," he replied. "Constance Lee Cumming."

Ghaz laughed so hard she snorted. "That's terrible!"

"I know. And it's not even original—I stole it off an actual queen, but don't tell anyone." He winked.

"Your real name doesn't happen to be Tyler Morris, does it?" Ghaz asked.

"It does—do I know you?"

"I'm friends with Emory!" Ghaz cried, immediately hugging him. "We have to take a photo and send it to her!"

After another brief photo shoot, we entered a narrow hallway crowded with people. A black guy was posing for photos on the stairwell, rocking a tight leather minidress and four-inch heels. As he leaned seductively over the rickety banister, one knee bent, his pink wig fell off, landing on Ghaz's turban.

"What are you going to give me for this, honey?" she yelled up, waving the wig.

"Hey!" someone shouted. "Bin Laden's back from the dead!" Ghaz frowned.

Like some Bond girl, the black guy slid down the banister and jumped off, executing a perfect landing in his stilettos.

"Ignore whoever that was, and dance with me," he said, reaching for Ghaz's hand and leading her into the living-room-turned-dance-floor, where an androgynous DJ was playing Robyn. Ghaz replaced his wig and they began frenetically dancing.

"I'm starvation nation," Umar told me. "Let's find the kitchen."

We headed down the hallway, through a doorway decorated

with sparkling streamers, and into the kitchen, where a pale red punch was being served from a whale-shaped plastic baby tub, a rubber duckie floating in it.

"Do you think that's hygienic?" Umar said.

"Maybe," Ghaz said, coming up behind us, a drink already in her hand, "but it's definitely not halal."

Umar stuck his tongue out as she toasted him and drank. Meanwhile, I was trying not to stare at the couple engaging in an intense make-out session next to the fridge, hands, legs, everywhere.

"Look at them," Ghaz whispered. "Hot."

When I turned sixteen, my mother asked if I wanted a vibrator for my birthday. Though I liked that she was sex-positive, the idea of my mother giving me a vibrator horrified me so I said no. I still hadn't bought one for myself. I'd only achieved orgasm four times. The first two times were on my own, and required a lot of labor; the others were with Doug. The second time I came with him, I almost told him I loved him. A few days later, I had my freak-out.

I couldn't think of sex without thinking of Doug.

"Brownies!" Umar exclaimed, zeroing in on a plastic-covered plate of brownies sitting on the laminate counter next to the stove. "There's exactly three left!" he said, handing them out. We insisted he eat the biggest piece, since he was so hungry.

Umar took a bite. "Mmmm . . . chocolate chips," he said happily.

I nudged Ghaz. "Look."

An actual Sikh guy had walked into the kitchen. His beard was several inches long, he wore a powder blue turban, and was in drag from the neck down, his sari so sheer you could make out the dark oval of his stomach hair. He'd tied the sari so it hit above his ankles, and was wearing embroidered leather sandals. His cheeks were hot pink from blush, and he'd pinned a gold and rhinestone brooch to his turban.

"He's kinda hot," Ghaz muttered.

He saw Ghaz, raised his eyebrows, and smiled.

"*Sat sri akal,*" he greeted her.

"*Sat sri akal, behen ji,*" she replied. "A sweet girl from the *pind* at a party like this?"

"Are you actually Sikh?" he asked. "Because you tied your turban terribly."

"I know," she apologized. "I'm Punjabi, but Muslim."

"Can't take you home to my parents then," he demurred.

Ghaz took a step closer. "Who said anything about parents?"

"Love marriage?" he said.

"Who said anything about marriage?"

The guy's eyes lit up, as most men's did when Ghaz started flirting with them. "Christmas for their balls," she called it.

"Let me get this straight," Umar said to me. "Our friend who is dressed like a Sikh guy is flirting with a guy who is Sikh but dressed like a girl."

"Yup," I said.

Ghaz brought him over to introduce us. "Meet my friends: Umar, though you can call her Tabitha, and Mars. This is Jug, short for Jugdeep, except tonight he's Jugni."

"You go to school here, Jugni?" Umar asked.

"Yeah. I go to Wharton, but I promise I'm not an asshole," Jug said.

We laughed.

"Lemme guess? You plan on saving the world's poor through microfinance," Ghaz declared.

Jug's eyes were practically shining now. "Actually . . . ," he began, and started laughing.

As Ghaz and Jug amped up their flirting, Umar enlisted me to help him hunt for food. As I opened a high cabinet, my hand began to tingle. Frowning, I lowered it.

"Do my hands seem okay to you?" I asked Umar, who was on his tiptoes, reaching for a bag of Doritos. "My fingers are all tingly."

"They seem fine," Umar said, holding my hands in his, his thumbs rubbing my palms. The tingling stopped. "Are you okay?"

"Yeah, though I do feel a little weird."

"Here, have some Doritos. They're expired, but they're Cool Ranch."

"Mars! Umar!" Ghaz exclaimed. "Guess what? Jug is captain of a bhangra team!"

"Respect," Umar said.

"Oh, it's on now," Ghaz said, pulling Jug's hand.

"What is?" he replied.

"Dance-off."

Ghaz borrowed Umar's phone and led Jug to the dance floor, the rest of us following, where it took her approximately forty-five seconds of flirting to convince the DJ to play a Bollywood bhangra song called "Sadi Gali," which I knew because Umar had played it a few times. Jug and Ghaz quickly cleared the floor with their dancing, Ghaz bouncing in a low squat, occasionally kicking her feet out as she moved in a circle around Jug, who was playing the female role, bouncing on one foot, head tilted, gesturing with sweeping hand movements. Then Ghaz leapt up and they began mimicking each other's steps, jumps, twirls, arm movements. Everyone was clapping and cheering on Jug and Ghaz's effortless bhangra synergy. I wasn't sure if I was more impressed by their moves or how well Jug's sari was staying on.

And then the same voice from before cried, "Bin Laden can dance!" Thankfully Ghaz didn't seem to hear. I scanned the room to find the douchebag, but this made me a little dizzy, so I headed to the wall, bracing my body against it. As I took a deep breath, I had a visual of oxygen as a blue musical wave flooding my nostrils, then bypassing my lungs to instead fold itself into a soft, rhythmic cushion around my heart. *See?* my heart said. *I know you're meeting your father's brother tomorrow but now I'm nice and protected. Thanks, oxygen!*

My organs were talking nonsense.

"I feel so light on my feet," Umar said, dancing up to me. His wig was crooked, an empty Doritos bag in his hand. "Like this body was made to groove."

The shadows on the opposite wall cast by the disco lights had begun swimming like minnows, in sync to the music.

"The brownies," I said suddenly.

"What?"

Worried he might freak out, I shook my head. "Nothing. We're all good. Everything's good."

Ghaz and Jug finished their dance-off, and Ghaz ran over to us. "What do you think his beard would feel like brushing against my outer labia?" she asked.

Before we could respond, the song "Chandelier" came on and Umar let out a cry of utter happiness. One moment he was beside us, the next he was on fire in the middle of the dance floor, shimmying and working it left and right, touching himself like he was his own greatest love, down to the floor and up again, one move flowing gracefully into the next, whipping his long black wig, glittery eyelids closed, lips parted as though expecting a kiss, grooving like no one else was watching, though everybody was, except for Ghaz and Jug, who had started making out. I tapped Ghaz on the shoulder because I knew she wouldn't want to miss it; we'd seen Umar dance plenty of times, but never with such utter abandon.

Ghaz released Jug and grabbed me and we laughed and hugged each other as we marveled at Umar.

When the song ended, Ghaz and I enveloped Umar in an ecstatic hug, and I saw him.

Doug.

Red hair, pale skin, leopard print leotard. I moved toward him, having no idea what I might say, only that I had to get closer, but he turned around, and it wasn't Doug after all. Not even close, except for the hair.

"Hey, guys," I told Ghaz and Umar, "I'm going to go outside for a bit."

I went back through the kitchen, where the hot-and-heavy couple were no more, down the steps into the backyard, selecting the plastic chair that seemed most stable. It was a cloudy night, no hint of stars, no glimpse of moon. I never paid much attention to the night sky until I started dating Doug. On our second date, he arranged a midnight picnic amid a grove of holly trees, and we lay on his New Mexican blanket and held hands and he talked to me about astronomy.

"Who died or broke your heart?"

I looked up, startled. I'd neglected to notice the drag queen presiding over the backyard from a rickety rocking chair a few feet away. She was a proper queen, a true glamazon, dressed in a low-cut, silver lamé jumpsuit, silver wedge boots, and an expensive wig of tumbling blond curls.

She smiled at me, her teeth white and shining.

"A few months ago, I ghosted on this really amazing guy," I confessed.

"Amazing how?" she said, flicking a speck of dirt off her boot with her bloodred pinky nail.

"He used to play this game, you know, where you'd make up dance moves based on real-life activities, except he would come up with totally insane ones. I mean, inane, not insane. I guess maybe a little insane, too." Sober Mariam would never blab like this to a stranger, but then I was far from sober.

"A queen's always on the lookout for new moves," she said, batting her rainbow lashes. "Show me."

"Okay." I lay down on the ground, my palms pressed together over my head, and began to wriggle back and forth aimlessly. "Snake in need of GPS."

The queen snorted.

I bent my arms at the elbow and started flapping them as I jerked my body about. "Electrocuted chicken."

"Mmmm hmmm," she said.

I squatted down, grunted, awkwardly kicked my legs up one at a time. "Fiddler on the Roof takes a crap in the woods."

She snickered. "Those are dumb as hell."

"I know!" I said, standing up. "He did it because it made me laugh. I can't believe I let him go. I'm so stupid."

"What's your name, stupid?"

"Mariam."

"*Enchanté*. I'm Enya Buttocks."

"Ha. Nice to meet you."

"How old are you?"

"Eighteen."

"That's okay then," she said, removing a cigarette and a Zippo decorated with crystals out of her clutch. "You're supposed to be stupid."

Of all the things anyone had said to me about what had happened with Doug, this was among the most comforting. I felt like hugging her, except I didn't want to mess up her outfit.

She lit the cigarette, crossing her legs as she blew the smoke behind one shoulder. "You'll fall in love again, sweetheart."

"Thanks. You're very elegant," I told her.

"Don't I know it. All this takes work," Enya said, her costume-jeweled hand gesturing from head to toe.

Umar came outside, drenched in sweat. "There you are! I lost one of my tits on the dance—oh, wow," he exclaimed, looking admiringly at Enya.

"This is Enya Buttocks," I said.

"I saw you dancing," Enya told him. "You were good enough to eat."

Umar blushed.

Constance Lee Cumming appeared in the kitchen doorway. "Enya!" he cried. "You're up."

"Showtime." Enya stood up, fluffing her curls, pausing to tell Umar, "Next time tie a bunch of rice in a knee-high stocking and stuff your bra with that," before sashaying away.

"Thanks!" Umar replied, taking her place on the rocking chair.

"Are you okay?" he asked me.

"Yeah. You?"

"Yeah. I had the best time dancing. I didn't even know I could dance like that."

"Well, now Ghaz knows, and she'll keep asking for it."

Umar frowned, picking at his lips. "Everyone's wearing so much glitter I feel like I keep eating it. Tomorrow morning, my shit is going to sparkle."

I laughed.

"Do you think only Tabitha Generous can dance like this?" he continued.

"You're the same person underneath the makeup and clothes."

"I can't stay hidden forever, Mars. I gotta dance. I gotta live."

"You will," I assured him. "You *are*. Come on, let's go see Enya's show."

Enya Buttocks had both hands on the fireplace mantel, her back to the cheering audience as she gyrated her hips almost to the floor, then shifted sideways, tossing her head back and kicking one leg into the air before flipping around to face us, legs spread widely, lip-synching to a song about a homeless woman and launching into a dance routine. Ghaz watched from on top of Jug's shoulders, his hands massaging her thighs as she drummed her palms against the ceiling and hollered with the audience.

When Enya cried, "Conga line!" we quickly got into

formation. As we danced out the front door, another queen, her enormous cleavage spilling out of her fur-trimmed dress, handed out balloons. Our merry, ballooned conga line danced down the middle of Forty-Second Street, singing the song's refrain with the wholehearted enthusiasm of the drunk and young.

La da dee la dee da

In front of me, Umar was doing an ass-shake, and I was laughing so hard I was worried I'd run out of breath.

As we danced our way back down the block, a cop car, its lights flashing, came to a stop outside the party house. Umar pulled out of line, alarmed.

"We gotta go," he said.

"Relax," Ghaz said. "They'll probably tell them to turn the music down."

"There's alcohol and we're underage. I'm leaving," he insisted.

"We can go to my place," Jug offered.

"Ah, we can't," Ghaz said. "We have to be up and out tomorrow; we have an important meeting in Ashburn, Virginia. I had so much fun, Jug."

"Me, too," he murmured.

As they locked lips, I realized Umar had already taken off. I tapped Ghaz's shoulder and pointed at Umar disappearing around the corner. I'd never seen him accelerate so quickly.

"Bye!" Ghaz told Jug, blowing him one last kiss.

We chased Umar down Spruce Street, until he finally

stopped in front of a Wawa, then doubled over and lay down on the sidewalk, his hairy legs splayed as much as his skirt would allow, his balloon still in his hand.

"I'm going to die," he gasped.

Ghaz kneeled next to him, resting her palm on his forehead. "Inhale sloooowly, exhale even slooooower. You really need to start playing tennis again."

"I'd still kick your ass," he said.

"Looks like someone's recovered," she said, giving him a gentle poke in the side.

He sighed, rubbing his feet. "My gladiator sandals are giving me blisters. And when the conga line broke up, someone grabbed my ass."

"It's not easy, being a woman," I said.

"What was that song we were dancing to?" Ghaz asked, humming the refrain.

I googled it. "'Gypsy Woman' by Crystal Waters. It came out in 1991."

"Old-school," Umar said. He cleared his throat. "I need to hydrate, stat."

I bought some Vitaminwater, and when I returned Umar and Ghaz were seated on the sidewalk, their backs against the window of Wawa. We drank our waters in silence, Ghaz and I leaning our heads on Umar's shoulders. It was nice to be outside, catch our breath, even if it was on hard cement.

"Well, that was a rollicking good time," I said.

"What?" Ghaz replied.

"Never mind. Why didn't you go home with Jug?"

She shrugged. "I really liked him, but I didn't feel like hooking up hardcore. Plus, can you imagine doing the walk of shame like this?"

We laughed.

Ghaz grabbed Umar, giving him a noogie on the head as he squealed. "And why have you been hiding those moves from us? You were amazing! You brought down the house!"

"Something was different about me tonight," Umar agreed.

"Oh, it was indeed, Tabitha Generous," she said.

"Those had to be pot brownies," I said. "My body was on its own trip, and I demonstrated a few of Doug's silly dance moves to a complete stranger named Enya Buttocks."

"But those brownies tasted so good," Umar said.

"That's because they had so many chocolate chips," I said.

"That's probably *why* they had so many chocolate chips," Ghaz deduced. "Should I ask Emory to find out?"

"No," I said. "It's better not to know. Then there's more possibility."

"You're right," Ghaz agreed. "Because maybe it wasn't pot brownies. Maybe it was something else."

"What?" we asked in unison.

She grinned. "The road trip effect."

We hailed a taxi, singing *la da dee la dee da* all the way.

Later, as we lay in darkness in our roach motel, I said, "You know what Doug told me once? Out in space, there are these two suns orbiting around each other, except they're spinning faster and faster and coming closer and closer. In a few years, they're going to crash into each other, and the explosion will be so intense we'll be able to see it from earth with our naked eyes. And from that explosion, a new star will be born, and it will be the brightest star in the sky."

"Mmmm," Ghaz said, rolling onto her side.

Umar started to snore.

It was weird, to think in the far reaches of the universe, two suns drew closer and closer in a cosmic dance of love, while down here some people tried to get as far away from one another as possible. My father from us, me from Doug, Ghaz from her parents. Then there was Umar, sometimes running away from his sexuality, sometimes running to it. And now me, chasing after my father. All three of us in flux, our friendship serving as an emotional anchor. If any of this ended in an explosion, I hoped it would be one that made us burn brighter, stronger than before.

Sixteen

"ONLY TEN MILES to Mera Lund House!" Umar sang.

He was referring to the Maryland House. Mera Lund means "my dick" in Punjabi. Though his wordplay was completely juvenile, it gave him such delight that Ghaz and I couldn't help but smile.

But when we entered the bright, airy food court, Umar's excitement quickly dissipated. "There's no more Roy Rogers."

"Roy Rogers? Are you kidding me?" Ghaz said.

"I love Roy Rogers. That's why I wanted to come to Mera Lund in the first place."

"You love anything that's fried in a vat," I reminded him.

He sighed. "I guess I'll get some Wendy's."

I got a table, and when they returned with their trays of

spicy chicken sandwiches and Frostys, Umar's forehead creased with concern. "You really aren't eating anything?" he said. He was like an auntie in that way, always wanting to make sure people ate.

"She's nervous about meeting Sanjeev Uncle," Ghaz explained. "She probably didn't even sleep last night."

I actually slept really well, though I suspected this was due to the alleged pot brownies.

Umar waved his fries at me. "You have to eat something."

I accepted a fry to appease him.

"So how long do you think Jug's hair was?" Ghaz asked. "Like, down to his butt?"

"Are you sad you didn't find out?" Umar said.

"Nah. A lot of times the promise of something is better than the actual experience. Like, when you leave it at a kiss, the sex could have been anything—soft, sweet, hardcore, kinky. But if you actually do it, then that's it. You know. But I did show him a photo of the billboard."

"What did he say?" I asked.

"He said, 'Wow! What did your parents say?'"

"Did you tell him?"

"Did I need to? Anyway, let's talk about you." Ghaz set her tray to the side and folded her hands. "Tell us, Mariam, what are your thoughts on meeting your uncle today?"

"I'm nervous."

"And what do you hope to accomplish?"

"Learn something about my father. Maybe gain some insight into myself."

"Hmmmm . . . you mean as to why you bailed on such a kind man as Doug?" Ghaz pushed imaginary glasses up her nose. "You know, it could have something to do with your mother, too. She never had another serious relationship, so you don't have anything to emulate, plus maybe you've internalized her reluctance to fall in love again. Thank you, that'll be two hundred dollars." She picked up a fry and dropped it onto her tray.

"Oooh, fry drop," Umar said.

"So, am I right?" she asked me.

Ghaz had no issue trying to force our hearts bare while keeping hers veiled. She'd give us the occasional glimpse—some Moroccan guy who'd broken her heart, a terrible thing her mother had once said, that she'd tried out bulimia in high school but was luckily really bad at making herself throw up—but the conversation, if you could call it that, would always end with her insisting all was "cool." Ghaz was both unabashedly open and fiercely guarded. She'd inform us immediately of the size and consistency of a pimple she'd found on her ass, but not if she was hurting.

"Well, everything you said makes sense," I agreed. "Now how about we turn the tables and play psychologist on you?"

Ghaz made a face. "That wouldn't be any fun."

Umar stood up. "I have to take a big Frosty dump."

"I love it when you talk sexy," Ghaz quipped.

Umar belched. "Meet you guys at the car?"

"Can you please change the station?" Ghaz asked.

We were listening to an NPR piece on how carbon emissions were contributing to rising nutritional deficiencies in many developing countries.

"I happen to find this interesting," I said.

"It's depressing," she replied.

"You can't avoid things because they're depressing," I argued. "Especially things that—"

"Hey, look to our left," Ghaz said. "Salafis!"

By that she meant ultraconservative Muslims. I glanced over. The father had a long beard and a white skullcap, and the wife was in a black niqab, only her eyes showing. There were two nerdy kids in the back, watching a movie.

"At least my parents aren't like that," she said. "They probably would have killed me by now."

"You know," Umar said, "my dad went over to this Salafi type guy's house for dinner, and they served the food on the floor because they said Prophet Muhammad used to eat on the ground so it's sunna."

"God. Did the guy get to work by camel, too?" Ghaz asked.

"Ha. Then the guy said something about how ISIS is doing bad things but some of their goals are good, and my dad got the hell out. I hadn't seen him so depressed in a while, and then he kind of stayed depressed. ISIS and Islamophobia are turning him into a big pessimist. The only thing that really cheers him up these days is his work, and his grandkids. He's way more playful with them than he ever was with us."

"Do you think it's true what your dad told you?" Ghaz asked Umar. "That's there's an FBI mole in every masjid?"

"Of course it's true. Probably more than one. And not only in the masjid. Didn't you hear about that thing a few years back, when the NYPD was spying on Muslim communities? They sent spies to infiltrate the Muslim Students Association at NYU and Columbia and even colleges out of state, like Yale and UPenn. One of the spies went on an MSA whitewater rafting trip."

Ghaz laughed. "Dude, who was the FBI mole on the MSA whitewater rafting trip? The quiet one taking notes in the back of the bus? Or was he like, 'Pass the s'mores, and hey, anyone want to build a bomb with me? Let's see some hands.'"

"You joke, but who knows?" Umar said. He took the civil liberties issue pretty seriously, given the stories his father told him about things that had happened to members of the masjid. He and my mother had even had a few conversations about it.

But Ghaz and Umar loved to push each other's buttons.

"Do you think the FBI has tapped our car?" she exclaimed. "Hey, FBI, CIA, NSA, if you're listening, no reason to be concerned! We're just three crazy Muslims, up to no good!"

Umar frowned. "That's not funny. This stuff is serious."

"I agree," I said, moving quickly to dispel any potential tension. "That was neither funny, nor accurate, as I am half Muslim and half Hindu and not really either."

"Mars the mutt!" Ghaz said. "I mean, the only proper Muslim in this car is Umar, and he loves cock."

I tensed, wondering if Umar was going to flow or blow.

"Mera Lund!" Umar cried, and we burst out laughing.

Seventeen

ASHBURN, VIRGINIA, IS VERY CLOSE to Dulles Airport. The closer we came to our destination, the less we spoke, listening instead to the roar of jet engines and the Australian-accented Google Maps voice announcing directions. As we entered my uncle's gated community, Ghaz attempted to lighten the mood.

"So," she began, "it appears Sanjeev Sharma has achieved the desi immigrant dream. Those gates keep the riffraff out—the only black people living here are like a middle-class version of the Obamas! Here to our right is the fancy clubhouse, where you can host your big desi functions. And here is a man-made lake with a spurting fountain, a sure sign that you have arrived.

And look at the paved path around the lake—perfect for those auntie and uncle evening walks, where you walk at your usual pace but move your elbows quickly and call it exercise. And the houses—such nice exteriors, two stories, attached garage, sure to impress your visiting relatives. Look, there is an auntie walking her dog. A lot of desis live here, but they are the assimilated kind—not the 'too much coconut oil in the hair, going around smelling like curry' kind, you know what I mean? What—not even one laugh?"

"Ha-ha," Umar said.

"I think I'm going to throw up," I said.

"You can still back out you know," Ghaz reminded me.

I shook my head. "We've come too far. If I leave now I'll never forgive myself."

"Those are some pretty nice tennis courts," Umar noted.

"We should have a code word," Ghaz suggested. "In case it doesn't go well and you need to leave."

"Like what?" I said.

"How about 'Enya Buttocks'?"

Umar and I looked at her quizzically. "That was a joke!" she exclaimed. "Man, I've never seen you two so serious. Mars, I understand, but Umar?"

"This is a momentous occasion," he replied.

"Tabitha," I said.

"What?" Umar said.

"If I need to get the hell out, I'll say, 'Tabitha.' That's the code word."

"Your destination is on the right," announced Aussie Google Maps.

We exited the car, stretched our limbs. Even though it felt morally dubious, I had instructed that we all dress in the kind of conservative, preppy attire that would garner auntie and uncle approval, because I wanted my uncle to have a good impression of my friends and me. Umar had chosen navy pants, a white polo shirt, expensive leather oxfords with no socks, and his navy butterfly scarf, the longer end thrown over his shoulder. He looked like a handsome desi metrosexual New England prep student. Ghaz was in a simple, deep purple dress. Though knee-length, she insisted it was modest enough because most Hindu families even let their daughters wear shorts. Her hair was pulled back in a ponytail, no makeup except lip gloss. I was wearing black pants and a striped button-down shirt, the same outfit I'd worn to most of my internship interviews.

The small American flag attached to my uncle's mailbox was crooked. As Umar paused to fix it, I reached for Ghaz's arm to steady myself. My mother didn't even know I was here. This could all go horribly wrong.

"It's going to be okay," Ghaz assured me, resting her hand over mine. "And if it's not, Tabitha's the word."

I nodded.

"All right," I said. "Let's do this."

As I rang the bell, I overheard Umar reciting *bismillah* under his breath. A woman who I assumed was my uncle's wife opened the door and greeted us with a nervous smile. Her dark brown hair was unevenly streaked with gray, her sunken eyes heavily rimmed with kohl. She was wearing a cotton *shalwar kameez* and gold bangles. Her red bindi seemed too small for her broad forehead.

"Hello," I said. "I'm Mariam."

"Yes," she said, toying with her bangles. "I'm Usha, Sanjeev's wife. Please, come in. I'll get Sanjeev."

The house was spotless, the hardwood floor so shiny and perilously slick that as we removed our shoes I was glad none of us were wearing socks. At the base of the curving staircase was a large, painted statue of the elephant god Ganesh playing a sitar.

Sanjeev Uncle stepped into the foyer, followed by Usha Auntie. The three of us stood before them in a row, our shoulders touching like we were lining up for prayer. My uncle didn't resemble my father, at least not based on the photo I had. He had a thick nose, a thick mustache. He was mostly bald, his scalp reflecting the light of the chandelier. Unlike us, Sanjeev had suffered no angst over today's outfit; he was wearing a plain T-shirt and rather ill-fitting pleated pants and flip-flops. His eyes lingered an extra moment on Ghaz, who folded her arms and widened her stance, her foot pressing against mine.

"Mariam is the middle one," Usha Auntie said to him in Hindi.

"Yes, I see the resemblance. Nice to meet you, Mariam," he said, reaching for my hand. Several red and yellow threaded bracelets circled his wrist.

He had a vigorous handshake, his palm sweaty against mine.

"These are my friends Umar and Ghazala," I said.

"Hello," Umar said.

"Namaste," Ghaz said solemnly, smiling beatifically and bringing her hands together beneath her chin, like a life-size cardboard cutout of an Air India flight attendant.

After a befuddled moment, Sanjeev Uncle and Usha Auntie said namaste back and then Sanjeev Uncle invited us to come sit.

"Usha," he said, "go get some chai, snacks."

Usha retreated and he led us into the formal living room. The furniture was overstuffed, with rounded, feminine edges, the color scheme cloying pastels. On top of a side table in the corner, small dark statues of gods and goddesses stood inside an engraved wooden altar. In front of the shrine were two trays, one displaying a brass candleholder, an incense burner, and a brass bell, the other one lined with apples, oranges, and grapes.

My stomach gurgled, but thankfully Sanjeev Uncle didn't seem to notice.

We sat on the sea-green sofa, me in the middle. Sanjeev Uncle took the lavender armchair, his fingers curving around the armrests, his feet up on the matching footrest. On his left hand was a large ring set with a deep yellow stone.

"Do you understand Hindi?" he asked us.

"Urdu," Ghaz replied.

"It's close to same to same," Sanjeev Uncle said, gesturing with a tilt of the head and an outstretched hand. "My two sons spoke Hindi when they were young, but as soon as they started school they stopped."

"They can speak a little," Usha Auntie corrected him, setting down a tray of neatly arranged cookies, papadum, and a bowl of fried Indian snack mix.

"No chai?" Sanjeev Uncle protested.

"It's coming," she said, returning to the kitchen.

"Any trouble finding the house?" he asked.

"No trouble," I said.

"Nice community you live in," Ghaz told him.

"Very nice," Sanjeev Uncle agreed. "We have all the amenities, even a grocery store. In fact, you can do most of your errands without ever leaving the subdivision."

Ghaz smiled. "Amazing."

She was being sarcastic, of course, but you'd only realize it if you knew her well.

"Mariam, you are in school?" Sanjeev Uncle asked.

"I just finished my freshman year at Swarthmore," I said.

"Very good. My eldest son, Mohan, is starting eighth grade, my younger son, Manish, is starting sixth. They are both attending their maths classes today, otherwise they would have liked to meet you."

Mohan and Manish. My cousins.

Usha Auntie came in, this time carrying a tray of chai, and Sanjeev Uncle told her, "Use the nice china, Usha, these are special guests."

As she turned back to trade up the china, he said, "And get those Danish cookies—in the blue tin. *Achha*, Mariam, what will you major in?"

"Not sure," I said.

"My son Mohan is already learning precalculus," he said. "You cannot succeed without science and mathematics. I've told him to study robotics. The future is robots."

I needed to start steering this conversation; I was here to learn about my dad, not get an aspirational lecture from an uncle who so far hadn't lifted a finger to help his wife.

"And your friends, they are also in school?" Sanjeev Uncle asked.

"Ghaz goes to NYU," I said.

"NYU." He nodded. "Big school, big city is not good. I went to college in Delhi, a big city, but I was very disciplined. Also, back then there was less to do. Only two channels on TV, can you imagine? You children are so easily distracted, *woh wala* video game, *woh wala* concert, *woh wala* restaurant. We used to stick to our books so that we could enjoy those things later. You know, my son once said to me, 'Daddy, I want sushi.' And not sushi only, but edamame and eel. I said, *'Bhai,* you're in kindergarten and you are already asking for edamame and eel? I couldn't even know these things until I came to the US.' I told him, 'You want edamame and eel, you finish that math workbook I gave you that you haven't opened.' So, he did, and I am a fair man, when he completed the book I took him for his sushi. A very good place, too, twenty dollars for a sushi combo plate. But he didn't like the eel. I told him, you see, dream and reality are very different. You were dreaming of eel, and now that you eat it you are calling it slimy snake. That is why your dream must stay attached to the reality, like your head must stay attached to your neck. This is how I taught my children the work ethic. My wife also works; she is a PhD in computer science, top in her field. Once a society loses its work ethic, it is lost. Black people, look what is happening to their community, half in jail, killing one another, why? No work ethic."

He might never stop talking. His racist comments were typical of a lot of desis, including my naani, but I wasn't about to listen to it. It was time to intervene.

"Excuse me, Uncle," I said.

"Now Indians like to point fingers at the blacks," he continued, "but even us, we are susceptible. You know there are Indian gangs in Queens, kids who don't study, sell drugs? Their parents didn't instill the work—"

"Uncle, if you don't mind," I said, firmer this time. "I was hoping we could talk about my father."

Usha Auntie, who'd joined us during Sanjeev Uncle's monologue, stood up. "Let's have some chai," she said. Her husband watched carefully as she kneeled on the carpet and poured it into porcelain cups with lily-white fairies painted along the rims.

"Give a little more in that one," he directed.

Usha Auntie took our milk and sugar requests. After we'd all been served a cup of fragrant chai, I repeated my request, keeping it deliberately open-ended. "I was wondering if you could tell me about my father."

"Yes. As I mentioned, I have had no contact with your father in many years."

"But he's in India."

"As far as I know."

Well, that was one question answered. "Do you have any photos of him?"

As Usha Auntie shifted uncomfortably in the next armchair, Sanjeev Uncle replied, *"Shayad ek ya do." Maybe one or two.* "But they would be at the bottom of some box in the attic."

Did he really not have a single accessible photo?

"But you knew she was coming," Ghaz said.

"Yes," he said.

"So you didn't think to, maybe, take out a few photos of her father?" she continued.

"How was I to know she would like to see photos? If she had told me before, perhaps Usha could have gotten them ready for her."

I patted Ghaz's knee, as a warning to keep cool.

"Okay, I know you can't tell me who he is now, or show me any photos, but maybe you can tell me, I don't know, what he used to be like?" I pressed.

"Rahul has never been in touch with you? No happy birthday, happy graduation, happy Diwali?" Sanjeev Uncle asked.

"No," I said, thinking, *It's not like you ever got in touch with us either, even though you lived a few states away, even though you're supposed to be a better man.*

He snorted, tapping the yellow stone of his ring against his teeth. "Why do you want to know more? You know enough."

Shoaib's point exactly.

An exasperated Ghaz threw her hands up. "Well, if you weren't going to look for photos, and if you weren't going to tell Mars—Mariam—anything, then why did you invite her to come here?"

Usha cleared her throat. "Tell her something, Sanjeev," she chided him.

"*Kya bolun?*" he demanded. *What should I say?*

"*Kuchh bhi,*" I said, which meant *whatever, anything.* "The truth."

"The truth? The truth is before he was a bad father, he was

a bad son," he said. "He did poorly in school, never studied. No work ethic."

Usha Auntie shot Sanjeev Uncle a look that made him pause, swallow whatever he was about to say, and begin again. "He was younger to me. He was talented at cricket— a very fast bowler. He could have been a cricket star but he couldn't apply himself to anything. He was not unintelligent, he thought he was better than all of us, speaking in this pukka sahib accent, quoting Yeats-Kates. He had no concern for any- one but himself. My mother spoiled him, even though he was always troubling her. He would disappear for one, two, three days. Once he went off to Manali with some foreigners he'd met without even telling my parents, you know, those hippie- shippie types. When he came back, he was growing a beard and saying, 'What is the meaning of work?' My father actu- ally beat Rahul with his belt for running away, but he had to stop when my mother threw herself on top of Rahul. My father wasn't quick enough; he accidentally gave her one lash. Your father, he saw our mother bleeding and suffering because of him, and he didn't even apologize."

"Tell something nice, too," Usha said. "It's her father."

"She asked for the truth! And what is the point in lying? He's already shown her what kind of man he is!"

"It's okay," I told Usha Auntie. "So how did he end up in New York?"

"One day he said, 'I'm moving to Bombay to become an

actor.' This was before email, cell phones. Months would pass, no word. Then one day, he calls and says he's going to New York for art school. How he got admission, how he paid for his ticket, I don't know."

"What kind of art?" I asked.

"No idea. He never shared anything with us, he never cared about us. We are a respectable Brahmin family; he knew how much it would upset our mother if he married out of our caste and religion."

"Sanjeev," his wife said gently, but he ignored her.

"*Bhai*, if you decide to marry against your family's wishes, then at least be a good husband and father. But what does Rahul do? He leaves his wife, his two children, returns to India, doesn't even pay a visit to our mother. By then she was in very poor health, all the stress he had caused her. One day I hear he's gone to Kerala to start a tea plantation, another time that he is guiding tourists on Himalayan treks. I kept telling my mother to come to America and live with us, the health care is better here, but she stayed, saying, *Nahin, mera Rahul ayega, mera Rahul ayega.*

"No, my Rahul will come, my Rahul will come.

"But he did not come once to see her, not even when our mother was on her last dying breath."

"Sanjeev," Usha Auntie persisted, and this time he waved her off. His resentment of my father clearly flowed long and deep.

"Family, obligations, responsibilities, they mean nothing to him. I took care of our parents when they became sick, I studied and I worked hard to make sure they lived a comfortable life, I paid for their medical care, bought them a better house, and when they died, who showed up asking for his half of the inheritance! 'What inheritance?' I told him. 'The house they live in I bought with my own money!' But he had no shame! Wearing a nice suit, stinking of whiskey—"

"Sanjeev, please," Usha Auntie pleaded.

"I told him, our mother didn't die of type two diabetes or high blood pressure, she died due to broken heart! And he had the nerve to tell me I need to relax! He is a scoundrel, through and through! I gave him one tight—"

"Sanjeev!" Usha Auntie cried, startling us all.

Sanjeev Uncle shut up for a moment, his compact body visibly tense against the lavender chair, a vein in his forehead throbbing with bitter blood.

"Usha, please," he said. "*Meri tang ki maalish karo*. My leg is cramping."

Usha Auntie left her chair and perched on the edge of his footrest so she could press his legs.

Though difficult to bear witness to, Sanjeev Uncle's diatribe had at least been informative. One, he clearly didn't know much about my father's life post–high school. Two, he couldn't stand him. Three, my father was also a dick to the family he was born into, not only the one he made. Four, my grandmother had loved him better anyway.

As Usha Auntie's small hands massaged his calves, Sanjeev Uncle's posture relaxed a little, though his vein still throbbed. Something about watching it move, like a pulsing, angry worm, was making me ill.

I needed to get out of here.

"Please, have some snacks," Usha Auntie insisted.

Umar reached for a cookie.

"Tabitha," I said.

Umar shoved the cookie in his mouth.

"I'm sorry?" Usha Auntie said.

"Tabitha is an incredible dancer," Ghaz replied, standing up and beckoning for us to do the same. "Who we are late to meet."

"Yes," I said. "Thank you, this was very informative."

Sanjeev Uncle took a deep breath. "Most welcome. You should visit India—your homeland," he said pleasantly, as if we'd been making chitchat about the weather.

"It won't be easy for me to get a visa," I said.

"Why? Your father is Indian."

"But my mother's heritage is Pakistani," I said, surprised I needed to remind him.

"Oh. Yes. Well, as your mother's side says, Insha'allah." He smiled broadly, pleased with himself for using the terminology of the other.

"Yeah, well, thank you and good-bye!" Ghaz said cheerily, and we followed her out of the room, through the shiny foyer where we put our shoes back on, and out the front door.

We were almost to the car when we heard Usha Auntie exclaim "Wait!" She hurried toward us, glancing back over her shoulder.

"I'm sorry," she said to me. "Please forgive Sanjeev. He had to bear the whole burden of taking care of his parents . . . It was very difficult on him."

The fact that my father had remained their mother's favorite must have made it even harder. "It's okay," I said. "My father hasn't exactly done right by me, either."

"I met your father only once," she said, "when my mother-in-law died. He could be very charming. A very good dresser, too. And . . . I'm sorry we never contacted you. Sanjeev said, if you wanted to know your father's relatives, you would reach out to us. We thought it was better to let you decide. Maybe we were wrong."

Now that I'd met Sanjeev Uncle, I doubted his presence would have had any positive effect on my life. His wife was nice enough, though. "It's all right. It was good to meet you. Take care, and say hello to my cousins."

"Oh." My mention of her sons made her suddenly emotional, and as she stepped back, her hand pressed a scrap of paper into mine. "Sanjeev thought it better not to tell you, because of the kind of man your father is, but I don't want to lie to you, now that you've come all the way here to find him. Your father's come back to the United States; he married an American. I knew you were coming so I wrote down all I know—his wife's name, the city's he in."

My father was in America.

"Thank you," I said, getting into the car. As we pulled away, she waved. I waved back, keeping my fist closed tight, paranoid the piece of paper might get lost or blow away, even though I was in the back seat with all the windows closed.

We drove past the tennis courts, past the spurting lake, past a different auntie walking her dog.

Umar broke the silence. "No room should ever have so many pastels."

"Well, thankfully we never have to see it again," Ghaz declared.

"I get why he can't stand my dad," I said. "I get why he thinks it's better for me not to know him. Maybe he's right. You can't really hate someone until you know them. I don't want to hate my dad. I don't want to hate anyone."

"Oh, Mars. Of course you don't. I'm sorry," Ghaz said.

"The thing is . . ." The thing was, Usha Auntie had given him to me. I literally had him in the palm of my hand. If you're in search of something, the closer you come, the more curiosity overrules caution, even if the destination might be dangerous, even if it might end in an explosion.

Maybe he lived far away, in Iowa, or California.

But if he lived somewhere on the way to New Orleans, or within easy driving distance, then surely it was a sign from fate that, for better or worse, I was meant to meet him.

I uncurled my fist, read Usha Auntie's small, neat handwriting.

Hannah Rae Tipple.

Nashville, TN.

"Hey," I said, "how do you guys feel about stopping in Nashville?"

Eighteen

"ACCORDING TO THIS TOURISM SITE," I read as Umar sped us down the highway, "Nashville is *more* than just country music."

"Thank God," Ghaz said. "I hate country music."

"Like what more?" Umar asked.

"Like Nashville offers free Roy Rogers to anyone named after one of the first four caliphs," Ghaz told him.

"Ha-ha," Umar said. "Hey, Mars, I was thinking, if your dad's married again he might have kids."

"Shit," Ghaz said. "You could have, like, a bunch of half siblings?"

"I bet they're hot," Umar said. "Half Indian, half white. Half anything is hot."

"Yup," Ghaz agreed. "Though when it goes wrong, it can go really wrong. But I'm sure yours are hot," she added quickly, lest I be offended on behalf of my imaginary siblings. "Hey— What if you never found out about them, and you went back to Swat, and fell for this hot half-desi, half-white dude, and you slept with him, and then you found out he was your brother?"

"And then I got pregnant and gave birth to a two-headed baby?" I replied.

"A *hot* two-headed baby," Umar said.

"That's, like, tabloid cover worthy—it'd give you even more notoriety than a billboard," Ghaz commented.

I shook my head. "Why do we spend half our time having inane conversations?"

"You know, I was thinking," Ghaz said, "meeting your dad can't be *that* much worse than meeting your uncle. I mean, your uncle was a pretty bitter, angry man. He was the good boy, but his momma never gave a damn."

"He was the good boy," Umar sang, mimicking a country song, *"but his momma never gave a damn."*

Umar had such a lovely voice they'd first asked him to deliver the call to prayer at his masjid when he was six. His earnest, melodic rendering moved his mother to tears, and prompted his proud father to buy him a new bicycle, which he never used because even back then he was a lazy mofo.

"Okay, Barry Manilow," Ghaz said to Umar. "So we've established that Mars's journey on this road trip is the search for her father. What about you?"

"What do you mean, what about me?"

"Think of every road trip book you've read, or movie you've seen. All the main characters have some sort of personal journey—discover something about themselves, or undergo some reckoning, experience some life-changing event."

"Seriously?" Umar protested. "Isn't going to places I've never been enough? Being on a road trip for the first time? And, hello, what about Tabitha?"

"Okay, you get some points for Tabitha."

"Yeah, like a hundred million points! What about you?" he said. "What's the purpose of your journey?"

"My journey is about having some fun and unwinding after my parents stuck me in my room."

Stuck was one word for it. Ghaz's ability to minimize what had to have been traumatic experiences was both impressive and unsettling. Her purpose may have been running from her parents, but it took more than physical distance to help you heal. Not to mention the fact that this was a round-trip journey. I promised myself I'd try to get her to talk about her feelings, after we met my father, when I could breathe freely again, without the choke hold of anticipation around my neck.

"That sounds like a cop-out," Umar told her.

"Hey, this road trip is happening because of me. I'm the catalyst for change. Now stop trying to change the subject."

I thought of one of my T-shirts. *Be the change you want to see*. I usually wore it to protests. I'd only gone to two all spring, though. After I dissed Doug, I withdrew into a lonely cesspool of shame and guilt and sorrow at how badly I'd behaved.

God. What if when I met my father it really was like looking into a mirror? What if I was incapable of being true?

No. I wasn't a terrible person. In fact, prior to Doug, honesty and loyalty were two traits I prided myself on. I had to make sure Doug was an anomaly. I never wanted to hurt anyone like that again.

She was the good girl, but her father never gave a damn.

I tuned back into the front-seat conversation.

"You can't be scared of being gay," Ghaz was saying.

"I'm not scared," Umar insisted.

"Then how come you've never kissed a guy? Every time we go to a makeup counter and some guy starts flirting with you, you blush and run away."

"Uh, what do you want me to do? Unzip his pants while he finds the right foundation for my skin tone?"

"I saw how you were dancing," Ghaz said. "Admit it. Admit that when you were dancing like that you fully embraced yourself as a sexual being."

"Come on," I interjected. "Every time he jerks off to his cub-bear porn he feels like a sexual being."

"You know what I mean," Ghaz said. "*He* knows what I mean. Don't you?"

"I felt a lot of things last night," he replied, "and most of them were over by morning."

"But you're not the same," she said. "That experience changed you, didn't it? Don't you want to kiss someone?"

"One day, yes. On this road trip, no."

"It's okay, Ghaz, we can give him another pot brownie and take him to a gay club," I teased.

I was kidding, but Ghaz clapped her hands yes, and Umar looked at her askance.

"No more drugs," he said.

"You don't need drugs," she assured him. She poked his waist and he let out a little squeal. "All the brownie and Tabitha Generous did was bring out something that was already inside you. A beautiful, proud, sensuous gay man."

"Yes. A beautiful, proud, sensuous, gay, *Muslim* man," Umar said.

How would Umar's dad react if he heard his son describe himself this way? Denial, fury, explosion. Napoleon on a moral rampage.

"Why not?" Ghaz demanded. "You are all of those things."

"Anyway, it's not the kissing I think about most," he confessed quietly. "It's being held."

"Oh. Oh! Our sweet Umar darling," Ghaz cried, enveloping him in such an enthusiastic embrace that he almost veered into the next lane.

Whoever Umar fell for one day had better be good to him, or he'd have Ghaz and me to contend with. For all our quibbles, we loved one another fiercely.

"I don't want to have to label my journey," Umar told Ghaz. "I want to enjoy the ride. Is that okay?"

"Fine," she relented. "All I'm saying is that if you meet a cute guy, you should be open to the possibilities."

"And what if the guy is Mars's half brother?" he joked.

"Go right ahead," I offered. "I have no issue with you sleeping with the father/uncle of my two-headed baby. Hell, you can even adopt my two-headed baby, as long as you teach it the work ethic."

"Keep the change!'" Umar bellowed.

Nineteen

WE COULD TELL WE'D ENTERED the south by
the guns and God billboards. *Repent Before It Is Too Late. Believe
in Jesus, He Believes in You. Guns Save Lives.* None of us had
been to the South, except Disney World, which didn't count, and
Ghaz's family trip to Atlanta, which she claimed didn't really
count, either. We spent the night in a motel near Roanoke, Virginia, run by Patels. The sight of a paan-chewing, bespectacled
desi uncle in the land of massive white crosses perched atop hills
gave us comfort, even if he did look us at disapprovingly when
we told him we would all share one room.

Ghaz and Umar passed out, and I Googled Hannah Rae
Tipple. I came up with nothing, so I invented her. Her Pinter-
est page contained photos of knitted scarves and homemade

jams and chintz curtains. She had auburn hair and large breasts and was an aspiring equestrian until she fell from her horse as a young girl, and now she had an Etsy store selling custom door wreaths. She was a fan of country music and had a separate closet for her cowboy boots.

Except how did someone like that end up with my father?

Maybe the boundless generosity of her love had rehabilitated him, though not enough to reach out to the two children he'd abandoned. There were thousands of Rahul Sharmas, so Googling him was useless, but there were very few Mariam Sharmas. If he Googled me, he could figure out I was a student at Swat. He'd see a photo of me from the local paper, smiling as I held up a garbage bag. *Mariam Sharma, West Grove High Senior, Organizes Community Clean-Up Day*. He'd know I was environmentally engaged, that I had inherited his face. Except maybe he'd never even Googled me. Maybe he'd exorcised me like my mother had him, and me turning up at his doorstep would make him angry.

"Mars?" Ghaz whispered, reaching for my arm in the dark. "You okay?"

"How did you know I was awake?"

"You think really loudly sometimes."

I decided to pull a Ghaz. "It's all cool, I promise. Go back to sleep."

Twenty

"LITTLE OLD LADIES DRIVE faster than you," Umar complained.

I gritted my teeth and said nothing. We'd already had to turn back after a few miles because Umar had left his lota in the motel room, which meant I'd had to merge onto the highway twice already. Though attempting to pass tractor-trailers on the steep ascent of a two-lane highway was the stuff of my nightmares, I was glad to be driving; it allowed me to channel my anxiety toward something concrete and life-threatening and in the moment. Still, it was a relief when we entered Tennessee and the terrain leveled out some.

"Dude," Umar said. "According to the Council on

American-Islamic Relations, Tennessee is the most Islamo-phobic state in the country."

"Awesome," Ghaz replied. "Is it the most homophobic, too?"

"It's not funny," Umar said.

"To you, maybe."

"I'm serious."

"What do you think's going to happen?" Ghaz asked. "Some guy's going to come up to you and call you a terrorist fag? Relaxi, taxi, you'll be fine."

"Repent, before it is too late," I said in an ominous voice.

"Kill 'em with kindness," Ghaz continued.

"Explain to them that we believe in Jesus, too," I said. "Or be like Sanjeev Uncle and tell them, don't worry, I have the work ethic!"

"Sing some Hank Williams Jr.," Ghaz suggested.

Umar groaned. "You guys are really helpful, thanks."

"Hank Williams Jr.?" I repeated.

"Umar loves him."

"What?"

"I don't *love* him, but yeah, I dig some of his tunes. I used to carpool to elementary school with our neighbor, and the dad played a lot of Hank Williams Jr.," Umar explained.

"Is he good?" I asked.

"If you like country."

"We're only kidding, you know," Ghaz said, reaching forward to muss his hair. "No one's gonna mess with you. And if they do, Mars and I are your superhero defenders."

Umar checked his hair in his vanity mirror, re-tousling it to his liking. "Meaning you'll disarm them with flirting and then Mars will tell them bad jokes and talk about the earth's impending environmental destruction until they get depressed and run away?"

I frowned. "First off, some of my jokes are pretty good—even you two connoisseurs of humor sometimes say so. Second, I bet Islamophobic homophobes don't believe in climate change."

"Okay, fine," he conceded. "Mars's superpower can be ghosting."

"Burn!" Ghaz exclaimed.

"Was that too much?" he asked me.

"Maybe," I said, "and anyway, if I ghost, how will that help you?"

"Enough, children," Ghaz said. "I've been meaning to make an announcement."

I held my breath and knew Umar was doing the same; with Ghaz an announcement could have approximately 0 to 50,456 consequences.

"I've figured out what I want to do with my life," she continued.

"We know—be a psychologist," Umar said. "Or is it now anthropologist?"

"Neither. I've realized I want to be an actor. I'm going to apply to transfer to Tisch," she said.

"That's interesting," I said, then wished I could take it back. *Interesting* was what people said when they didn't want to say what they really felt, which was, *Isn't it ridiculously hard to actually make it as an actor?*

Umar was less circumspect. "What's your backup plan?" he asked.

"What do you mean, backup plan?" she replied.

"You know there aren't many roles for desis out there, except maybe a doctor extra on a hospital show," I pointed out.

"Times, they are a'changing. What about Mindy Kaling? Aziz Ansari? Hasan Minhaj?" Ghaz shot back.

"They're comedians," Umar said. "I mean, you can be funny but you're not a comedian."

"Wow. Thanks for your support." Ghaz slumped against the seat, pouty-lipped, chin to chest, folding her arms over her knees.

I immediately felt repentant. If I told Ghaz I wanted to be a turtle farmer, she'd buy me a book on turtles. She would never piss on anyone's dreams.

"You might have to do some side jobs for a while to help pay the rent until you make it big," I said. "But I think you'll be an awesome actor."

"You're only saying that because you feel bad."

"No, I'm saying it because I mean it. Right, Umar?"

"I think so, too," Umar said. "I swear. I said backup plan because you know, it's practical to have one, even though you won't need to use it. Because, remember, your dreams must be connected to reality, like your head must stay attached to your neck."

"Chill, my naysaying friends," Ghaz said. "I actually *do* have a backup plan."

"What?" we asked.

"Astronaut."

As Umar and I shared a moment of confused silence, Ghaz broke into laughter. "Who's a comedian now, witches?"

Twenty-one

SOMEWHERE ON I-40 BETWEEN Knoxville and Nashville, Umar announced that he was starving.

I was still driving; I had insisted on it, even though my butt cheeks were going numb. Behind the wheel, I remained too focused on not killing us all to think about much else.

"Shouldn't we wait?" I said. "I think we're less than an hour from Nashville."

"I might eat my face before then," he said.

"Oh, not your beautiful face!" Ghaz piped up.

"We're, like, in the middle of nowhere," I protested. "And we just passed a rest stop."

"Look," Umar said, pointing at a roadside sign. "Lots of options at the next exit."

The first thing we saw after the exit was a McDonald's.

"McDonald's!" Umar exclaimed.

"Sick," Ghaz complained.

"Come on!" he protested. "Those golden arches never looked so good."

"We can eat McDonald's anywhere. Let's make a rule—on this road trip we eat local," she proposed.

Umar groaned.

"I'm serious. Keep driving, Mars."

Umar reluctantly relinquished his dreams of fries and a Big Mac and I kept driving, away from the gas stations and fast-food restaurants clustered around the exit and down a wide road that led past overgrown fields and abandoned buildings and a plethora of churches. Zion Baptist, Assembly of God, Missionary Church of God. I didn't know the difference between any of them, except they all probably believed homosexuality was a sin, but then so did most of the people at Umar's masjid.

We finally arrived at the town, a few ugly buildings grouped together on opposite sides of the road. I slowed down and we surveyed the scene. A gas station, a dollar store, a discount tobacco shop, a Chinese takeout called Great Wall of China.

"Chinese?" I said.

"There," Ghaz said. "On the other side of Western Union. Ivy's Family Restaurant."

"Do you think they have fried chicken?" Umar said.

"If they do, I bet it's better than Roy Rogers," Ghaz replied.

"Let's do it," he said.

The front of Ivy's Family Restaurant was a wall of mirrored windows, which allowed us to watch our dusty Prius pull into a parking spot between a white PT Cruiser and a freshly waxed, cherry-red pickup truck with wheels as high as my thighs. Ours was the smallest car in the parking lot. Outside, the humidity was so intense you could practically carve your initials into the air.

As she stepped out of the car, Ghaz said, "Well, fiddledeedee," in a high-pitched, Southern accent, waving an imaginary fan. "It's hot as balls in Tennessee."

"What's fiddledeedee?" I asked.

"You still haven't seen *Gone with the Wind*?" Umar cried. "You're hopeless, and Ghaz, you could get us shot, so be quiet."

"Yeah," I agreed. "How about not offending the locals?"

Ghaz stuck her tongue out but shut up, and I led the way inside.

Ivy's interior had no natural light, due to its mirrored windows. Instead, it was lit by unflattering long fluorescents, like in hospitals and cafeterias. A bell chimed when the door opened, prompting everyone inside to look up at us, Umar the fabulous with his stylishly draped scarf, Ghaz the long-legged beauty, and me, plain and prim. There were only a few customers: three pimply teenagers in bright blue sports jerseys emblazoned with a snarling tiger; a father, wide-faced, square-jawed, with a forward comb-over and a closely shaved beard in the shape of a narrow strip along his jawline, who was eating something smothered in gravy while his young, blond son had brought his own Big Mac meal. In the corner was a guy dressed in a camouflage hat and shorts. He had beady eyes, a shaved head, an intense tattoo on his upper arm of a dagger with a cross-shaped hilt. He had tucked his napkin into the neckline of his tank top, and his entire meal consisted of a large plate of fries smothered in ketchup, which he was stuffing into his mouth with his fork.

"Scary camouflage man sure likes his fries," Umar whispered.

We were the only nonwhite people, and likely the only non-locals, but their expressions seemed more curious than hostile. They didn't look up at us for long, but still, we made sure to smile, in an attempt to seem both nonthreatening and completely at ease.

A woman came out of the kitchen wearing a neon pink T-shirt, white cotton shorts, and orthopedic shoes. Her name tag read *Sylvia*. "How y'all doin'?"

"We're good, how about you?" Ghaz said.

"Oh, I'm good, sweetheart, thank you for asking."

She was so warm and friendly I relaxed, chiding myself for being paranoid.

"Only the three of you today?" she said.

"We're enough, believe me," Umar joked, and Sylvia laughed.

"Right this way," she said, grabbing three menus and leading us to a table that was thankfully on the farther side of the room from scary camouflage man. "Where y'all visiting from?"

"New Jersey," I said. "Not too far from New York."

"You know, I've never been to New York," she told us.

"Oh, you gotta go," Ghaz said.

"I know, sweetheart. It's on my bucket list."

"What else is on your bucket list?" Umar asked.

"Well, let's see." She began counting on her fingers. "The Grand Canyon. One of those Caribbean cruises where you can watch the world go by and drink all day by the pool. I've always wanted to try fly-fishing, ever since I saw *A River Runs Through It*. Oh, and going to one of the honky-tonks in Nashville and riding the mechanical bull. I've come close to doing it, but I get so nervous. I don't know why—the guys who control the bull usually throw the men off but are nicer to the ladies."

"You probably need to get drunk first," Ghaz suggested.

She grinned. "Believe me, when I do it, I'll have to ask my friends to take a video because I'll be so drunk I won't remember! I'm so old I just hope I don't fall and break my hip."

"You don't look old," I said. She didn't—mid-forties, maybe. My mother's age.

"Oh, bless your heart," she said. "I've got three grandchildren."

"No way," Umar said.

"I think the Lord sent y'all in here to boost my ego today!" she said. "Anyway, enjoy your meal. Emma will be over shortly to take y'alls order."

"I love her," Umar said after she'd walked away.

"I know, she's so warm and fuzzy," I said.

Ghaz held up the menu. "Fried chicken, chicken-fried steak, fried okra, fried pickles, fried shrimp, fried catfish. This is why people in the South are so overweight," she said, switching to Urdu.

"Eat local," Umar reminded her.

It was true that everyone in the restaurant, except the teenagers who'd already left, were not exactly the picture of health.

The dining experience went swiftly downhill after Sylvia. Our server Emma was sullen and curt. Umar's fried chicken was too dry, the gravy too salty, Ghaz's fried shrimp was mostly bread with a hint of shrimp, my green salad a bed of wilted iceberg. Ghaz pronounced her coffee undrinkable. Umar began to eye what little remained of the kid's Big Mac.

Scary camouflage man finished all his fries. The blond kid did, too, and ordered a gloppy soft-serve hot fudge sundae.

When we walked up to pay at the register and Sylvia asked us how we liked the food, we lied and told her it was delicious.

"My favorite is the fried catfish," she told us. "Have y'all ever had catfish?"

"I have," Umar said. "It's good."

"Not pretty to look at, but darn good to eat," she declared.

"Like eels," Ghaz said.

"I've never tried eel."

"They're delicious," Ghaz told her.

"Well, I'll have to add that to my bucket list, then. Y'all have a lovely trip. Come back again one day. Maybe by then I'll have ridden that bull."

We left a big tip, partly because of Sylvia, partly to leave a good impression on behalf of all desi people.

"God, I'm so full," Ghaz announced as we stepped outside. "Fried foods always make me feel a little sick."

"Dude, you're in the wrong part of the country then," Umar said.

Ghaz made a barf face. "I have to do yoga."

"What, now?" I said. "It's like a hundred degrees."

"Hot yoga, baby. Extended triangle pose is good for digestion. Pop the trunk."

Most people would have done their triangle discreetly, but not Ghaz. Instead she unrolled the fuchsia yoga mat she'd bought in Philly right along the side of this country road in small town Tennessee, because Ghaz always had be a little performative. After centering herself in mountain pose, she spread her legs apart and twisted toward the street, one arm reaching toward the sky.

A pickup passed. The driver's tanned arm hung out the window, his fingers drumming against the door to a country song, a cigarette dangling from the corner of his lips. Seeing Ghaz, he slowed down to stare.

"I'm sure this is a first for this town," Umar said.

I opened the car door. "Let's sit in the AC. I'm sweating."

We kept an eye on Ghaz in the rearview mirror. After she finished with one side, she rose gracefully, rested again in mountain pose, switched feet, and bent forward from her lithe waist, twisting to face the parked cars.

"What the fuck!" she yelled.

We swiveled in our seats. Ghaz was standing up, hands on hips, her face contorted with anger. There was no one else around, nothing we could see that might cause such alarm.

"Do you think she's being dramatic?" Umar asked.

"We'll find out," I said. "She's walking back to the car."

Except instead of joining us inside, she lifted the trunk, took out the softball bat and ran.

We got out, rushed toward her. She was at the end of the row of parked cars, waving the softball bat at a silver pickup truck like she might smash the bumper.

"Ghaz!" I cried.

As soon as she heard me, she stepped back, dropped the bat on the ground, and covered her face with her hands. Her whole body was shaking. I comforted her as Umar picked up the bat, holding it safely out of her reach.

"What is it?" I asked, rubbing her back. "What happened?"

"Look at the back of the truck," she sniffed.

TITAN, it said in bold letters. My eyes moved downward, and I understood.

There, below on the bumper, a sticker.

Guns Don't Kill People, Muslims Do

"Oh, man," I said.

"Okay, that's frigging disgusting," Umar said. "It must be scary camouflage man's truck. But why the hell did you pick up the bat? Were you trying to get us all arrested—or killed? That's not the way to handle things."

"Umar, give her a break; she didn't actually do anything," I said.

Ghaz wiped her eyes. "No, he's right. It's not the way to handle things."

She started running, this time toward the restaurant.

"What are you doing?" I yelled, chasing after her and grabbing her arm. "You realize scary camouflage man probably has a gun!"

"Yeah, we are not going back in there," Umar said.

"Screw him and his gun!" Ghaz cried, spit spraying from her lips. "He needs to know how hurtful that is!"

"Ghaz, please," I pleaded. "Nothing good will come out of this."

She yanked her arm away and dashed into the restaurant.

This time, when we entered, everyone looked up and kept on looking.

"Who owns the silver Titan pickup truck?" Ghaz cried, chest heaving.

Umar and I watched scary camouflage man, bracing for him to stand up and reveal his weapon of death. I could hear Umar praying under his breath, the first Quranic sura my grandmother taught me, and the only one I still remembered.

Alhamdu lillahi rabb ilalameen . . .

But scary camouflage man said nothing, did nothing, only watched us over his ketchup-streaked plate.

Sylvia stepped forward, wiping her hands with a towel.

"It's mine," she said.

No.

"Yours?" Ghaz asked.

"Yes. Everything all right, sweetheart?" she continued.

Sylvia. Warm, fuzzy, grandma Sylvia.

Maybe she'd borrowed the truck from a racist friend.

"That's . . . your truck?" Ghaz said.

"Yes, darlin'. What's the matter?" Sylvia asked with such concern, though surely by now she'd figured it out. What if we'd walked in wearing headscarves and skullcaps? Would she have greeted us with *sweetheart* then?

"Your bumper sticker," Ghaz said.

Sylvia neatly folded the hand towel, setting it down gently on a table before stepping forward. "But it's not meant for you, dear."

"But I'm Muslim," Ghaz said. "We're Muslim."

After Ghaz dropped the *M* bomb, there was a moment of uncomfortable silence, and then the blond kid said, "Daddy, you said Muslims are dirty. They don't look dirty."

"Shut your mouth, boy." The father reached over and smacked the kid across the head.

"You seem like good people," Sylvia said.

"So are most Muslims," Ghaz replied.

"I'm sure some are," Sylvia said. "I don't have a problem with Muslims *personally*. It's the *religion* that's the problem."

She said this as though it made perfect, logical sense.

"It doesn't fit in with the values of this country," she continued. "I'm not a racist. I believe anyone can be a good American—black, brown, yellow, blue—as long as they have American values. Now, you don't have to be Christian to live here, but you have to understand this is a Christian nation, and everything that means."

Ghaz made this crazy noise like a cat dying.

Even though I knew there was no point in arguing, that you could respond to her in a hundred different ways, point out her logical fallacies, offer facts and statistics, appeal to her humanity, and none of her uninformed, bigoted beliefs would change, I couldn't stay quiet.

"But what you're saying *is* racist!" I exclaimed.

"She's right," Umar chimed in.

There was a squeaky noise behind us. I turned to see scary camouflage man had stood up, a frown on his square-jawed face. I thought he'd say something, but instead he walked out of the restaurant.

Sylvia's eyes narrowed slightly. "Is it right to kill—"

"Please, stop," I interrupted her. "We came in to tell you we were hurt by your bumper sticker, not to get into a debate. Guys, let's go."

As we headed to the door, Ghaz turned around. "You know what are American values? Tolerance and secularism."

I pushed her out the door before Sylvia could reply. What we needed to do at this point was get the hell out of there, but when I opened my purse I couldn't find the car keys.

"No, no, no," I said.

"Please tell me you didn't lose them," Umar begged.

"They were in here—"

"Oh my God, you guys," Ghaz said. "He's coming."

Scary camouflage man was heading toward us. We all froze, and then Ghaz and I stepped forward to shield Umar, but he pushed his way to stand between us, resuming his whisper-prayer.

As far as I could tell, scary camouflage man's hands were empty. Surely this guy couldn't be crazy enough to cold-bloodedly shoot us in broad daylight.

Please don't let him be crazy enough to shoot us in broad daylight.

"No need to worry," scary camouflage man said, his gruff voice matching his face. "I just wanted you to know not everyone 'round here thinks like that. I served in the army for twelve years, and I know that truth is way more complicated than what can fit on a bumper sticker."

Umar's sigh of relief was embarrassingly audible.

"Thank you," Ghaz said.

Scary camouflage man nodded. "Y'all take care," he said, and walked away.

When I opened my purse again my less-panicked eyes immediately spotted my keys at the bottom.

None of us spoke until we got back on I-40. If there was a bright side to this, I wasn't so scared of the speeding trucks anymore; they seemed a lot less dangerous than humans.

"We don't want to be stereotyped, but I guess we stereotyped camouflage man," Umar said.

"Yup," I agreed. "I hope he wasn't too offended."

"Sylvia seemed so nice," Ghaz said.

"It's not like racist people snarl all the time and have horns on their heads," I replied. "Like she said herself, she doesn't even consider herself racist."

"True. But seriously, Ghaz, why the softball bat?" Umar demanded. "Were you trying out for a Beyoncé video? I can't get arrested! And I definitely don't want to get arrested in a small town in the most Islamophobic state in America."

"I know. When I saw the bumper sticker, I got so frigging angry. Come on—I was never actually going to hit the car, or anything else for that matter."

"It's fine," I said. "I mean, it's not fine, but you know. Next time you get that angry, take a walk. Without any sports equipment."

"Yeah," Umar said. "What happened to kill 'em with kindness?"

"Do you think we should have argued with her more?" she asked.

"No point," I said. "We wouldn't have changed her mind."

I didn't belong to the Muslim Student Association at Swat, but Doug and I and a few friends had gone with them to Berks County to counterprotest a group that was opposed to settling Syrian refugees. The signs they waved were as disgusting as Sylvia's bumper sticker. They'd shouted things like "Terrorists go home!" "Stop sharia now!" They'd also taunted members of our group, asking one girl in hijab if her father gave her permission to be outside, and another girl in hijab, who was black, if she wore it to cover her kinky-ass hair. Of the protests I'd been to, it was the ugliest by far. I cried in Doug's arms that night, for the first and last time.

We turned quiet again, Ghaz holding child's pose in the back seat, Umar's forehead pressed to the window. I knew that he was having a one-sided argument with Sylvia inside his head, telling her all the reasons she was wrong, a mental exercise that would bring him no relief because he'd never see her again, she'd never apologize, there would be no resolution.

Something needed to be done.

I took the next exit, pulled into a McDonald's, and parked in an empty corner of the lot.

"What are we doing?" Ghaz asked.

"I don't think I can eat," Umar said.

"We're going to scream," I said. "All of us."

"What?"

I explained how this climate change scientist had given a talk at Swat, and someone had asked him how he personally dealt with the fact that no matter how many studies came out, the deniers kept denying and ecological disaster loomed ever closer, and he said he screamed. It was some primal therapy thing, and at the end of the Q&A he had us all do it, close our eyes and scream and scream, and afterward I felt lighter, because when do you ever scream, like really really scream?

"So you want us all to scream to help us process what happened with Grandma Bigot?" Umar said, peeling his forehead from the window.

"Yup."

"It's not so simple," Ghaz objected.

"I'm not claiming it'll fix anything," I said. "Only that it'll help."

"Ah, why the hell not? I'm down," she said. "Let's Edvard Munch it up in here."

"Good. Everyone close their eyes," I said. "Now, all that anger, all that frustration, all that hurt and fear, all the stuff that's riding on the surface but also the things you keep way underneath, all of it, let it rise up and let it all go, from the deepest darkest depths, push it all out. Let the scream start from your belly, not your throat. Don't hold back. Ready? One, two, three."

Ghaz and I got into it right away. Umar's scream was weak at first, but listening to Ghaz and me unleash the beast compelled him to do the same, and soon the entire car was reverberating with the resounding pain of Grandma Bigot and having your parents lock you in your room and deadbeat dads and homophobic dads and lost loves and the rising temperatures of oceans and islands of floating trash, of the trials of being young and trying to find your place in such a screwed-up world. If anyone else heard, I bet they understood, because one of life's sad truths is that not all of us receive love but every single one of us knows pain. After a few minutes, we fell back, spent, breathless.

"I do feel better," Umar said. His window was foggy from his breath, and he had tears in his eyes. "Well, less mad and more sad."

"That was a good idea, Mars," Ghaz said. "I love you guys."

"I love you, too," I said. "And Ghaz, please sit up and put on your seat belt. It's a four-lane highway now, in case y'all haven't noticed."

Twenty-two

GHAZ HAD FOUND US a one-bedroom Airbnb in Nashville close to Vanderbilt University, a popular spot for off-campus housing, judging from the small, boxy apartment windows displaying Vanderbilt paraphernalia, the tiny patios decorated with plastic outdoor chairs and charcoal kettle grills, beer cans sticking out of the grass. Our apartment was small, the bedroom separated from the living room by a sliding glass door, and the décor was sparse, but so were our needs. In the kitchen was a sign that said *I Believe in Nashville*, with red-and-white stripes and a blue center circle with three stars in it.

"That's not the Confederate flag, is it?" I said.

"No, silly. The Confederate flag has an *X*," Ghaz said, pulling up a photo on Umar's phone. "That's probably the Tennessee flag or something. Do you really think there'd be a Confederate flag hanging in the kitchen of an Airbnb?"

"I would hope not," I said. "But after a day like today . . ."

"Wait till tomorrow," Ghaz said. "Family reunion of a lifetime."

"At least Hannah Rae Tipple can't be that racist, if she married my dad," I said.

"It's so weird that you have a stepmother," Umar said.

"Maybe she'll be like Julia Roberts," Ghaz offered.

"What?" I said.

Ghaz rolled her eyes. "*Stepmom?* You really need to watch more movies. Bollywood, Hollywood—you're missing out on entire cultural conversations."

"Have you seen any of the Harry Potter movies yet?" Umar asked, smacking his forehead when I replied in the negative.

Stepmother. A woman named Hannah Rae Tipple was my stepmother.

The road trip effect was starting to feel more akin to *The Twilight Zone*.

I still hadn't told my mother. We'd been texting, but I'd ignored her call last night, because it felt devious to have a conversation with her and not speak of my quest for my father. But it was equally devious to avoid her. I'd never kept a secret from her, not any that mattered.

I couldn't meet my father without telling her first.

"Earth to Mars." Ghaz waved her hands in front of my face. "Return to orbit."

"I'm here," I said.

"I'm hungry," Umar said.

"Shock and awe," Ghaz replied.

We walked arm in arm to Hillsboro Village, a compact but cute neighborhood with brick-paved sidewalks, and cafés and clothing stores catering to young people with a taste for frills and lace. It was only half past seven, but a lot of places were already closed. We walked until we hit a major intersection. Across the street a sign indicated the start of Vanderbilt University's campus.

"Let's eat at that place Fido," Ghaz suggested. "It has great Yelp reviews."

As we headed back toward the café, we passed a guy playing guitar in front of Pancake Pantry, which Ghaz informed us was one of Nashville's most popular breakfast establishments. He was dressed in skinny jeans and boots, indigo geometric tattoos up and down his arms, his long hair parted in the middle.

I kept my secrets because I wanted you to stay

But it was keeping secrets that drove you away

Oh, for cryin' out loud.

"Hey, guys," I said, falling back. "I'll meet you inside."

I sat down at one of the empty metal tables outside Fido and called my mother. She answered on the first ring, as though she'd been waiting.

"Hi, Mom."

"Hi, Mariam. All well?"

"Yes, we're about to have dinner in Nashville."

"Is it nice?"

"Well, Tennessee has been kind of intense, which I'll explain later, and so far Nashville is hot and small and quaint, but we haven't seen much."

"Good. And Ghazala? How is she?"

"She's okay. We still haven't really talked about the stuff that happened with her."

"She's reluctant?"

"There's that, and also because . . . well, I've been taking up a lot of space."

"How so?"

Noting my hesitation, she said, "If you'd rather not tell me, it's okay."

Ever since I could remember, even if my door was ajar, my mother would knock and wait for me to tell her to come in. I hadn't realized how rare her respect for privacy and distaste for emotional intrusion was among desi parents until I'd become friends with Ghaz and Umar.

"I saw Sanjeev Uncle," I said. "My father's brother. We had chai with him and his wife at their house in Virginia."

She was quiet, but only for a moment.

"Was it a successful visit?" she asked.

"That depends on how you define *successful*."

"The definition is yours and yours alone."

I summarized the visit, the perfect house in the perfect subdivision, Sanjeev Uncle the bitter chauvinist, Usha Auntie the kind, obedient computer scientist wife. I told her he had long been estranged from my father but spared her the details he'd revealed—it was nothing she didn't already know.

Umar stepped outside to check on me. I gestured at the phone and waved him away.

"Did you ever meet him?" I asked.

"Sanjeev? No. It seems I didn't miss out on much."

I laughed. "No. But there's something else. As we were leaving, Usha Auntie came out and told me my father remarried some American woman and was living in Nashville. So, that's really why we're here."

"Ah," my mother said.

After a moment of fraught silence, she cleared her throat. I hated that sound because it meant she was about to deliver unwelcome news. *I know I said we could stop for ice cream but we no longer have time. Alex, the beloved neighborhood stray cat, was hit by a car.*

"What is it?" I asked.

"I knew."

"Knew? You mean you knew he'd come back to the US?"

"I did. An acquaintance emailed me several months ago. I don't know how she knew."

"Why didn't you tell me?"

"Why would I?"

Why would she, when we never spoke of him, when we'd erased him from our life, our conversations, when I'd never told her I wanted to find him.

"I don't know. I feel like it's something most people would tell their kids."

"I'm not most people, I'm your mother. He knew how to find you if he wanted to reach out. And I didn't realize how badly you wanted to meet him."

"Do you remember the book he gave you? *The Brothers Karamazov?*"

"I'm afraid I don't," she said.

Of course she didn't remember. That was why it had remained on our bookshelf.

"Well, he gave it to you, and signed it, and I found it when I was a kid and kept it in my nightstand drawer, because, I don't know. It was a piece of him, of the two of you, however far removed."

"Oh."

"Are you upset?"

"Why would I be upset? I can understand why it's important for you to meet him. When are you going to see him?"

"Tomorrow."

"Are you feeling strong about it?"

"I feel strong and utterly terrified at the same time. Sometimes I think nothing makes any sense."

"So little of the world makes sense. It's only that most people either construct a narrative in which it does or try to ignore it."

When it came to my father, both options seemed impossible. "Are you going to tell Shoaib?"

"Would you like me to?"

"He'll freak out. He hates our father."

"I'll leave it to you to tell him when you think the time is right."

"How is he?"

"Shoaib? He has a new girlfriend, and has started drinking a protein shake that smells like old socks."

I laughed. "I miss you tons."

"I miss you. Take care. And don't forget to take care of Ghazala."

"I know. I'll call you soon."

I arrived at the table at the same time as the food.

"We got you a veggie burger," Ghaz said.

"Did you tell your mom you're meeting your dad?" Umar asked.

"Yup. She says she understands."

Ghaz shook her head. "I'd love to hear my mother say that to me, just once. 'It's okay, *beta*, I understand.' Anyway, it's good you got that secret off your chest. I know how open you and your mom are."

"What if, after all this, my dad isn't even there?" I ventured.

"He might have already abandoned Hannah Rae Tipple."

"Wouldn't that be anticlimactic," Ghaz said.

"This veggie burger is delish," I said.

"Please, how good can a veggie burger be?" Umar said.

"Try it," I countered, but he refused.

"So are we hitting the town tonight or what?" Ghaz said.

I shook my head. "I need to crash soon."

"So do I," Umar said.

"Not even a movie?" Ghaz protested. "There's an independent cinema across the street. Ten bucks says they're playing a film about a white hipster couple with a broken marriage, or something depressing with subtitles."

"Sounds like a scream," Umar said. "I'll pass."

"Me, too," I agreed.

Umar was asleep on the couch in front of the TV before I'd even finished brushing my teeth. In the morning, he would be annoyed that he'd forgotten to floss. Ghaz and I shared the double bed, which took up most of the bedroom. She smelled like the jasmine *ittar* Umar wore every day. It was a subtle scent that revealed itself in close proximity, which is why Ghaz liked to say that you wore *ittar* for your lover.

And if not for your lover, then for your best friend lying tucked against you in a strange bed in a strange city which your estranged father now called home.

I'd thought she was asleep, but after a while she said, "Mars?"

"Yeah?"

"I swear I wasn't actually going to hit the pickup truck with the bat."

"I know," I assured her. "Though you might need to reassure Umar. You know how sensitive he is, underneath all those jokes."

"Yeah. I'll talk to him tomorrow. But I've been thinking, picking up the bat, holding it in a menacing way, that's not me. That's something my mother would do, except she usually does it with a frying pan or a shoe. Or maybe it is me. Maybe my true self is emerging."

"You are not like your mother."

"If you're worried you're like your father, can't I be worried I'm like my mother?"

I propped myself up on an elbow. A party had commenced down the street, an urgent bass line, youthful voices drunkenly hailing one another. "It's different. My father remains largely a mystery. You know your mother well, and therefore you can also know you're not like her."

She sighed, throwing her arm over my waist. "Then why did I do it? The road trip effect?"

"You were angry about Sylvia's bumper sticker. But maybe it was more than that. Maybe you're angry at your parents, too."

Ghaz murmured noncommittally into her pillow.

"Ghaz. Of course you're feeling anger and resentment. They shut you up in your room and said terrible things. And you haven't talked to us about it at all. You're keeping it all inside."

She lifted her head from the pillow, burying her face into my shoulder instead. "I'll talk about it later, but not now. I don't want to, really, I don't. The bat thing was weird, but it won't happen again, I promise."

"All right," I said, stroking her hair.

"Mars?"

"Yeah?"

"Yesterday in the car, remember you said whenever you were feeling stressed about something, Doug would sing you some song from *Monty Python*?"

"'Galaxy Song.'"

"Will you sing it to me?"

"*Whenever life gets you down, Mrs. Brown. . .*" I sang, even tra la la'ing the waltz part like Doug used to. By the time I finished, Ghaz was asleep. I kissed the top of her head, willing her dreams to bring the peace her heart wouldn't allow.

Twenty-three

FOR A MERE THREE dollars ninety-five cents, a website had provided me with Hannah Rae Tipple's address, phone number, and date of birth.

"That's some serious stalker shit!" Ghaz exclaimed.

"It's all from public records," I said, but she was right. First, I invaded Hannah Rae Tipple's privacy, and now I was about to show up at her house, with my two best friends in tow. That morning, Umar and Ghaz had taken an excruciatingly long time deciding what to wear. Ghaz tried on three outfits, all black. Umar finally settled upon navy pants, an ivory short-sleeved ikat shirt, his lucky navy butterfly scarf, a red slim-fitting corduroy jacket, and his cherry-red sunglasses.

"A corduroy jacket?" Ghaz objected. "In the middle of summer?"

"Don't hate me because I'm stylish," he shot back.

"Are you saying I'm not?" she said, modeling her dress. It was black, ankle length with a cinched waist, embellished throughout with lace, with a high lace neck.

"Um, what is that?" he replied. "A black doily? How do they market it? Goth tea party to funeral wear?"

Ghaz stuck her tongue out. "It's modern Edwardian, thank you very much."

"So like . . ." Umar considered this. "*A Room with a View* meets *Edward Scissorhands*?"

Ghaz responded by hurling a pillow at him.

"Are you guys ready yet?" I demanded.

They turned toward me. "Are you ready?" Umar asked.

I was wearing the same interview outfit I'd worn to meet my uncle.

"Please," I begged. "Can we go?"

"One sec," Ghaz requested. She went into the bedroom and came out with a long string of pearls. "Put this on. Ah—*très* chic."

Forgetting how slowly the South moved, we made the mistake of getting into the drive-through line at Starbucks.

"God," Umar complained. "They should call it a Drive and Wait Forever to Get Through."

Ghaz let out a loud laugh. "They should call it, Coffee Insha'allah."

"Which means we'll never get our coffee." Umar looked back. "Should we bail?"

"There are only three cars ahead of us," I snapped. I usually enjoyed *The Ghaz and Umar Show*, but one, I was nervous, and two, there was something frenetic and slightly desperate to their interaction today. I suspected that it had to do with yesterday's incident, like they were trying to prove that Grandma Bigot hadn't dampened their style, as if the more jovially they behaved, the less it would hurt.

"Okay, sorry. No more jokes," Ghaz said.

"On the bright side, whoever your dad is, at least he's going to be interesting," Umar offered. "I mean, art school, your mom, tea plantation, Hannah Rae Tipple in Tennessee? This is not the typical life of a desi uncle."

"Yeah," Ghaz agreed. "It's like that ad campaign—the Most Interesting Man in the World. Your dad is the Most Interesting Desi Uncle in the World."

"Do you get to hold that title if you abandon your family?" I said.

"Hmmm. Good point. Correction—he's the Most Interesting Desi Uncle Dickwad in the World."

"In the *world*?" Umar said.

"Okay," she conceded. "The Most Interesting Desi Uncle

Dickwad in Tennessee."

"Try putting that on a sash," Umar said.

We sipped iced lattes and ate muffins as we headed south through Nashville. To my anal-retentive driver chagrin, the drivers in Nashville seemed not to realize when the light turned green, or that their cars were equipped with turn signals. After a while I realized it was because half of them were too distracted texting or talking on their cell phones.

"Idiots," Ghaz swore when I pointed this out. "Who *texts* and drives?"

We drove through a long stretch of congested shopping district, upscale strip malls with parking lots that seemed too small for the number of cars clogging the road. The traffic finally calmed and the landscape opened up to gated complexes and stately churches on large, corner plots, transitioning to wealthy country estates, wooden fences running along manicured rolling hills, grand mansions set so far back that from the road you caught only a teasing glimpse of their glamour.

"This is serious old money," Ghaz said as we turned into Hannah Rae Tipple's pinkish-red gravel driveway and drove up to the wrought iron black gate. I rolled down the window and stared at the fancy intercom.

"Are you sure we shouldn't have called first?" I said.

"And what if your father had told you he didn't want to

meet you?" Ghaz replied.

"He could still say that."

"Well, we're here now," Umar said. "At least he'll have to say it to your face."

"Right," I said.

"Just press the buzzer and say you're here to see the Most Interesting Desi Uncle Dickwad in Tennessee," Ghaz instructed.

"What?"

"Kidding! Ask for Hannah Rae Tipple. It's her house. But first, deep inhale, hold it one, two, three, now exhale it all out. One more time. Okay. Go."

I pressed the red button. Nothing.

I was about to press it again, when the voice came through.

"Who is it?" it demanded. The voice was female, the tone unmistakable. Hannah Rae had a sullen teenager in the house.

"We're here to see Ms. Tipple," I said.

"I'm Ms. Tipple," she said. "You mean you're here to see Mrs. Tipple."

"Well, you're technically both Ms. Tipple," I said.

"Politically correct, I got it."

The voice withdrew, and the gates slowly opened.

The long, picturesque driveway, bordered with shade trees, led us past well-tended meadows and a stretch of lush, emerald lawn before coming to a split. To the right was a circular driveway in front of the main house. It wasn't as large as you'd expect based on the size of the property, but impressive nonetheless—pristine white with a pillared entrance and tall windows with dark green shutters. To the left was a massive barn, whose white and green palette mimicked the main house.

"Dude, this is like a proper estate," Umar said. "The kind of places with horses and a guest house."

I parked at the far end of the circular driveway. As we exited the car, Ghaz stopped and said, "Listen."

In the near distance, you could hear a mad cacophony of bird sounds. Curious, Ghaz began walking toward it, while I called for her to come back. But then Umar decided to follow, so I did, too. It didn't take long to discover the source. Between the house and the barn were a series of huge, domed white aviaries, housing a variety of exotic birds. The aviary closest to us was home to a green parrot. He had his own fake tree and an elaborate wooden structure with ladders and hanging toys.

As we approached, a few of the birds began making weird croaking noises.

"Look," Umar said, pointing at one with a large, colorful beak. "That one's totally Toucan Sam."

"Toucan Sam isn't a real bird."

We spun around. A teenage girl stood behind us. Her hair was dyed a striking platinum white. She was tall and skinny, dressed in frayed cutoff jean shorts that barely covered her butt, ankle-length cowboy boots, a ribbed white tank top with a black string bikini top underneath.

"Who the fuck are you guys?" she said.

"I'm Mariam, and this is Ghazala and Umar. We're here to see Mr. Sharma."

"No shit." She stepped forward then stood with her feet in first position as she assessed me. Her mouth kept making a clicking noise, and when she spoke again I realized it was the sound of her tongue piercing striking against her teeth. "And here I was thinking this was going to be another boring-ass day. Follow me."

"She's, like, a trashy Taylor Swift," Umar said as we walked behind her, maintaining enough distance so we could talk. "But rich trashy."

"Do you think they had slaves here?" Ghaz asked.

"I doubt there were any cotton fields," Umar said. "The property line is right over there."

"But they had to have domestic slaves," she insisted.

"Okay, Ghaz, there's enough complicated history in this situation as it is," I said. "I really don't also want to be thinking about the ghosts of enslaved people on top of everything else."

"You can't separate histories," Ghaz argued, but stopped because the teenage girl had bounded up the front steps of the house and was waiting for us at the main door. The stairs were shaped like a corset, narrowing at the waist and widening again.

"Fiddledeedee," Ghaz muttered under her breath, and I elbowed her.

The daughter, aka my stepsister, led us into the foyer and instructed us to wait. The walls were covered in deep orange wallpaper patterned with lions, the floor was shining marble, and above our heads glittered a pendant chandelier. Hanging over the fireplace was a gilded mirror, on the mantel an enormous golden candelabrum. Two oval-backed, velvet chairs flanked the fireplace, set atop a gorgeous antique rug decorated with stags.

"It kind of reminds me of the Beast's castle," Umar said.

"If it ain't baroque, don't fix it," Ghaz said.

"What?" I said.

"Look at those," Ghaz said, gesturing at the historic portraits of mostly ugly white people that lined one wall.

"He's kinda cute," Umar said, pointing to one man with slightly messy, thick chestnut hair and a beard.

"He was a slave owner," Ghaz stated. "Man—right when you walk in the house, it's like, meet our generations of rapey slave owners!"

"What about our ancestors?" I said. "A lot of Muslims used to be slave owners, too."

"The only reason the Prophet didn't forbid it is because it would have been too upsetting to the economies of the world," Umar explained. "That's why he encouraged people to free their slaves. It had to be phased out slowly."

"Daenerys Targaryen didn't do it slowly," Ghaz said. "She white-woman saved the day in less than a season."

"She—" Umar was cut off by the arrival of my stepmother. The first thing you noticed about Hannah Rae Tipple was the massive creature on her shoulder, a bird with stunning blue feathers and yellow-ringed eyes. The bird stood completely still as it regarded us, as did Hannah Rae, who was tall, fit, blue-eyed, very blond, dressed in beautifully tailored cream pants with a matching linen blouse, a chunky gold bracelet, leather espadrilles. She had Botox face, her skin stretched and smooth and semi-paralytic. But you saw where her daughter got her beauty.

"Hello," Hannah Rae said. "I'm Hannah Rae and this is Sherman."

"Hello!" the bird echoed.

"Hi," I said, figuring I should get right to the point. "I'm Mariam Sharma. I'm Rahul's daughter."

"Oh," she said. Though the work she'd done on her face limited her facial expressiveness, there was no mistaking the surprise in her light eyes.

"Didn't know your husband had a kid, did ya, Hannah Rae?" her daughter said.

"Athena, hush," Hannah Rae said.

Athena gritted her teeth. "It's A.T., Mom."

"Whether you're Athena or A.T., you still have no license to be rude," her mother reprimanded her in a lilting Southern accent.

Behind her, A.T. made a face, clicking her tongue ring extra loud.

"Well," Hannah Rae said, turning back to me. "This is . . . unexpected. Rahul did mention to me that he had children from a prior marriage, but I don't know much about it—about you, I mean."

"He left us, my pregnant mother and me, when I was two," I said.

"Of course he did!" A.T. snickered.

"Athena, go to your room this instant!" Hannah Rae said. At the sound of his owner's raised voice, Sherman opened his sharply curved beak and grunted loudly, twisting his face toward her.

"It's okay, Sherman," she assured him, scratching his head. "And you, young lady, to your room."

"Oh, come on," A.T. protested.

"Now. I mean it."

"Fine!" A.T. cried. She thudded up the curving staircase, stopping halfway to yell, "Why can't you admit you married a loser?"

"You're grounded," Hannah Rae called back, and A.T. let out a piercing scream before running the rest of the way up the stairs. Sherman spread his gigantic brilliant blue wings and descended to the floor, where he started dancing in a circle around Hannah Rae.

"It's his protective circle," Hannah Rae explained. The heated exchange with her daughter had made her flush red, forehead to collarbone. "Shall we go sit down? Dorothy!"

A middle-aged black woman stepped into the foyer. Her hair was in braids, tied up in a tall, stylish bun at the top of her head. She was wearing a maid's apron over her jeans and T-shirt.

"Dorothy, we have guests," Hannah Rae said.

"I see that," Dorothy said.

"Would you please bring some sweet tea and savories to the drawing room?" Hannah Rae requested.

"Sure thing."

Hannah Rae entered the drawing room first, followed by Sherman, then us. It was a stunning room, with high, arched windows and two-story double French doors that opened onto a stone patio. We squeezed together on a silk settee, Hannah Rae taking the divan across.

"So you've come here to see him?" she said.

"Yes," I said.

"How long has it been?"

"Since he left when I was two."

"Oh."

With a grunt, Sherman hopped onto her lap. She leaned against the divan's curved side to make room and he rolled onto his back like a puppy so she could tickle his tummy. His tail was even longer than his body.

"Why now?" she questioned. "If I may ask."

"Why not?" I replied, not about to confide in a woman I barely knew.

Dorothy entered with iced tea and a plate of mini-quiches. She looked at us curiously, probably trying to figure out who we were. I smiled; she smiled back.

"Dorothy, will you please go get Rahul? He's out back playing croquet," Hannah Rae said.

"Croquet?" Umar whispered.

After Dorothy left, an awkward silence ensued. We watched as Sherman nudged Hannah Rae's shoulder.

"Darling," she told him, "I know you want a massage, but now is not the time."

Sherman cocked his head.

"Okay, my spoiled little chick," she conceded, and began vigorously scratching around his neck. Sherman released a high-pitched squawk, resting his head against Hannah Rae's stomach as she moved on to the front of his chest. Then he lay back, his head nestled against her elbow.

"Oh, you want to play puppy now, don't you," Hannah Rae cooed. She toyed with his talons, which were as big as her hands, continuing to scratch his tummy and his neck as he rolled back and forth, his massive beak occasionally nipping at her fingers.

"That looks like a strong beak," Umar noted.

"Oh, yes," Hannah Rae said, still in her bird-puppy voice. "You can crack coconuts with this beak, can't you Sherman?"

Sherman crawled up to her shoulder, stood erect. "Hi! Kisses!" he said, and made a kissy noise.

"You rascal!" Hannah Rae laughed, planting a noisy kiss on his coconut-cracking beak.

I couldn't have imagined this any weirder than it already it was.

We heard singing.

"Main pal do pal ka shayaar hoon . . ."

I'm a poet for only a moment or two.

I didn't know the song, but Umar and Ghaz were already humming along.

"Pal do pal meri kahaani hai."

My story only lasts a moment or two.

A man stepped through the French doors. He swept his arm forward, hailing Hannah Rae.

"Hi! Kisses!" squawked Sherman.

Hannah Rae nodded toward us, and he turned, his arm still in the air.

His eyes met mine.

My father.

His face had become pudgier, his cheeks rosy. He had a double chin and a gut that hung low and round over his cotton pajamas. He was unshaven, his hair tied back and slightly greasy. He was wearing a blue silk bathrobe, his pajama shirt parting at the last button to reveal a slice of hairy stomach, significantly paler than his face. On his feet were pink furry slippers a size too small, his toes, long and skinny like mine, curling over the edge.

His eyes were lively, amused.

"What do we have here?" he said in a thick British-Indian accent. "'I wander'd in a forest thoughtlessly, / And, on the sudden, fainting with surprise / Saw three fair creatures, couched side by side.'"

What the hell.

"Rahul, this is Mariam," Hannah Rae said. "Your daughter."

He brought his thumb and forefinger to his jaw, pinching his chin. "Mariam, my daughter?"

"Yes," I said. The utter surrealness of this situation was at least allowing me to maintain a state of relative calm.

"Excellent," he said, walking to the mahogany bar, humming the same song as he went. The back of his robe was decorated with a dazzling peacock's tail. "I think this calls for a drink."

Hearing this, Sherman flew off the couch and went over to join him.

"Rahul! It's ten a.m.," Hannah Rae chided.

"Then it's noon somewhere over the Atlantic," my father stated. He held up a bottle with a blue label. "And it isn't scotch. Normally I am a scotch man, but this! A single malt French whiskey, so fine, aged in cognac barrels." He faced us, the bottle to his chest, one end of his bathrobe's waist tie dangling toward the floor. "Children?"

"I think I'll pass," Umar said stiffly.

"No, thank you," I demurred.

"I'll have a sco—French whiskey," Ghaz said.

"On the rocks?" he asked Ghaz.

"Neat," she replied.

He nodded approvingly, pouring a generous amount of whiskey into a glass of etched crystal. He held the glass out to Ghaz. She waited for him to bring it to her, but he didn't move, so she got up instead.

"So kind of you," she said, her voice saccharine.

My father arched his eyebrows, one higher than the other. He knew she was telling him to fuck off.

"Sherman," Hannah Rae said. "You know I see you."

Sherman grunted at my father's feet.

"I can't, my feathered friend," my father apologized. It was the first time since he'd spoken that he sounded sincere. "Your mother doesn't like it when you drink. But what about your mother? Hannah, my dear fairy, my maiden Idun, can I wet your lovely lips?"

"Only a tiny bit," Hannah Rae said.

He did her the courtesy of walking over, bowing and kissing the back of her hand as he delivered her drink. Hannah was blushing, the corners of her lips turning up as much as her Botox allowed. I couldn't tell if she was embarrassed, or enjoying this theatrical display of affection, or both.

"Do you like birds, Mariam? My wife," he said, reaching into his bathrobe pocket for a lighter and Dunhill cigarettes, "she adores birds. She was an Amazon parrot in her past life, and before that, a Tasmanian emu, and before that, a pterodactyl. But in this incarnation, she is the golden apple of my life."

"Don't mind him," she said to us. "He's . . . eccentric."

An eccentric who seemed completely unfazed that the daughter he'd abandoned sixteen years ago had shown up unannounced.

Except now he was looking at me while sitting rather daintily on the divan's golden-edged arm, one leg crossed over the other, furry slipper flapping against his foot. I waited for him to say something, but instead he blew a smoke ring that held its shape for an impressively long time before dissipating. Umar coughed.

"Rahul," Hannah said, "your daughter has come to see you after all these years. Don't you have anything you'd like to say?"

"Fairies, come take me out of this dull world, / For I would ride with you upon the wind . . . / And dance upon the mountains like a flame," he recited.

In all the ways I'd imagined this meeting, it had never been like this.

"Anything besides poetry." Hannah Rae was starting to sound annoyed. For some reason, this made me feel better.

"You know, if he doesn't want to say anything—" I began.

"Well," Ghaz said harshly, "not saying anything is saying something, isn't it?"

"What should I say?" my father replied, spreading his arms wide. "She came here to meet her father, but I am but a shell of a man, a shadow of a shadow of a shadow. It is only by the good graces of my wife that my heart still beats."

"Oh, Rahul. Why must you be so dramatic?" Hannah Rae protested. "Why don't you start by asking her how she is?"

"I haven't asked her in sixteen years," he said, returning to the bar and his beloved French whiskey. "I would be a hypocrite to start now."

"Do you have anything you want to say to him?" Ghaz asked me. I could smell the alcohol on her breath.

"Yes," I said. "I'd like to know why you never got in touch with us, never asked how we were. Weren't you even curious?"

He tilted his chin, his body sagging some, a puppet whose master had slackened the strings. Then he took another sip, and, buoyed, leaned his elbows against the mahogany bar. "Because you were better off without me," he said. "Hasn't coming here convinced you as much?"

That was it. What else could I say? He knew what he'd done, he was unremorseful, and he had justified it to himself long ago. There was as little point arguing with him as there was with Sylvia.

Ghaz couldn't keep it in any longer. *"Behenchud chutiya,"* she swore at him.

My father raised an eyebrow. *"Meey ghar aake, meri* whiskey *peeke tum mujhe gaali deti ho?"* he said. *You come to my house, drink my whiskey, and give me insults?*

"Aapka ghar nahin, aur aapki whiskey *bhi nahin. Biwi ke*

paisay, biwi ki whiskey." *Not your house, not your whiskey. Your wife's money, your wife's whiskey.*

Instead of riling him up, this seemed to amuse him. "What a fiery capitalist your friend is," he said. He shook his tumbler, the ice globe clattering against the crystal.

"You were right," I said. "We *are* better off without you."

My father raised his glass. "I'm a wretch, Mariam. When I die, even the vultures won't deign to pick the meat from my bones."

"The vultures are going extinct," I said.

My father looked at me. The corner of his lip twitched, and then he burst out laughing.

Next to me, I heard Umar murmur *what the hell.*

I couldn't stay here anymore. My father, Hannah Rae's coddling of him, this house, her daughter's angst, my father's laughter, the ghosts of slaves, it was all too much too much too much.

"Tabitha," I said.

Ghaz shot back her drink. "We're leaving," she announced.

"A wise move," my father said.

I felt Umar's fingers circle my wrist. "Come on, Mars."

We ran into A.T. right outside the drawing room, eavesdropping. She smiled at me, her former petulance replaced by sympathy.

"At least you get to leave," she said. "My mom's still married to him!"

Behind us, Hannah Rae cried, "Athena! Back to your room!"

Athena hurried away, but was standing on the central landing of the steps as we entered the foyer. "Hey," she called out. "If it makes you feel better, my real dad doesn't give a shit about me either."

I'd never been so relieved to walk out of a house.

When Umar gestured for the keys, I gladly gave them. Like Usha Auntie, Hannah Rae also felt obligated to follow us out to the car. She stood a few feet away, feeding Sherman cashews from her pants pocket.

"Mariam," she said as Umar opened the door for me. "I'm sorry. I know it all must seem very . . . unusual."

Unusual was one word for it.

"All right, I have to ask," Ghaz said to her. "How did you two end up together?"

"I've always been interested in reincarnation," she explained, "and I started taking classes with a new yoga teacher who recommended—anyway, long story short, I went to India. I was by myself, but I took a tour of holy places, you know, Varanasi, Bodh Gaya. Your father was one of the guides, and he was so charming. We hit it off. By the time we got to Rishikesh, we were . . . like infatuated teenagers. We couldn't keep our hands off—I mean—"

"Hands off!" Sherman cried.

Hannah Rae blushed. "We both abandoned the tour, and

went farther up into the mountains, and your father showed me such beautiful places. He was so knowledgeable, he taught me about all the native Himalayan birds, which of course for me was like a dream. Then we went to Rajasthan, and in the desert outside Jaisalmer we had a priest marry us, walked around the fire seven times. I know it sounds crazy, but it was so romantic, and exotic, and he was attentive, and sweet. And it's silly, but doesn't every girl dream of being with a prince, even if he is penniless?"

"Excuse me?" I said.

Hannah Rae looked at me quizzically. "Your father comes from a royal family. Their palace and their lands were confiscated by the government when India got its independence. They were left with nothing. Your father was supposed to be the next Raja of Totapur."

Umar started to choke, Ghaz laughed out loud, and I felt my heart sink. My father was a scoundrel, through and through.

"What?" Hannah Rae said.

"*Totapur* means *the city of parrots*," Ghaz explained.

"Yes, he told me. And he showed it to me on a map, it's in Uttar Pradesh," she said.

"It's not true," I said. "His family's not royal; he's not a prince."

Hannah Rae was quiet for a second. She had impeccable posture, even with a blue-winged giant on one shoulder. "I suppose I always took that story with a grain of salt. I don't know . . . We still have these moments, when it's like it was in India. And Sherman really likes him. But now, so much of the time, he's—"

"I'm sorry," I said. My hands were trembling, and I lowered myself sideways onto the car seat, clasping my hands in my lap. "I can't hear this."

She nodded. "Of course. Of course. Forgive me. I'm sure y'all need to get going."

"Yes," Ghaz said, "we do."

"Would you like me to keep in touch?" she asked.

"No," I said. "Unless he dies, I don't want to know."

"Yes," she replied, her eyes weighted with sadness, "I understand."

We'd almost reached the gate when I told Umar to stop the car.

"Here?" Umar said, but he braked.

I opened the door and ran through a field of wildflowers until I was out of breath, then lay on the ground. Closing my eyes, I willed myself to slowly fade to black, to sink to safety, where I could think, but the conditions were all wrong, the sky too bright, the ground too hard, my mind spinning like a Tilt-A-Whirl.

"Mars!" Ghaz said. I opened my eyes, the sky replaced by my friends' faces, hovering a foot above mine. "You okay?"

"I don't even know how you process something like that," I said.

They lay down on either side of me.

"I kinda felt like we were in a movie," Umar said.

"Or a tricked-out Tennessee Williams play," Ghaz suggested. "He was like . . . a Shakespearean Shashi Kapoor meets the Dude."

"Why are you trying to bring down the Dude?" Umar objected.

"Who's the Dude?" I asked.

Ghaz groaned. "That's it. At some point on this road trip we are watching *The Big Lebowski*. And did you see the charming in him? Because I didn't. Golden apple of my life? Barf."

"Shoaib," I said suddenly.

"What about him?" Ghaz asked.

"He didn't even ask about Shoaib. God, does he even know my brother's name? He didn't ask about my mother, either."

"Are you surprised? He's a total narcissist. Probably the only way he can live with all he's done is by shutting himself off emotionally," Ghaz said.

"Yeah, he's clearly a very unhappy man," Umar agreed.

"But man, that French single malt was delicious," Ghaz said.

I shook my head. "The next Raja of Totapur?"

"White lady got played," Ghaz remarked.

And my mother? My iron-cored, steely-eyed mother? Had she gotten played?

"Something about him . . . all those dramatics," I said. "It was like almost nothing he said was real. I'll never know who he really is, and I don't want to. At least I know that now."

"See? That's a positive development," Ghaz said.

"Yeah," Umar agreed. "Think of it this way—on the bright side, after Grandma Bigot and your father, Tennessee can only go up from here."

Twenty-four

UMAR WAS HUNGRY, and we went straight from the Tipple estate to eat some of Nashville's famous hot chicken. Even at eleven a.m., there was a line out the door. Thankfully, unlike the line at Starbucks, it moved quickly.

Umar kept wiping the sweat from his forehead with the edge of his scarf, which always grossed me out a little because I was pretty sure he hardly ever washed his scarves, unlike his ass. At least he took them off when he ate.

Forty-five minutes later, Umar and Ghaz were in the throes of a culinary orgasm. Every few bites, Umar would make an enthusiastic proclamation. *Delish! Roy Rogers has nothing on this. So good.*

"This is amazing," Umar said. "My parents would love this."

"Screw your principles," Ghaz told me. "Have a bite."

I wasn't disgusted by meat like some of my vegetarian friends, and I used to love it growing up: I still remembered this goat and okra curry my grandmother used to make. But six years of abstaining had made me lose interest. I wondered if it was the same way with sex. I really enjoyed hooking up with Doug, but when Ghaz complained about being hard up and horny, I couldn't relate. Ghaz said it was because I'd never had amazing sex, but with Doug it had been pretty amazing.

It sounded like Hannah Rae and my father had once had amazing sex.

Sick.

"Earth to Mars," Ghaz sang out.

They'd consumed their chicken like good desis, relishing every last bit of meat and cartilage, leaving only a carcass of slender bones resting atop a slice of grease-soaked white bread. I'd eaten less than half my fries and pimento macaroni and cheese but was already feeling ill.

"I'm back, I'm back. What were you talking about?" I asked, offering Umar what remained of my food.

"I'm so full I can't," he said, before taking a bite.

"I was saying we should hit up the honky-tonks tonight," Ghaz said.

"I hate country," I said.

"You and half the world's population," she countered. "The point of a road trip is to expand your horizons. Have either of you ever been to a honky-tonk before?"

We shook our heads.

"Exactly."

"You guys go," I said. "It's not that I'm anti-new experiences—I know I won't be up to going out tonight."

"Yeah," Umar chimed in. "Let's get a couple of pints and watch a Lifetime movie."

Ghaz regarded me with the intensity of a mind reader. "Hmmmm. You're obviously upset about your father; even though you knew he was a wastoid, it was another thing to witness his full wastoid-ness in the flesh. You were concerned that you might have inherited some of his less desirable traits, but I think we can safely say you're nothing like him."

"Nothing at all!" Umar piped up.

"You feel sad for yourself, sad for Hannah Rae Tipple, sad for your father. You feel sad for the polar bears and the polar ice caps."

"They *are* melting at an alarming rate," I said.

Umar snickered.

"What did I miss?" she pressed.

That was Ghaz—she'd keep prying and poking until satisfied that I'd laid my heart bare.

"Well, I'm debating what to tell my mother, though I know she won't ask herself. Do I tell her he didn't even mention my brother? And, I don't know, I guess I thought that when I saw him, we would have a connection, like there's an invisible rope that binds a father and daughter together, even if they've never met, even if the father's an asshole. I thought I'd feel some tug of emotion, some subconscious memory of attachment, if that makes sense. But I didn't. All I saw was a stranger, a selfish narcissist who happened to be my father. Blood doesn't mean much if it's not tied to love. Like my brother: he can be such an ass, and so many things about him drive me insane, but we grew up together, we've looked out for each other, I love him. But my father, he was nothing to me, and I realize now he never will be."

Umar broke the contemplative silence that ensued by saying, "Now do you see why she doesn't want to hit the honky-tonks?"

As she considered my words, Ghaz chewed on her bottom lip, leaving teeth marks. "There was a part of you that was hoping that meeting your father would offer some sort of reconciliation, or healing. But now you know you never really had a father, and you probably never will. So, what you need to do is mourn him."

"But like you said, I never had him," I objected.

"But you were thinking you might." She snapped her fingers. "I know what we're doing tomorrow!"

Umar and I exchanged a wary glance. "What?"

"We're having a funeral. For the father you'll never have."

"Is this so you can wear that black doily dress again?" Umar said, protesting as Ghaz punched him in the arm.

"I'm serious," she said. "I think it'll be good for Mars. A step toward moving on."

Once Ghaz was convinced of an idea's brilliance, she'd cling to it tenaciously. Umar and I had learned to pick our battles, and who knew? Maybe it would be a little cathartic.

"Where would we have a funeral?" I asked.

"A cemetery," Ghaz replied. "Where else?"

Twenty-five

AFTER HOT CHICKEN, Ghaz and Umar decide to explore the city more and I returned to our Airbnb to call my mother. Since she'd always been deliberately opaque about my father, I wasn't sure how much detail I should share, and if hearing of my father's pathetic state would make her feel better, or worse, or nothing at all. My mother's emotional journey in relation to my father remained even more of a mystery than my father himself.

In spite of the heat, I headed outside to make the call. Sometimes tough conversations felt easier if you were unconfined.

She answered on the first ring.

"How are you?" I greeted.

"Came home early from work."

Because you were distracted by today's events? I thought, but didn't bother to ask. She'd never admit it anyway. "Drinking a glass of wine?"

I could sense her smile. "Opening a bottle as we speak."

"Old world or new?"

"Australian Shiraz. Very new."

I pictured her, sitting at the kitchen island, elbows braced against the gray granite, her silvery hair tied back in a loose bun because she couldn't stand to eat or drink with it down, swirling her wine, waiting.

"So I met him."

"All right."

My mother listened quietly as I briefly described the house, the grounds, the aviaries, Hannah Rae, and her beloved bird. I described the bloat of his face, the bathrobe, the pink furry slippers. I said he quoted poetry and had started drinking mid-morning, that he seemed uninterested in me, or in making any kind of amends.

"I almost feel sorry for him," I said. "He's very unhappy, but it's not for me to worry about. He's made his choices. He didn't even try to engage with me; it was like he was acting out some play, like we were all second fiddle to his dramatic stage presence. Anyway, we won't be having any kind of relationship."

"Are you okay?"

"Yeah. I mean, it was difficult. He was actually even worse than I expected." I hadn't meant this to be funny, but laughed anyway. "I'm glad I met him, though. It was something I felt I needed to do."

"I'm sorry to hear it didn't go well. I hope it brought you some closure."

I'd been thinking of how Hannah Rae had described my father as charming, romantic, a good lover, how she claimed to have once been giddy in love with him. Had this been the pattern with my mother? Had she been as taken with him as Hannah Rae was? I couldn't imagine her being anything but levelheaded.

"I have a question," I said.

"Go on."

I had walked down the street to a local park, where children were climbing all over the undulating body of a mosaic dragon sculpture. Parents watched, smiling, as their children chased one another underneath the arches of the dragon's body, and I suddenly felt overwhelmed by the magnitude of what my father had missed.

"Mariam?"

"Yeah?"

"You were going to ask me something."

"Right. Now that I've met him, I keep thinking—why did you marry him? I know you prefer not to talk about it, but I'd like to know."

"Ah. I thought you might ask this." She paused, and I could hear her breaking her one-glass rule by pouring more wine. "He was the opposite of my parents, spontaneous, nonjudgmental, poetic, unconstrained by expectation, or what people might think. He made everything an adventure, even going to the bodega for ice cream in the middle of the night. I was infatuated, I knew he wouldn't make a good long-term partner, but I was only twenty-four. I didn't want a long-term partner. I cared that he was good for me then. A few months after we started dating, I got pregnant. I always insisted that we use protection, but one night, the condom broke. There was no morning-after pill back then. I thought, what are the chances?"

"You were pregnant with me," I said.

"Yes. When I found out, I wanted to terminate the pregnancy. I was young and I had misgivings about your father, but when I told your father, he was ecstatic. He said we'd live in a cottage in a magical wood, and make art and raise lambs. And when he saw I wasn't convinced, he called my mother. I hadn't even told my mother about him, can you imagine? But my mother agreed I should have the baby, and get married, and . . . I couldn't fight them both. Your father, he would sing 'Mary Had a Little Lamb' to my belly, and part of me thought, maybe it could work out between us. Maybe having a child, starting a family of his own, would give your father stability."

"Oh, Mom. Do you think you would have been happier if you hadn't had me? Maybe you would have met a better man, wouldn't have been a single mother."

"Nonsense," she said brusquely. "Not at all. I am content with the choices I made. I am happy with the life I have."

"You sure?"

"Mariam. I may keep my emotions somewhat cloaked, but do I ever say things I don't mean?"

"No, you do not."

"But listen to me carefully—I have never, not for a single moment, regretted that I chose to have you, but if, at the time, I'd chosen to have an abortion, I wouldn't have regretted that either. Do you understand?"

My mother was staunchly pro-choice, and I understood the message implicit in her words: that if I was to find myself unexpectedly pregnant, I should not look to what she did but instead do whatever was right for me.

"Don't worry, I'm not going to have a baby at twenty-four just 'cause you did," I teased her.

"I'd rather you say you're not going to have a baby at twenty-four because you're careful about protection."

"Believe me, you really don't have to worry. Is everything else okay? Shoaib isn't driving you too crazy?"

"He likes to press your buttons far more than mine. You know he doesn't mean half the things he says; he's trying to goad you."

"Well, that's really immature."

"He is a sixteen-year-old boy. How are Ghaz and Umar?"

"Honestly? We're having fun, and at the same time we're all a little emotionally screwed-up."

"Would you like to elaborate?"

"Yes, but I think I have enough to process for one day," I said.

"I need to go lie down and try to think before Ghaz and Umar come back. I love my friends, but it's hard to get lost around them. In thought, I mean."

She laughed. "Okay, go get lost. Anyway, I've got work to do. And Mariam?"

"Yeah?"

"I love you."

"I love you, too."

Twenty-six

TO GHAZ'S DISMAY, we spent our second night in Nashville on the couch, so when she woke up the next morning insisting upon funeral preparations, Umar and I felt obliged to play along. A few hours later, we arrived at the historic Nashville City Cemetery, bordered by a busy road on one side and railroad tracks on the other. As we walked through its black iron gates, we were greeted by a sign that said *In Memory of the Confederate Soldiers*.

"Ugh," Umar said. This had become his standard response to anything with the word *Confederate* in it.

"Should we spray paint *black lives matter* over it?" Ghaz suggested.

"And get arrested for vandalism? No way," Umar protested.

"Hey, look at that beautiful magnolia," I said.

In one corner of the cemetery was a majestic magnolia tree, framed by deep blue sky, so tall it dwarfed the slim, pillared tombstones surrounding it. The city had an abundance of magnolia trees but this was the most impressive one I'd seen.

"Pretty," Umar said, taking a photo.

"Let's do this before we melt," Ghaz said. "We need to find the right spot."

We walked by another massive tree, a weeping willow half the height of the magnolia but twice its breadth, its wispy, hanging branches swaying gently in the breeze.

"How about there?" I said.

"It's very apropos," Ghaz replied. "But it's almost too dramatic. Let's keep walking."

We followed her deeper into the cemetery, along the paved paths, each of which had a name, marked by wrought iron street signs. Though the cemetery itself was serene, its nineteenth-century graves were now subject to twenty-first-century industry; the birdsong and rustle of leaves competing with the sounds of eighteen-wheelers whizzing past, the whir of heavy machinery from nearby industries, the pounding of a jackhammer.

"Here," Ghaz declared, stopping in the shade of a small willow tree next to an old-fashioned streetlamp, at the corner of two paths named Walnut and Cedar.

I couldn't see why this particular spot resonated with her, but figured it was as good as any other.

Ghaz stood and faced us, clearing her throat. She was wearing her black dress from yesterday, even though she said it stank. She'd parted her hair in the center, dark waves tumbling past her shoulders.

"Dearly beloved," she began, "we are gathered here today to mourn the father Mars will never have. Even though her real father is alive, he's as much a father to her as a male grizzly bear who eats his young."

Umar and I glanced at each other, trying not to laugh.

"To varying degrees, we all wish our parents were different. But on this road trip, Mars has come to realize that her father is incapable of being a parent. And so, we stand together underneath this small, lovely willow tree, to put to rest Mars's hopes for a paternal relationship, and to help her move on and live an even more fulfilling, amazing, and irrevocably awesome life. And now, Mariam Sharma will read a eulogy to the father she never had."

This morning, while Ghaz and Umar slept, I'd gone to a French café in Hillsboro Village and sat at a window table to write my letter. After the first half hour, all I had written was the beginning of a poem—

Elegy to My Father
Normally, I'm a scotch man

but this!
a single malt French whiskey
so fine
Aged in cognac barrels

Then I'd sat there grieving that these were the words of my
father that I would carry my entire life—not *I'm sorry*, or *I missed
you*, or *forgive me*—and a solitary teardrop had fallen poetically
into my mug, salting my hot chocolate. When I finally began
to write the letter, I did so not because I believed in its power
of catharsis but because I didn't want to disappoint Ghaz, who
wanted so badly to help me heal.

Ghaz and Umar had folded their hands in front of them,
bearing such solemn expressions that I almost wanted to laugh.
A yellow-and-silver freight train creaked along the side of the
cemetery, and I waited for its deafening screeches to fade before
reading.

"I wasn't sure who to address this letter to," I began, "because
if you had stuck around I'm not sure what I would have called
you. Abba is a Muslim thing, and you're not. Pitaji is what Hindus say, but it seems pretty formal. Maybe Dad, but for some
reason that sounds weird. So, I decided to call you, the father I
would have wanted but will never have, Poppa."

Umar sniffed.

"To be honest, I haven't spent much of my life thinking about
what it would have been like to have you. I don't even know what

we would have done together, because I don't know what fathers do, I mean, except from TV, or what I've seen or heard from my friends. For most of my conscious memory, it's been me, and Shoaib, and Mom. I can't imagine it any other way. I can't even say it would have been better, only different; just because a father sticks around doesn't mean he's going to be good at it. Of course, there were moments—I hated any time in school when we had to draw or talk about our families because even if their father didn't live with them, most of the kids at least knew where their father was.

"But I did think about you. I kept your photo hidden in my drawer, and I wondered if I was like you. I wondered if you'd ever reach out, if I'd die without having met you. I wondered why you left us, concocting stories, like maybe you'd embezzled funds and were wanted by Interpol and had to go into hiding forever. I wondered if you had another family, and if you were good to them. I wondered who took that photo of you, if you loved her, if she loved you. When I dumped Doug, though, I started thinking about you a lot more. The way I treated Doug made me ashamed, and I wondered if I was a lot like you after all. Did I inherit some of your nature? If I looked like you, was I predisposed to act like you? So, that's why I went to see your brother. He really isn't a fan, but I guess you know that already.

"Of course I couldn't not meet you. It was like the stars were aligning—the road trip, your brother emailing me back, every-thing. I wasn't expecting fireworks, but I guess I expected you to be more interested in me, in my life, in my mother and Shoaib. I thought you'd, if not apologize, at least try to explain why you left. I thought we'd look at each other and feel something, the tug of shared DNA, but there was nothing.

"And deep down I thought maybe we'd go for a long walk, and I'd tell you how I was mean to Doug, and you would tell me not to worry, because I wasn't like you, that I was capable of healthy, committed relationships, that it was a momentary blip. It's crazy, to think I was hoping to get this reassurance from you, but see, the thing is, even though you left us and never looked back, I thought you were a better person than you are. But you've run away from all forms of responsibility your whole life, and you'll never be Poppa to me, or anyone. I feel sad for you, but I'm now okay with you not being in my life. I need to focus on the people I love, who've been there for me. I need to focus on being kind, and that means surrounding myself with people who are kind. It's good I met you, because I can stop all that wondering. I think most of the time, it's harder not to know. Knowledge can be painful, but it comes with a sort of peace. So here—in this cemetery, underneath this lovely weeping willow tree—I lay you, the father I never had, to rest. Let me go my way, and you yours."

Halfway through, my voice had started trembling, but not

enough to make me stop. There was something about the act of reading aloud, of giving voice to your pain, that was undeniably powerful.

"That was really beautiful," Umar said, dabbing his eyes with his scarf. "And you're not like him, you know."

"I know."

"So now," Ghaz said, resuming her role as funeral MC, "we must bury the letter."

"Bury the letter? How?" Umar asked. "Did you bring a shovel?"

"Uh, no. But we could use our hands?"

"No way," he objected. "It'll take forever to get the dirt out of my fingernails."

"They're painted black!" Ghaz had insisted on painting our nails black for the occasion.

"I second Umar. No hand-digging," I said.

"Okay. But we need to do something, you know, for finality," Ghaz explained.

"Why don't we burn it?" Umar suggested.

"Yeah, that makes sense. My father's Hindu so he's probably going to be cremated," I said.

"Awesome. Who has a lighter?" she asked.

We stared at one another.

Ghaz groaned. "I guess we go get one."

"There are only warehouses around here," Umar pointed out.

"We can head back. There's a gas station near our Airbnb."

As we walked toward the entrance, a maintenance truck was heading down the main path toward us. Even though it was a public cemetery, and we were doing nothing wrong, we collectively tensed, because we were three brown people in an otherwise empty cemetery dedicated to Confederate soldiers. The truck slowed down as it approached, and we all smiled, Ghaz adding a finger wiggle wave, and the two old white men inside waved back.

As we passed through the gates, I happened to look down. Beneath another plaque in memory of Confederate officers and soldiers, something else had been laid to rest, an empty forty-ounce bottle of malt liquor in a brown paper bag. *King Cobra*, the label read.

The juxtaposition made me smile.

Twenty minutes later, we were at the gas station near our place, huddled between the ice freezer and the back wall of the convenience store. Ghaz handed me the lighter.

"Good-bye, Poppa," I said, lighting a corner of the letter. As we watched it burn, an old Mustang pulled up. Two cracked-out peroxide blondes emerged, one younger, one older, dressed in denim miniskirts and skimpy tank tops and platform heels, black mascara streaked like claw marks beneath their eyes.

They observed the three of us standing around the burning letter, which now lay between us on the asphalt. The older woman took a swig from a two-liter of Mountain Dew and nodded, as if to acknowledge that we were, all of us, up to no good.

"Ashes to ashes," Ghaz said, using her foot to brush the letter's remains behind the ice freezer.

She and Umar hugged me, and I hugged them back. As silly as it was, it had helped. Being made to describe my sorrow had forced me to give it a form, and giving it form gave it borders. It was a deep sorrow, yes, but it was small in comparison to the good things in my life, like the two friends who were chasing each other, laughing, into the convenience store because one of them had decided he really wanted some Mountain Dew.

Twenty-seven

"HELLO, FRIENDS," our Lyft driver, Ed, greeted us as we entered his car. A unicorn dangled from his rearview mirror. "Off to the honky-tonks this fine eve?"'

"Yes," Umar said. "Should we not be?"

"Ah, it's not my kinda thing. But if you're visiting Nashville you have to check them out. You know, when you visit New York for the first time, you gotta see Times Square."

"I hate Times Square," Ghaz said.

"There's a few things you like about it," Umar corrected her.

"Oh yeah? What's that?" Ed asked.

"Some of the billboards are nice," Ghaz said, but since she left it at that, so did we.

"How long have you been a Lyft driver?" Umar asked Ed.

"Three years."

"What's the craziest thing that's happened?" Ghaz inquired.

"Well," he said, "that depends on what you mean by crazy—like crazy terrible or crazy weird?"

"Mmm . . . crazy weird."

"I got a ride request from Franklin, and before I picked him up he called me and said, 'You got three hours?' I said sure, and when I picked him up he was wearing sweatpants and a lounge robe, and he had his hair pulled back into a ponytail so tight I was like, that has to be hurting his face. He got into the car with a laptop and some other techie equipment, and he had me drive around for three hours straight while he worked on his computer."

"What was he doing?" Umar said.

"He told me he was a fixer—that if a celebrity got into trouble, they would contact him and he would fix it."

"Fix it using his computer?"

"I guess so. He kept getting phone calls, and I heard him speak in at least four different languages—French, Russian, English, and German."

"Dude, that is shady," Ghaz said. "I wonder what he was doing."

"I have no idea. I thought it was better not to know too much. But at the end of the three hours, we stopped at a taco truck on Nolensville and he bought me lunch, which was pretty cool. I've got tons more crazy stories. A lot of the city may be turning into this fancy high-rise condo-boutique hotel-land, but there's still some Nashville weird going on."

"Nashville weird," Ghaz repeated.

"And here we are," Ed announced, pulling up to a corner of Broadway.

The honky-tonks went on for several blocks, flashing lights and loud music, the bars' balconies packed with bodies, the sidewalk thronging with people, a mini Las Vegas of country music. Not only did all the honky-tonks have live bands, some featured a different band on every floor, the musical cacophony extending on both vertical and horizontal axes.

"And here we are," Ghaz said. We still hadn't left the corner. "Let's do this."

"Um, this is, like, the heart of whiteness," Umar said. He sounded nervous, and I knew he was looking at the overwhelmingly white crowd and fearing a sea of Sylvias.

"Look, there's a black guy," Ghaz pointed out.

"You mean the bouncer?" Umar said.

"Hey, a piano bar," she said. "That sounds like a good place to start."

Relieved that Ghaz had zeroed in on a destination, we plunged into the chaos of the sidewalk, weaving our way through the drunken revelers toward the piano bar.

The centerpiece of the bar was a stage with dueling pianos. The piano players were two fratty-looking guys in T-shirts and baseball caps. They were talented, bringing their own unique style to the audience song requests, like a high-speed rendition of Elton John, or a jazzy version of Prince. The stockier piano player could do a great falsetto.

We sat at a table near the players, where there was some floor space to dance. On either side of the stage stood two bouncers, their arms folded across their chests.

"Bouncers?" Ghaz said. "How bad can things get at a piano bar?"

Umar nudged us, gesturing at a bachelorette party. The young bride was in a skintight white dress and cowboy boots, torn white veil pinned to her big blond hair; the bachelorettes were dressed in matching tight black tank tops that said *I'm Poppin' Bottles*.

Five seconds later, another bachelorette party walked by, the bride in a gold sequined dress and a sash that said *Bride and Bitches*, the bachelorettes in skimpy black dresses, capital *B*s glittering on their chests.

"I guess bachelorettes like the honky-tonks?" Umar said.

No sooner had he said this than a third bachelorette party passed, the girls in matching white tank tops that featured their individual titles. *Too Hot to Handle. Slayer. Dancing Queen. Bridezilla.* The two brides before had looked pretty young, but Bridezilla looked like she was sixteen. A plastic penis-shaped whistle hung from her neck.

"Someone go tell Bridezilla about statutory rape," Ghaz said.

So far, everyone had used the dance floor as a crossing point, but then two women next to us started dancing. One looked like she was in her forties, the other maybe twenty years younger. Though the piano player was crooning a heartfelt rendition of Adele, they were dancing like they were in a hip-hop club.

"What's their deal?" Umar asked.

"I think they're mother and daughter," Ghaz guessed.

It was a strong possibility. They were both blond, with the same narrow face. They both wore Daisy Dukes and cowboy boots, except the mother had on a tube top and a Mardi Gras–style necklace of shiny purple beads, the daughter a more modest short-sleeve T-shirt. The mother started grinding low to sad Adele, holding her drink high and tossing her head back as she hooted.

"How are they so wasted?" I said. "It's not even nine p.m."

The daughter started freaking the mother from behind, spilling her drink down her mother's tube top.

"Good thing she's drinking something clear," Ghaz said.

The mother ran her hand sexily across her wet cleavage, then licked her fingers.

"I think they call this a white trash train wreck," Umar said.

We were mesmerized.

Mother and daughter were approached by a guy. Like most of the other young men we'd seen so far, he had the clean-cut, fresh-faced look of white boys raised on meat and corn and athletics. He was good-looking, bearing a resemblance to Matt Damon. His T-shirt said *IDF* in bold letters.

"Oooohh," Umar said. "He's pretty hot."

"Do you see his T-shirt?" I said. "Doesn't IDF stand for Israeli Defense Forces?"

"He looks more *Friday Night Lights* than IDF," Umar said.

"Maybe it stands for something else, too," Ghaz said.

We assumed IDF would make a move on the daughter, but he hit on the mother instead, and now they were grinding, the mother's arm hooked around the back of his neck as she humped his thigh. The daughter seemed thrilled that her mother was getting some. She started to dance a circle around them, egging the couple on. Then the mother lifted her arms over her head and attempted to shimmy backward while maintaining crotch-to-thigh contact. She fell on her ass, then her daughter laughed, and IDF helped her up. He started twirling her around, which seemed a bad idea given how drunk she was.

A waitress appeared with a tray of three shots that IDF gallantly handed to mother and daughter.

"Dude, I don't think they need any more alcohol," Umar said.

They all downed the shots and the mother and IDF resumed their seesaw grinding. The mother seemed more and more off balance, and suddenly, she stopped dancing. We leaned back in our chairs, alarmed, as she came careening toward us, mouth agape, eyes popping out. At the last moment, she veered to the empty table next to us and proceeded to puke all over one of the chairs, covering it in a white, watery vomit gravy.

"Oh my God," Ghaz breathed.

The mother stood up, shook her head a little, picked up a used napkin from the table, and wiped her lips. We assumed she'd go to the bathroom to wash up but instead she turned around and danced her way back to IDF, who grabbed her ass and drew her closer.

A second later, they were making out.

"I'm sorry, I can't watch this anymore," Umar said. "We gotta go."

We waited until we were back on the street before bursting into laughter.

"I can't even . . . what *was* that?" Ghaz cried.

"Nashville weird?" Umar said. "Or honky-tonk normal?"

"I think we've seen enough," I said.

"Come on. One more bar," Ghaz begged, insisting we go to a bar called Tequila Cowboy, because she'd decided she was in a tequila mood.

From the entrance, we could see packs of bachelorette parties roaming the bar in matching outfits. The age range of the patrons was impressive, from the barely legal brides to a geriatric sitting at the bar one whiskey away from the grave, and everything in between.

"Is it me or are the guys here generally better looking than the women?" Ghaz said. "That almost never happens."

"It's true, a lot of these women are busted," Umar agreed.

"Some of the guys are cute in that corn-fed kind of way. But almost everyone is straight."

We headed to the bar, passing a wasted white frat boy dancing badly by himself, thrusting his hips at any woman who came within a certain range. The bar smelled like spilled beer with a hint of bile. The bartender had knotted her T-shirt right underneath her ample breasts, exposing her pierced belly button and taut stomach. She poured Ghaz a shot of tequila, then lined up a row of beer bottles between her thighs, leaned forward, and snapped off their caps one by one, handing me the one that had basically been in her crotch.

"That's what I call a fishy beer," Umar said.

"You guys!" Ghaz cried, gesturing upward with her empty shot glass. "I think there's a bull upstairs!"

On the second floor was a mechanical bull, a crowd watching as a dyed blonde, wearing black lingerie underneath a transparent white lace dress, climbed on. With a whoop, she began riding it before it even started moving, and when it did move she tumbled off immediately but recovered quickly, jumping up from the mat and shouting "Yaaaaaahh!" as the crowd cheered back.

Umar shook his head. "The shit you get away with if you're blond."

"In a transparent dress," I added.

"So this is Sylvia's bull," Ghaz said. "I'm gonna do it."

"Are you serious?" I asked.

"Hell, yeah," she said, pushing her way through three guys in black Harley-Davidson T-shirts and getting in line.

Another woman went next, her heft making it difficult for her to climb onto the bull. She was thrown off in seconds, and the button-down shirt frat boy who followed lasted only a few seconds longer. As Ghaz approached the bull, the crowd grew quiet. She had her yoga face on, slight frown, intent eyes. She rested her hands against the bull's flank for a moment, did a round of deep breathing, and climbed on. The bull started to move, more slowly than for the others, and I suspected the male operator was going easy on her. As the bull began to buck back and forth, Ghaz squeezed her thighs tight, gripping the strap and trying to move her body with the bull instead of against it. The crowd began to cheer. Emboldened, she smiled and lifted her arm. The bull jerked backward, and she fell off, but she'd managed to stay on for about thirty seconds, which was impressive in bull time.

When Ghaz got up, she mouthed something at us.

"Take that, Sylvia."

As she made her way back to us, Ghaz was in her element, accepting people's high fives, briefly flirting with the two guys who hit on her, accepting a shot from a guy in a turquoise-beaded cowboy hat.

"I hope that isn't roofied," Umar said.

"Come on, Ghaz," I said, taking her hand. "Let's get out of here."

Outside, a musician jammed on an electric keyboard, the sidewalk so crowded you either had to be pressed against a bar window or move with the tide of flesh that threatened to topple you if you paused for a selfie. A party pickup truck rumbled by, the back of it set up like an open-air limo, Justin Timberlake blasting from the speakers, the bachelorette party holding red plastic cups and dancing on couches.

"Literally a party in a pickup truck," Umar said. "That's a first."

As if not to be outdone in the parade of vehicular debauchery, the party pickup was followed by a party pedal tavern, the bachelorettes swigging from cups as they pedaled halfheartedly, thongs visible above their jean shorts. The bride was wearing a penis hat, and holding up a photo of her fiancé on a stick.

"That is so not sexy," Umar said. "That is, like, where sexy goes to die."

"Oooh, look!" Ghaz exclaimed. "Karaoke!"

"Ghaz!" I cried. "Haven't you had enough?"

"Come on, last bar, I promise," she pleaded.

Like the piano bar, the karaoke bar offered a variety of musical genres beyond country. Ghaz ordered another tequila, me another beer, and we stood in the crowd watching women with names like Amber and Brandi sing "Like a G6" and "Proud Mary." Amber was talented, Brandi not so much.

A group of bros near us started laughing and high-fiving one another. One was wearing a shirt that said, *I've got the dick. You make the rules.*

"Hey, where did Ghaz go?" Umar asked.

"Bathroom?" I ventured. "Either that or she's making friends."

I hoped it was the former, because I'd wanted to leave even before I saw the unsmiling man sitting in the corner of the bar, underneath a string of Christmas lights that flashed haphazardly, his T-shirt emblazoned with the American flag. I tried to keep an open mind, reminding myself of not-so-scary camouflage man, but something about his presence and posture made me think of a man stockpiling weapons for the rise of the white supremacy army.

A black woman took the stage. I was very happy to see her. Ghaz reappeared, her smile so broad you could spot her crooked tooth. She'd clearly been up to no good.

"Where were you?" I asked.

"Signing Umar up for karaoke," she said triumphantly.

"What?" Umar said. "Hell no."

"Come on, you have such a beautiful voice."

"What if I get booed?"

"No one's booing her," she said, pointing at the woman on stage, who was singing something that sounded like country meets spiritual.

"Yet," Umar said.

"You'll be fine!" Ghaz insisted. With each tequila, the pitch of her voice increased exponentially. "Channel your inner Tabitha. If I rode the bull, you can sing karaoke. Even if this isn't our scene, we can still contribute to it, right? We have to think, like, our presence here can make it better. We have as much right to be here as anyone else. Yes, Mars?"

"I think it's more a question of do we want to be here? But you have a point. You got chops, Umar. Surely this is a crowd who could appreciate that."

Umar sighed. "Fine," he said, "but only if you promise that after the song, we're done with the honky-tonks."

"Yay!" Ghaz hollered, kissing both of Umar's cheeks and attracting the attention of the people around us, including two ruddy-cheeked older men. One looked at her admiringly, but the other, with a shaved head and reddish beard, his sunglasses perched in the center of his forehead, bore an expression bordering between curiosity and hostility. I stepped in front of Ghaz protectively.

Ghaz pointed at the group of bros nearby. "Does his T-shirt say, *I've got the dick. You make the rules?* What is *wrong* with people?"

"At least he's ceding power," I quipped.

"Do you think that shirt gets him laid?"

"Ummm, do you see how wasted people are getting? You could be a one-armed leper and you'd probably get laid."

Then, over the loudspeaker: "Next up is Muhammad. Do

we have a Muhammad in the house?"

"That's you," Ghaz said.

The bar had become quieter. I pretended not to hear the snickers.

"Muhammad? Are you serious?" Umar said. "Do you want to get me shot?"

"Last call for Muhammad," the announcer said.

Somebody booed, followed by laughter.

"Go! Show 'em what you got!" Ghaz urged, giving him a push.

As Umar went forth, I hissed at Ghaz.

"Why did you do that? He could get killed! Or beaten up. Are you crazy?"

"It'll be fine," she insisted. "Watch."

I don't know what Umar overheard as he walked to the stage, but by the time he arrived his hands were shaking. Whatever people's preconceived notions, he was one of the best-looking and best-dressed gentlemen in the bar, if your taste veered toward well-tailored cloth and textured scarves. As he stood in the spotlight, clutching the mic, the decibel level in the room lowered so dramatically you could hear the bartender making a drink.

When the first bars began to play, Umar smiled at Ghaz, and Ghaz hooted. I didn't recognize the song, but everyone else did, because they were hooting, too.

I gave Ghaz a questioning glance. "Hank Williams Jr.," she mouthed.

When the crowd heard Umar's beautiful voice, they cheered, swaying and singing with him. A group of Japanese tourists near us raised their beers. It must have been a honky-tonk anthem, judging from the intense audience enthusiasm and the fact they knew every word. With each verse, Umar became more confident, until he was strutting his stuff like a karaoke superstar, singing with a melodic glee that inspired much dancing and beer spillage.

Every time he sang the refrain *Hank, why do you drink?* the entire bar went wild, replying in unison "To get drunk!"

I looked back at the American flag man. Though still stone-faced, even he was nodding along to Umar's heartfelt rendition.

When Umar finished with a bow, the crowd responded in an uproar, people high-fiving him and slapping him on the back as he made his way toward us.

"You're a rock star!" Ghaz shrieked, giving him a smack on the lips.

"Thanks," Umar said. His smile vanished. "Can we get out of here?"

When we left the karaoke bar, Ghaz and I were euphoric, proud of Umar, sailing on the energy of the audience, but Umar kept walking fast, pushing past pedestrians, not stopping till we'd reached the end of the street, to a small plaza that bordered a river. Then he sat down on a bench and put his head in his hands.

"What is it?" I said.

He looked up at Ghaz. "Never ever do that again."

"But it went so well! They loved you!" she protested. "Muhammad singing country—talk about challenging stereotypes!"

Umar shook his head.

"Ghaz," I said. "Let's listen to him. He clearly had a different experience. Umar, what happened?"

Umar was too upset to respond, his obvious distress finally piercing Ghaz's "everything is awesome" tequila goggles. She kneeled in front of him, directing him to breathe deeply, breathing with him until he was ready to talk.

"So I'm walking up to the stage," he said, "and everyone's looking at me. A few people smiled, but a lot of them were hostile. Some guy says, 'Better give him a pat down first,' and people laughed like it was so funny. And I hear this guy, the one with the red beard and sunglasses on his forehead, say to his friend, 'First black music, now a raghead.' Then, as I'm singing, I see him singing along, lifting his beer high, and, when I'm walking back, he wants to give me a high five. And I wanted to tell him off, but what did I do? I high-fived him, with a big, fake smile on my face, like it's all cool. But it's not. It's not cool."

"It's all right," I said.

"No, it isn't."

"But," Ghaz began gently, "how can you change people's hearts and minds if you don't engage with them? At least now red beard has one positive association with the name Muhammad."

"Engage with them?" Umar objected. "I felt like a performing monkey! Look at me, my name's Muhammad, but hey, don't worry, I like Hank Williams Jr., same as you! Let's be friends!"

"I'm sorry," Ghaz said. "I didn't mean for you to feel that way. I thought it would be cool and exciting and, I don't know, subversive. But I don't always make the best decisions when I'm drunk."

He sighed. "You do realize you gave new meaning to 'lip-synch for your life'?"

"If it helps any, you were brilliant," I offered.

"Yeah, I know I was fabulous," he said, tossing his scarf over his shoulder. "That's not the issue."

Ghaz gripped Umar's arm, planting a series of kisses on his cheek. "What can I do to make you feel better?"

"Take me someplace where I can stuff myself with greasy food."

"I think this place called Prince's Hot Chicken Shack is open late," she offered.

"I'm down for that," he said.

But I was hungry, too, and I'd had enough.

"Um, hello," I said, "have you forgotten that I'M A VEG-ETARIAN."

"Whoa," Umar said.

"I think you mean, vege-terrorist," Ghaz said.

"Osama bin Lettuce," Umar said.

"Kohlrabi Wahhabi."

"Jihadi Jackfruit."

I rolled my eyes. "You guys are idiots."

We ended up at a Greek diner instead.

Twenty-eight

AS WE DROVE THROUGH southern Tennessee, Ghaz read us an email from her fourteen-year-old sister.

Ammi and Abba say we're not supposed to contact you, but I thought I should let you know Ammi's been really sick, some mornings she won't even get out of bed. And some of the uncles have stopped shaking Abba's hand after Friday prayers. A lot of people blame Ammi and Abba for what you did, even though anyone who knows them knows how religious they are. You really hurt them, and our whole family. Ammi's stopped going to the masjid because she's too ashamed to show her face. I don't like going anymore either because I know everyone's either looking at me and wondering if I'm like you or feeling sorry for me because of what you did. Ammi says she hopes by the time it's time for me to get married people will have forgotten about what you did. Insha'allah I'll meet a guy who understands siblings can be very different. Anyone who respected themselves and their body wouldn't pose naked on a billboard for the whole world to see. Anyway, you should know Ammi and Abba and all of us are really suffering. I don't know if you still care about us but if you do please don't bring any more shame on us. Your sister, as if you care.

"I'm so sorry," I said.

"She doesn't mince words, does she?" Umar said.

Silence. I glanced back. Ghaz chewed her bottom lip as she stared out the window, her knees tucked into her chest, her feet pushing against the back of my seat. We followed her lead, quietly watching the world go by at seventy miles per hour. The landscape was lush and green and monotonous, except for the occasional sun-bleached billboard.

We passed one that asked, *Where Will You End Up? Heaven or Hell?*

Even with the AC on high, my skin was slowly roasting from the sun streaming through the windshield. In the highway median, lanky weeds undulated wildly in the wind from passing cars. We drove by a small cemetery on a grassy slope bordering the highway, a faded billboard for *America's Best Value Inn* towering above the tombstones.

Even the dead couldn't escape capitalism, and no one, it seemed, could ever really escape their families. They'd continue to haunt you, through technology or memories or an aching for what once was, like the pain of a phantom limb. I wondered if Ghaz would ever have a healthy relationship with her family, if Umar would after he came out. It made me feel helpless. I could try to ease my friends' hurt, but nothing I could do or say would change their families' attitudes. I'd seen it in my own naani, this stubborn clinging to notions of right and wrong that superseded even love.

We had been listening to a Belle and Sebastian playlist, and the song "The Party Line" came on. It was the kind of song that made you want to dance from the very first note. I thought maybe dancing would be inappropriate given Ghaz's sorrow, but she was the first one to start bopping her head, Umar soon joining in. I turned the volume up, and it was on.

All three of us loved to dance. Umar's and Ghaz's moves were more graceful and fluid, mine were staccato, like a robot's, but a cool robot's. At least I liked to think so.

Umar had an amazing ability to groove and steer at the same time. He had solid dance-driving skills. I was doing my robot arms, and Ghaz was sitting up now, embellishing her moves with Bollywood gestures.

Ghaz hooted, and I knew that, despite all that had happened

and whatever lay ahead, we were lucky to have music and dancing and one another.

After the song ended and we'd caught our breath, I asked
Ghaz how she was feeling.

"You mean about my sister stabbing me in the back?" she
said.

"You two have always been very different," Umar pointed out.

"Yeah—she's been a Goody Two-shoes since she could talk.
She would tell on me all the time. 'Ammi, guess what I saw Ghaz
do, guess what Ghaz said, blah blah,' and then as my mother
yelled at me, she'd stand behind her and stick her tongue out.
She's always wanted to define herself in opposition to me, like
we were in some sort of competition. My brother and I are much
closer, but it's only a matter of time before he gets completely
brainwashed. My whole family's right-handed. I'm left. It was
doomed from the beginning."

"But you still love them," I said.

"Loving your family and liking them are two very different
things."

"They might come around," I said.

"Will they?" Ghaz said. "Will Umar's family come around
to him being gay? I mean, *really* come around? Will his parents
ever say, 'we'll throw you and your husband a wedding as dope
as your sister's, with a nice *mehndi ki raat* and a fancy reception, because you deserve it just as much'? Will my mother ever
say, 'sorry for the things I said to you, for calling you a slut, a

whore, a filthy prostitute'? She won't, because she thinks I am those things."

"Oh, Ghaz," I said. I'd heard enough about Ghaz's mother that I should no longer be surprised by these revelations, but I always was.

"What kills me is that she portrays herself as the powerless, weak one. 'Look at me, look at how sick I've gotten, how depressed you've made me'. But she was unhappy before I was even old enough to do anything wrong."

"My mother's the opposite," I said. "She doesn't dare feel sorry for herself. But I don't know, I think there's a balance. It's okay to sometimes think your life is hard, or unfair."

"You know what I once heard my sister say?" Umar said. "She's like, 'I totally accept that there are gay people, but why can't they keep it quiet? I don't go around flaunting my heterosexuality everywhere.' Oh, and she also said gay men could never be as good parents because two good gay men still could never equal one good mother."

"Well, you'll have to prove her wrong," I said.

"Can we take the next exit?" Ghaz requested. "I think I need to scream."

"I could eat some fries," Umar said.

"You have an unhealthy relationship to grease," I told him.

"Relaxi, taxi, it's a road trip. Road trips run on grease."

"Let's see where we are," Ghaz said, searching on Umar's phone. "Hmmm . . . we are about to pass Pulaski, Tennessee, which is apparently where the KKK was founded."

"Hell no," Umar declared.

"Come on, I'd never! Let's stop at the next rest stop."

When we pulled into the rest stop parking lot, Ghaz said she didn't feel like screaming anymore, so we got out for a pee and sugar refuel. The challenge of summer in the South was not only the sun's intensity, but its weight. The moment you left the car's air-conditioned cocoon, you felt it bearing down on you.

"Damn, it's hot," Ghaz complained. "Imagine the slaves having to pick cotton in this."

While in the South, it was hard not to view everything through the lens of history, even the sun.

We walked toward the rest stop, past a white rape van and a line of trucks with brightly colored cabs: purple, cobalt blue, fire-engine red. The few people milling around were old, with alarmingly thick middles.

"People here really like their poly blend," Umar noted.

"Spoken like a true clothes snob," I said.

"I'm not a snob. Some items from my wardrobe are from Target."

"What do you think is harder?" I said. "Being Muslim or being poor?"

"Being a poor Muslim," he said.

"Being a poor, trans, lesbian, black, Muslim woman," Ghaz said. "That's probably the hardest."

"Being poor isn't an excuse for being racist," Umar argued.

"I wasn't excusing it," I said. "I was only reminding you—us—that we're also privileged."

"What a cute rest stop," Ghaz said, pointing to the rest area's main building, made entirely of stone, bluegrass playing through its outdoor speakers. Inside, a life-size cardboard cutout of Dolly Parton welcomed us to Tennessee, which meant several minutes of posing and selfies. There was no food available, but the old lady at the information desk directed us to the one-room building next door, which featured wall-to-wall vending machines. It smelled like chemical cleaning supplies, but Umar was immediately in heaven, doing a circuit of the machines and proclaiming the possibilities.

"Peanut M&M's! Twix? Cheddar potato skins! Raspberry shortbread? Goldfish! Swedish fish! Jalapeño poppers?"

Ghaz stood in front of the broken gourmet coffee machine, frowning at it as if that might get it to work.

"Cheetos? Starburst?"

"No Starburst," Ghaz said, so vehemently that we both turned to look at her. She shrugged. "It's personal."

Umar settled on Snickers for all.

We returned to the main building, which had a cozy room with rocking chairs next to a stone fireplace decorated with a wreath and featuring a wall of information about the Civil War. No one else was there so we took it over. As we had our sodas and Snickers, the combination of chocolate and caffeine and the rocking motion of the chair allowed Ghaz to relax a little.

"Sorry I snapped in there," she said to Umar.

"It's okay," he said. "You know, that stuff that's happening with your parents, it's going to happen to my parents, too, when I come out. I bet there will be men who stop shaking my dad's hand in the masjid. They all see me as the sweet boy who does the breast cancer walk with his mother every year, who will be a successful doctor like his successful parents. Imagine the gossip when they find out otherwise. At least my dad, he only cares about the respect of people he holds in high regard, but my mom, she wants it from everyone. She loves the admiration from the community, being the model Muslim family. From white people, too. When the local paper wrote an article about my parents' charity missions, she was so psyched. There was some other Pakistani guy who came out; he's much older than me so I don't really know him. Some people started saying, 'I always thought he was a little strange'; other people wondered if it was because of something his parents had done. My parents had a party a little while after everyone found out and I heard people say stuff like, 'Such a shame. Very handsome, too. Such a waste.'"

"Screw the community," Ghaz said.

"It's my community, too. And if you leave the community, how can you ever make it better? Anyway, even if I did distance myself, there would still be . . ."

"What?"

"Allah."

I glanced around to make sure we were still alone. I knew I

shouldn't care, but people got kicked off planes for simply saying the Arabic name of God.

Ghaz groaned. "Oh, Umar, come on."

"The Quran says—"

"The Quran also says a woman's testimony is worth half a man's," she cut in.

"Ghaz," I said softly, "let him talk."

Umar folded his Snickers wrapper into one-fifth its size as he spoke. "You know I grew up thinking homosexuality was a sin. I was, like, eight when I realized I liked guys."

"How did you know?" I asked, realizing we'd never talked about it in detail.

"I don't know . . . I always found men more aesthetically pleasing. I wanted to look at them more. But I knew it was wrong, so I tried not to think about it, but then puberty hit, and I'd be in the masjid at Friday prayers and I'd see this guy I thought was beautiful, and I'd feel so guilty: here I was in the house of Allah admiring other men. I started to hate myself. My mother was always asking me why I was so sad. But I also kept thinking, Allah wouldn't have made me this way if He didn't want me to be this way. Who I am is Allah's will. But I didn't know how to reconcile this with the fact that according to Islam, it's a sin to have sex with other men. I still don't really know."

"I'll tell you how," Ghaz said. "Forget about Islam. I say pull an Ayaan Hirsi Ali and never look back."

"Come on," I objected. "Even you don't mean that."

"I don't want to leave Islam. I love Allah. I love the Prophet," Umar said.

"So what will you do, Umar?" Ghaz said. She was starting to become agitated again, as she was wont to do about Umar's insistence on maintaining his faith. "Get to Cornell, go to the gay party Thursday night, and attend *jumma* prayers with the MSA the next day?"

"Maybe Cornell has a progressive MSA," I said.

"What does Islam give you, besides guilt?" she continued.

"Lots of things," Umar replied. "A sense of peace. Guidance. Community. Identity. Come on, Ghaz, even you like some parts of it."

"Yeah," she retorted. "Like eating all day on Eid."

"And I've been reading this book by a gay Muslim scholar," he added. "There's really only one part of the Quran that addresses homosexuality, the story of Prophet Lut, and he argues that you can interpret it so that what it's condemning isn't homosexual sex, but male on male rape."

Ghaz threw her hands up. "This is what I don't get! If Allah is all-knowing blah blah, and the Quran is the word of Allah, then why would He leave us with a book that was like, interpret it this way and homosexual sex is a grave sin, but interpret it this way and it's cool? Why wouldn't He say straight out that it was okay? You know why? Because it was a text meant for a desert tribe in the seventh century. Applying it in a way that makes sense to the twenty-first century is ridiculous, and forces you to jump through all these interpretive hoops. And anyway, the Abrahamic God is a total douche."

"You'll never understand," Umar argued.

They could go on like this for a while.

"So how will you reconcile it, your faith and your sexuality?" I asked, hoping to steer the conversation to some sort of resolution.

"Well, I figure, what's repeated the most in the Quran? That Allah is all-forgiving, all-merciful. Before you eat or start a journey, you even say aloud that He's merciful. So I don't think it's a sin, but I figure that He's so merciful that, even if it did turn out to be a sin, He'd forgive me."

"Umar! The fact that you even think Allah might have to forgive you! I need to get some air." Ghaz rose so vehemently that her rocking chair continued to sway in anger after she'd gone. I reached over and stopped it with my hand.

"What's with her?" Umar said. "Why is she acting so militant?"

"You know it isn't really about you. She's upset about her sister's email and she's taking it out on you."

"Yeah." Umar rocked back with a sigh, lifting the frayed edges of his scarf and gently laying them in an *X* across his chest.

"I'll go find her. In the meantime," I said, gesturing at an illustrated panel depicting *The Confederacy's Last Gasp in Tennessee*—in which the Union and Confederate armies faced each other, only a few feet between their pointed rifles, the

Confederate side depicted as both larger and more organized—"you can learn about the Civil War."

Ghaz had climbed up the small hill behind the vending-machine building and was sitting in the shade of a lone tree, her long legs to one side, one hand toying with her necklace as she gazed toward the horizon. Her hair was loose, and she wore no makeup, and her eyes were dark and sad. There were still moments, like now, when her beauty gave me pause.

"Hey," I called out as I walked up the hill.

She crossed her legs to make room for me in the shade. I reached for her hand, and we listened to the sizzle of crickets and the distant strains of bluegrass music.

"Can I ask you something?" Ghaz said.

"Of course."

"What did you really think of the billboard?"

I wasn't sure what question I'd been expecting, but this wasn't it. "Well, you looked beautiful."

"That's a cop-out. And you always think that. You were thinking it a second ago when you were walking over here."

"How do you know?"

"Ninety percent of the time, you're an open book. Come on, tell me the truth."

"Honestly, I don't have a straight-up answer. On the one hand, I've never been a fan of the Brooklyn Attire campaigns, the way they sexualize young girls, turning them into some sort of empty vessel for a man to fill with his fantasy. I'm not a fan of how women's bodies are used as commodities to sell practically everything. I mean, you hardly ever see men selling watches half-naked on their knees. But I also don't believe that a woman's worth should be measured in what she does or doesn't wear. The people who think women should remain fully clothed, who equate being covered with female modesty, they're also sexualizing women's bodies. It's two sides of the same coin. My point is, I don't have an answer to your question because it's complicated. All that really matters anyway is how *you* feel about it."

"How I feel about it," she repeated. "I don't know. I had this idea that the billboard would change my life, that maybe some talent agent would contact me and tell me I was the next big thing, but the few agents who contacted me offered to represent me only if I pay them first. God, I even thought maybe some Bollywood director would see it and insist I star in his next movie. Instead, I had to deactivate my Facebook account yesterday because I was getting friend and message requests from random desi men, some were creepy stalker, some gross lewd, some *you bring shame to Muslims and are going to hell*. And then there's the fallout with my family. If I'd at least been paid some decent money maybe I'd feel better about it."

"How much did they pay you?"

Ghaz sighed. "Three hundred bucks."

"That's it?"

"Yeah, I mean, they have this open call, and they get all these excited nonprofessional young girls, and you feel honored just to have been picked. If I'd asked for more money they had a hundred other girls willing to take my place.

"Ugh," she said, tossing her head as if to clear out the sadness. "In more pressing concerns, I was mean to our darling Umar."

"It's okay. He understands you're hurting. He wants you to talk about it, too."

"What's the point in talking about it more than we already have? It's not going to change the past, or who my parents are."

"No," I said, "but it might make you feel better."

"I want to do some tree pose. Will you do it with me?"

As I trembled next to Ghaz, I marveled at her ability to be completely steady and rooted to the earth even on one leg, transitioning into a more complicated version I didn't dare attempt. When she was finished, she said, "I can't believe he still worries that Allah thinks it's a sin. I wish I could unburden him of his guilt."

"I know," I agreed. "But he's got to figure that out with his God. No one else can do it for him."

Twenty-nine

UMAR WANTED TO EAT barbecue for lunch because Alabama was famous for it so once again I'd capitulated to the carnivores. We were in Big Bertie's BBQ, inhaling the pungent aroma of vinegar and meat. The restaurant's dozens of award ribbons and framed press clippings covered an entire wall in the restaurant. There were four different types of barbecue sauce on the table: white, hot, traditional, and Hawaiian. Umar had already sampled them, pouring them onto his plate and dipping in with his finger, since neither our utensils nor our waitress had arrived yet.

"Is it because we're brown?" Ghaz speculated.

But it was lunchtime, and the restaurant was crowded. Next to us was a group of eight white, middle-aged men, employee ID badges clipped to their button-down shirts, conversing in thick Southern accents. There were a lot of white people, a few black people, us, and a stooped, elderly Asian woman who limped behind a cleaning cart, clearing off and wiping down tables.

"Oh, man," Ghaz said as the woman passed us. "I really wish there was dim sum in her cart instead of dirty plates."

"You're telling me," I muttered.

"Gimme your phone," she said. "I need to check email."

As Ghaz and Umar got sucked into the internet abyss, I tried not to think about the amount of antibiotic-laden pig that was being consumed in this establishment and instead focused on those doing the consuming. It was nice to see multigenerational tables, with kids, parents, and grandparents eating together, and that the old people weren't all staring at some ugly carpet in a nursing home, which Umar said was his mother's biggest fear. It had always been a pain to take my grandmother out to eat. She only ate halal meat and disliked vegetarian, so we'd have to go to an Afghani or Iranian or Turkish or desi restaurant, which would have been fine except no matter what she'd ordered, she'd proclaim that she could make it better at home and all we were doing was needlessly wasting money, and the amount we'd spent on the check would have better invested in gold.

Behind me was a table of women, dressed in hats and floral dresses like they were attending a high tea, and when they burst into laughter I leaned back, trying to eavesdrop.

"Those Asians, I tell you," one woman said.

"They are industrious people," another said.

I assumed they were referring to the very industrious Asian woman bussing the tables, but then the first one said, "The last time she did my nails, as I'm walking out the door, she yells 'You got boyfriend?' I love her. For Christmas, I'm going to get her a wok."

I hoped she was kidding.

"Shit!" Umar exclaimed, looking down at his phone. "Remember how an uncle was murdered a few weeks ago while walking to Fajr prayers? Yesterday, some guy beat a Pakistani woman in Ohio with a crowbar so badly she almost died. He said he did it so she wouldn't give birth to more terrorists, except she was like a seventy-year-old grandma."

"Seriously? Even being a grandma can't save you?" Ghaz said. "What the hell. We're not safe anywhere."

"How come you don't consider yourself a Muslim but when it comes to stuff like this you say, 'we'?" Umar asked.

"I'm not religious, but that doesn't mean I don't feel solidarity for my community if they're attacked. That could have been my mother. Besides, if they come for us, they're coming for me, too."

"When they do, show them your billboard," Umar said.

"What is that supposed to mean?" Ghaz bristled.

"It was only a joke."

The waitress, a droopy-eyed brunette, her lips a startling shade of fuchsia, arrived with our utensils. "Y'all ready?" she said, not glancing up from her pad as we ordered.

"So much for Southern hospitality," Ghaz breathed after she'd walked away.

"Hey, listen to what my mother wrote," Umar said. *"Maybe you shouldn't go to the IANA convention. What if something bad happens?"*

"Like what?" Ghaz said.

"Like a bunch of guys with machine guns standing outside pointing their guns at you in a menacing manner," I offered.

"Yeah, but we can't act all scared. That gives them power," Umar objected. "That's what they want, to subdue us, for us to cower in fear."

"I'm not saying we aren't the victims of Islamophobia," Ghaz said, "but the Muslim community also needs to deal with their own racism. You know the kinds of things our parents say about black people that make you wish you were deaf. And they're all like, 'Muhammad Ali! Such a great Muslim,' like that somehow proves that the community isn't racist."

"We're all racist on some level," I said.

"I'm not," Umar protested.

"Oh, come on. I'll ask you a question, and I want you to answer it honestly. If you're walking down the street at night, and are passed by a young black guy or a young white guy, who would you be scared of?"

"What are they wearing?" Umar asked.

"Oh, please, like you'd look at their clothes first," Ghaz interjected.

"It *is* Umar," I said.

"We're all conditioned by society to be racist," she continued.

"Maybe, but that doesn't make it right," I said. "What about the people 'conditioned' to see a brown guy with a beard and get scared because they think he's Muslim?"

"We can't only fight Islamophobia," Ghaz stated. "We have to fight all kinds of discrimination."

"No one's disagreeing with you," Umar replied. "I don't see IANA making statements condemning violence against the LGBTQ community, unless it was a Muslim who did it."

Our food arrived: beef brisket for Umar, pork ribs for Ghaz, and a salad for me.

I groaned. "This salad has bacon on it."

"Here," Ghaz said. "Have my mac and cheese."

"There's bacon in that, too," Umar pointed out.

The party of women behind us got up, hugging one another effusively amid peals of laughter. The middle-aged corporates also stood, shaking hands across the table.

In the midst of their good-byes, Umar's prayer app went off, the call to prayer blaring loudly from his phone.

Allahu akbar Allahu akbar

Aaaaaallahu aaaakbar Aaaaaaallll—

It took Umar till the fourth *Allahu akbar* to shut it off. The women and the corporates now stood in complete silence. The entire restaurant was staring at us, including the elderly Asian woman.

"No need to be alarmed," Umar announced. "It's only the call to prayer."

"You're not helping," Ghaz whispered.

"I don't know what to do," he whispered back.

"Let's talk to one another normally, like we're normal," she replied.

"We *are* normal," I said.

We picked up our forks and played with our food. No one approached us, though when the other tables resumed their conversations, it was with lowered voices. People kept glancing in our direction.

"I can't eat," Umar murmured.

Ghaz set down her half-gnawed pork rib. "Eat, both of you!" she insisted. "You don't want them to think you don't like their food."

"There's nothing here I *can* eat," I reminded her.

The waitress returned.

"Y'all enjoying the food?" she asked.

"Delicious," I said.

"You know those ribs are pork?" she said to Ghaz.

"I know."

"Thought I'd check—I know your kind don't eat pork."

"Actually, she does eat pork," Umar said. "Thank you, though."

"I'll leave the check here. And listen, I wouldn't be playing that Allah song if I were you. A lot of people around here won't take kindly to it."

"It's a free country," Ghaz said, because of course even in the Deep South she couldn't keep her mouth shut.

"Yes, it is," the waitress replied evenly.

I squeezed Ghaz's arm under the table, trying to signal it wasn't worth it.

"Your kind?" she said after the waitress left.

"I think she was trying to be helpful," I said.

Ghaz snorted, and said we should leave no tip, but Umar insisted on leaving twenty-five percent, and even bought a bottle of the Hawaiian barbecue sauce.

"What the hell, Umar?" Ghaz cried as we got into the car. "I thought you silenced that app!"

"I thought I did, too!" he replied.

"God," I said. "If this stuff is happening to us, what's happening to women who wear hijab?"

"They get knifed in the street," he replied.

"Oh, relax. The number of Muslims being killed has to be way less than the number of black people killed by cops," Ghaz said.

"Some of those black people might be Muslim," Umar reminded her.

"I used to think the world would end with nuclear war," I

said, "but now I'm leaning toward slow, painful, ugly decline."

"Not a bang, but a motherfucking whimper," Ghaz grumbled.

"I can't win," Umar said. "Some people don't like me because I'm gay, some people don't like me because I'm Muslim, and some Muslims don't like me because I'm gay."

"And I bet some gay people won't like you because you're Muslim," I stated. "Just because you're queer doesn't mean you aren't prejudiced."

"It could be worse," Ghaz reminded him.

"Yeah," I agreed. "You could be gay and Muslim *and* a refugee living in a garbage-strewn, makeshift camp, no country willing to take you, haunted by the memory of your entire family killed before your eyes."

"Damn, woman," Ghaz said.

"That is true," he conceded.

"You could be that," Ghaz continued, "but instead you're a rich kid on the road trip of a lifetime. Look on the bright side, right?"

As if on cue, a giant pickup truck with monster wheels merged in front of us, the large Confederate flag attached to the back fluttering in the wind. Hanging below the rear bumper were two giant metal balls.

"Wow," Ghaz said. "Look at those truck nuts."

"Is that really what they call them?" I said.

"Yeah. They're testicles for your truck."

I was speechless.

Umar groaned. "You guys, I don't know. Maybe it's time to turn around and head home."

"No way!" Ghaz said. "NOLA or bust, remember? If we turn around, truck nuts wins! What we need to do now is take a deep breath, relax, put on the Boss, and crank up the volume."

Bruce Springsteen took us all the way through western Alabama, down a bucolic highway that had no billboards and hardly any vehicles, only woods and open road leading us toward a beautifully layered sunset, teal-gray expanse of sky, a narrow band of wispy pink clouds, a horizon edged in deep gold. It was nice to be in nature, sans people, because people could be pretty awful.

By the time we entered Mississippi, it was dark. We filled our tank, stopped at a Taco Bell, eating it so quickly we all felt sick, and when we returned to the car Ghaz announced we were going to play a game of post–Taco Bell Truth or Dare.

"How is post–Taco Bell Truth or Dare different from regular?" I asked.

"More farts," Umar said. "My question is, how many dares can you do inside a moving car?"

"I guess that means you want truth," she responded. "Umar, please tell us about the first time you came. Not, like, in a dream, but purposefully."

"Ummm . . . I honestly don't remember much about the first time. Well, I do remember that I was scared to masturbate because a teacher at Sunday school had told us masturbation was haram and would make your eyesight weak, so when I first did it I turned the light back on to make sure I hadn't gone blind. But other than that, I don't really remember."

"Fine, then tell us about an interesting time when you came," Ghaz said.

"Interesting . . ." Umar clucked his tongue as he thought. "I mean, it's silly."

"Even better," I said.

"Okay. So, there was this guy in the community, Wasim. He was, like, five or six years older than me. His mother was Kashmiri and he had light skin and hazel eyes and black, black hair, even thicker than mine. Terrible dresser, but beautiful face. His family's house was super modern, boxy with lots of glass, and once in a while they'd have a party, which everyone would be excited for because they'd have yummy Kashmiri food, and I'd be excited for because Wasim would be there. I mean, all the girls had crushes on him, too, he was like Imran Khan with greener eyes."

"Who's Imran Khan?" I asked.

"Famous Pakistani cricketer heartthrob of his time," Ghaz explained.

"Anyway, we go to a party at his house—I must have been eleven or twelve—and the boys are in Wasim's room playing video games. Wasim is playing this assassin in medieval Rome, and I'm cheering him on like the other boys as if I care about the video game, but all I really care about is that I'm sitting cross-legged on the bed and he's on the floor right in front of me, and sometimes as he plays he kind of jerks back, and whenever he does, his hair brushes against my bare toes. I had to work so hard to play it cool, because every time it happened I'd get a shiver up and down my spine."

I noticed Umar's shoulders do a little shimmy, as if reliving the physical memory of his experience.

"And then?" Ghaz said. "Please tell me it ends with you two on a Ping-Pong table."

"What? No! Wasim's mother came to tell us to come down for dinner, but I stayed after everyone left. I'd noticed a laundry bin in the corner, so I opened it and stole a pair of Wasim's dirty boxers. I stuffed them inside my *shalwar*, and when I went home that night I held them to my nose and, you know, jacked off. Because I had them stuffed in my own crotch, they smelled like a combination of him and me. It was the closest we ever got."

"See," Ghaz said, "if you did that with the stolen underwear of a girl, I'd be grossed out, but since it's a guy, it's kind of sweet."

"What happened to Wasim?" I asked.

Umar shrugged. "Graduated from college, became a biologist, got married young, moved to the West Coast. Last time I stalked him online he had a receding hairline." He ran his hand through his own locks, reassuring himself of their longevity.

"Mars, do you remember when we first met Umar?" Ghaz said. "He wouldn't have been able to say the words 'jack off' without his cheeks turning that sweet shade of pink. We really brought out the potty mouth in him."

"It was always there," Umar said. "It was waiting for the right audience. All right, Ghaz, your turn to spill your tea. We know you have something good."

"Same question? Well, I think the first time I came is pretty interesting," she revealed. "I was ten, and you know what made me horny? The Quran. We used to learn the stories of the Prophets in Sunday school, and one day we learned the story of Yusuf."

"Ah." Umar nodded.

"I don't know it," I said.

"Yusuf is the same as Joseph; you know, his treacherous brothers throw him down the well, yadda yadda. So, he ends up in Egypt, and the minister buys him and brings him home, and he's so smoking hot that Zulaikha, the minister's wife, is totally beside herself with desire. She wants him so bad that one day she can't take it anymore, and she locks the door of the room and is like 'Come over here, hot stuff,' and he wants her, too, but of course he remembers Allah and says 'I can't, it's a sin,' and runs away. She chases after him and grabs his shirt and the shirt tears in her hand, and Yusuf makes a break for the door and when he opens it, who's standing there but the minister."

"Uh-oh," I said.

"So the minister is standing there wondering what the hell is going on, and Zulaikha freaks out and says, 'Yusuf tried to seduce me!' And Yusuf says, 'No way, she was jumping me.' But when the minister sees that Yusuf's shirt is torn in the back, he knows his wife is lying, and he asks for Yusuf's forgiveness."

"The lustful woman trying to corrupt the virtuous man," I said. "Classic."

"Oh, but that's not even the best part," Ghaz went on. "So after this happens, word gets out in the 'hood and all the ladies start talking smack about Zulaikha. That she's so full of lust and *ishq* for her slave she can't see straight anymore, yadda yadda. And when Zulaikha hears the goss, she's like, screw you bitches, and invites them all over for a banquet. She gives them knives and veggies to chop, and then she asks Yusuf to come into the room. When he comes in and the ladies see how insanely hot he is, their knives slip and they all cut their hands and stand there bleeding, staring at him lustfully. And Zulaikha's like, 'Now you *b*'s see why I'm crazy for him!' and Yusuf's like, 'I'm outta here,' and after that he goes to prison, you know, where he interprets the dreams."

"Oh yeah," I said. "For the pharaoh, right?"

"Exactly. Anyway, I listened to Sister Fatima tell us this story from the Quran, and that night in bed I kept thinking about it. It was the first time I'd ever heard the word *lust*, and it was the first time I learned that sexual desire can be so powerful that you can tear someone's shirt and cut your own damn hand, and I kept wishing I could see Yusuf because I wanted to feel it, too. Only for a sec, though, because I didn't want to get into too much trouble like Zulaikha did. So, I started imagining him in front of me, and I got this tingling feeling between my legs, and I put a pillow underneath my torso and started rubbing my crotch against it, faster and faster, and while I'm coming, who walks in but my mother. And she yells, 'What are you doing?' and I say, 'I was thinking about Prophet Yusuf,' and she slaps me and tells me I'm dirty and makes me do *wudu* and pray and ask forgiveness from Allah for having impure thoughts and she took my pillow away."

"Oh, Ghaz," I said. To me, the idea of your own mother hitting you was so foreign and incomprehensible and sad, but Ghaz spoke of it like it was simply a fact of childhood. "How many times has she hit you?"

"Not a lot," Ghaz said. "Not a little, either."

"My mother could never hit me," Umar said. His mother doted on him, still babied him even though he was almost eighteen. "And my father doesn't need to hit, he employs a different kind of intimidation." His phone began to vibrate. "My sister," he said.

Umar pulled over so he could talk. I looked at Ghaz in the rearview mirror. She was humming along to "Get Lucky" by Daft Punk, not seeming at all disturbed by the story she'd relayed. Outside, Umar was making funny faces at his phone, probably FaceTiming with his niece and nephew.

"Ghaz, have you ever thought about seeing a therapist?" I asked gently. "The stuff that's happened with your mother . . . it has to be rough on you."

"I guess. But I've never known it any other way."

"Yeah, but that doesn't mean it made you feel good."

"But it's made me resilient. I'm cool. Besides, you know what my ultimate rebellion is going to be? To be happy."

I didn't doubt Ghaz's determination to be happy, but she couldn't keep running from her past, or pretending everything was cool. But what else could I do except keep bringing it up and hoping she'd one day let us in?

Thirty

AFTER A LONG DAY in the car and confessional conversations, by the time we arrived in the infamous party capital of New Orleans even Ghaz declared herself too beat to hit the street. It had already been such an emotionally intense trip I wasn't sure I had the energy to party much longer. I wasn't a huge partier anyway. Plus, I needed time and space and solitude to process what had happened with my dad, and the fact that my mother had known my father was back in America but didn't tell me, and the Sylvia incident and all else that followed, but this was impossible because we kept moving, and with each day came some new incident or revelation.

I needed to withdraw for a bit, decompress.

But first, New Orleans.

Umar had spent hours Googling in the car and found us a cool hotel for seventy-nine dollars a night in downtown, "normally one forty-nine," he informed us proudly. It was a historic building, with a lovely stone courtyard and tall, beautiful windows. Umar had booked the room with one king bed because it was cheaper, but since we didn't want to be charged for an extra person, I volunteered to wait across the street as they checked in.

I stood in a shadowy part of the sidewalk where I could observe Ghaz and Umar enter the small, ornate lobby, walking up to a stern, bald man sitting at the fancy antique writing table that stood in for a reception desk.

They were holding hands, a handsome, fashionable couple, Umar with his cropped hipster pants and wavy, rock star hair, Ghaz in a black skirt embroidered with black flowers and a white button-down vest-shirt and a string of pearls and cheetah-print Converse. As I watched them, my heart ached a little. I wanted them to be happy. I wanted us all to be happy. So much uncertainty lay ahead. At least I had the comfort of knowing that no matter what, my mother, and even my supremely annoying brother, would be there for me.

Umar and Ghaz checked in and disappeared through the hotel's inner courtyard. When Umar texted me the room number, I decided to stay out for a while longer. It was nice to be alone, on a quiet street lit by a beam of pale moonlight.

The bright side of all this road trip distraction was that I'd obsessed less about Doug. If we were still dating, I'd be calling him each night, recapping the day's highs and lows. He was such a good listener. It was what had first attracted me to him. A lot of guys cut women off, or listen only so they can respond, but Doug listened like he cared about what I had to say, because he did. It might sound like a silly thing to fall for someone over, but it was a special quality. My high school boyfriend had loved to hear himself talk, and preferred me to remain quiet and nod. Doug was always asking me what I thought, how I felt.

My mother would have liked him.

My phone buzzed. **Earth to Mars! R U in a vampire trance in the middle of the street??**

When I got to the room, Ghaz was in downward dog, Umar sprawled on the bed, watching *The Big Bang Theory* and eating potato chips. The bed was the room's crowning centerpiece: an enormous, intricately carved wooden four-poster with a damask canopy.

We played rock, paper, scissors to see who'd sleep bitch, and I lost. I lay awake, listening to Umar's intermittent but heavy mouth-breathing, and at two a.m., I texted Shoaib.

Everything cool?

Yeah why?

No reason. I miss home.

Well, I had to hire another feminazi to lecture me

haha

They don't come cheap

Ur an idiot. Hows ur girlfriend

We broke up

Why

Too clingy, and kinda dumb. Whats the point of a girl-
friend if she can't do ur math homework

Plz tell me u didn't ghost

Nah, had a talk with her

I never thought Shoaib would have the moral high ground on me.

Good. Mom ok?

She's always ok. Ghaz ok?

Not really.

Ghaz moaned and turned over, flinging her arm across my chest, sleeping beauty in distress. A tendril of hair lay across her cheek, the strands splaying with each breath. Her face was clenched, her lips moving, forming words I couldn't make out.

I should go, I told Shoaib.

later

I rested my hand on Ghaz's forehead. "Ssshhh," I said, over and over, until her jaw relaxed. At some point, I fell asleep, because I woke up to sun streaming through the curtains and Ghaz tickling my feet.

"Wake up!" she cried. "Brand-new day! Don't you love this room?

"The water pressure sucks, though," she added, before jumping on top of Umar and pummeling his side. "Umaaaar *utho*! Partying is better than sleep!"

"What time is it?" Umar asked.

"Almost noon."

"Are you serious? I have to head to the IANA convention," he said. "I have to show my face."

"We can all go," Ghaz offered.

"What?" I said.

"Come on, Mars, have an open mind," she told me.

"I do have an open mind, but religious conferences are not my thing."

"Did you guys even register?" Umar said.

She shrugged. "What, is some burly bouncer going to kick us out?"

"But you can't be seen with me," he said. "Like, three of my cousins are supposed to be there. Plus, what if Ghaz runs into someone she knows? Her parents will freak if they find out she's at the biggest gathering of Muslims in the United States."

"Biggest gathering of Sunni Muslims," she reminded him.

"He's right," I agreed. "It's a bad idea."

"I'll wear a disguise," Ghaz said.

"Oh, really? What are you going to go as?" I said. "Santa Claus?"

"The Burqa Avenger," Umar suggested.

"The Easter Bunny," I said.

"Oh, I know—you could walk around as Zulaikha, with a torn piece of shirt in your hand, all hot and sweaty, like, 'Yuuuuuuusuf? Anyone seen Yusuf?'" Umar said. "Oh, and

Mars could dress as the minister, and walk behind you all pissed off, going, 'Has anyone seen Zulaikha?'"

"Lemme guess," Ghaz said. "Our darling Umar will play Yusuf?"

"I can't help the effect I have on women."

Ghaz leapt forward and pinched his burgeoning love handle. "Not if you keep this up. Come on. You're too hot to get fat."

"Shut up. It's the Southern five; I'll lose it when I cross back over the Mason-Dixon," he said. "But seriously, what are you thinking when you say you'll wear a disguise?"

"You really don't know?" she cried.

"What?" I said. "Drag again?"

Ghaz laughed. "Yes, I'll attend the IANA convention dressed like a drag queen. No one will notice."

"Sissy that walk!" Umar cried.

As she started to sashay around the bed, Umar announced, "*As-salaam alaikum*, Brothers and Sisters. Our next queen likes to slay the infidels—on the runway, that is. She prefers it haram with her cherry on top. May I introduce you to America's hottest new queen . . . Sharia Law!"

Ghaz struck a pose, lips in a pout, one slender arm curved around her head, hip thrust forward, and we all burst out laughing.

"Salaams, everyone, I'm Sharia Law," she purred. "Every Republican legislator's biggest wet dream."

"Work it, Sharia!" Umar said as Ghaz attempted an acrobatic

leg split that ended with her splayed on her back, wincing.

"That part of the act needs work," Umar noted.

I helped her up. "You're obviously not going to go to IANA as a drag queen. So what, then?"

"Think about it. What will no one expect the shameless naked billboard girl to be wearing?"

"Versace," Umar replied.

Ghaz threw one of the bed's silk cushions at him. "I'll wear hijab! I don't think anyone will recognize me then."

"Ah." Umar nodded. "I see."

"So we're really going to this thing?" I said.

"Seriously, though, why do you want to go?" Umar asked Ghaz.

"I don't know," Ghaz said. "To check it out. I'm curious to see what's up. I haven't been since I was little. I may be an atheist, but I'm a *Muslim* atheist. And I'd say Mars didn't have to go, except I want company, since Umar can't hang out with me."

"Can we discuss this further over brunch? I'm starvation nation," Umar declared.

We went to a breakfast joint across the street and had the most decadent brunch of my life: eggs Benedict po boys, stuffed French toast, bananas Foster. By the end of it, I was wishing my jeans waistband was made of elastic. If brunch was like this, I both anticipated and feared dinner.

Back in the room, we began to get ready for the convention. As Ghaz rummaged through her suitcase, she let out a shriek, holding up a bottle of Big Bertie's Hawaiian BBQ sauce she'd found amid her clothes. "Very funny, Umar!" she cried. "What if it had opened?"

Umar grinned. "Meet the new face of Big Bertie's distinctive BBQ sauce collection: Sharia!"

Annoyed as she was, Ghaz couldn't resist. "Big Bertie's sweet and tangy Hawaiian BBQ sauce," she said, caressing the bottle, "is guaranteed to get you lei'ed."

Umar and I groaned appreciatively.

"You guys are clowns," I said.

"You love it," Umar replied.

He was right. I did.

As Ghaz got ready, Umar and I lay on the bed, Umar searching Yelp for the best restaurants in town. I was impressed he could even read about food after the meal we'd consumed.

"I can't make a decision," he declared, tossing his phone aside. "There are *too* many good places to eat."

"Hashtag firstworldproblems," I said.

Umar reached across me for the book on the nightstand. "*The Brothers Karamazov*. Hmmmm." He flipped through the pages. "Not exactly a summer beach read, is it?"

"My dad gave it to my mom a long time ago," I explained. "I kept it out because I'm going to leave it in the guest lending library downstairs."

"Oh." He gently flipped the book over so it was faceup on the bed, smoothing out its cover. "Are you sure?"

"Yeah," I said. "I've been holding on to it because I felt like it was a piece of him, but I don't need to carry it anymore."

He nodded. "I really admire you, Mars."

I paused, waiting for a punch line, but there was none. "Thanks. If only Doug could say the same."

"Okay!" Ghaz cried, turning away from the mirror, one of Umar's scarves, a pale gray cotton, covering her hair and pinned tightly around her face. "Does it look okay?"

"Sister!" Umar exclaimed. "*Masha'allah*, you look so beautiful, so pure."

"*Jazak Allah khair* and shut the hell up," Ghaz replied.

It was true. I wasn't sure about beautiful and pure, but she did look pious, and decidedly non-billboard.

"I don't like having my ears covered," she said.

"Can you hear okay?" I asked her.

"What?" she said.

"Can you hear?" I said, louder, and she started laughing.

Aside from her gray hijab, she had on her doily funeral dress, a black cardigan, her long necklace of pearls, and her cheetah-print Converse.

"You look like the long-lost Muslim cousin of the Addams family," Umar told her.

"Oh yeah? And you . . ." She studied him. He'd used a little gel today, his hair cresting like a wave over his forehead, and had on fitted cargo pants embellished with dark leather and brass zippers, a simple black T-shirt, his green-and-black checkered scarf. "You look like AllSaints and Odin New York threw up on a member of Hamas."

I didn't get the reference, but Umar said, "Ha-ha."

"Hey—what about me?" I asked.

Umar threw his arm around Ghaz's shoulder and together they assessed me.

Ghaz had told me to dress modestly, but my long-sleeved button-down now had stains on it, so I'd paired my jeans with one of Umar's shirts, navy blue ikat with a Nehru collar. It hung loosely off my shoulders, hit unfashionably past my hips.

"Try tucking your shirt in," Umar suggested, so I did.

"Now you look like a dyke," Ghaz pronounced.

"A dyke with excellent taste in menswear," Umar said. "But yeah, untuck."

"Should I change into my other pair of jeans?" I asked.

"I don't know," Umar replied, "did you also steal your other pair from the closet of Bilbo Baggins?"

"Umar!" I cried. "That is not helpful. And is this an Islamic convention, or a fashion contest?"

"Fashion contest," Ghaz said.

"What?"

"Ignore her," Umar said. "You're right, you don't have to be fashionable for this."

"Do I have to stay if I don't like it?" I asked.

"Don't you know?" said Ghaz. "You have to stay until you've been converted."

Thirty-one

DESPITE THE STICKY HEAT, New Orleans had this
energy that made you want to eat, drink, dance. Everywhere
you turned there was music, *good* music, playing in restaurants,
bars, and hotel lobbies, audible from the street. It was even being
piped out from the speakers at the convention center entrance,
foot-tapping jazz greeting the hundreds of brown people making
their way across the plaza.

"Someone's definitely going to complain about the music,"
Ghaz said.

"Really?" I said.

"You can't have a gathering of this many Muslims without a
few buzzkills in the mix," she explained.

After allowing Umar a five-minute lead time, Ghaz and

I headed inside. A huge banner stating *Welcome to the 52nd Annual Islamic Association of North America Convention* greeted the attendees. The lobby was crowded with people hugging, mingling, talking on their phones, taking photos. Most people seemed either desi or Middle Eastern, and the attendance spanned generations, from tiny infants to senior citizens stooped over canes. Scattered amid the brown were a few African Americans, some in traditional African dress. There were a couple of women who read as white, all of them in hijab.

As we ventured farther in, I realized how few women were showing their hair. Nearly every woman, and even a few little girls, wore headscarves.

"A lot of floral," Ghaz observed, referring to the patterns of the loose, flowing dresses popular among the women.

Many of the female attendees were dressed up. They'd chosen scarves to complement their outfits, and wore nice shoes, long necklaces, bracelets over their sleeves, eyeliner, mascara, lipstick, blush.

And here I was, in baggy jeans and flip-flops and an oversize shirt and no makeup except clear lip gloss, my hair exposed. I had hoped to be wallpaper, but I definitely stood out.

As I contemplated making a run for it, Ghaz put her hand on my back.

"Impressions so far?" she said.

"Has hijab always been so prevalent?" I asked.

"It's become more and more popular since 9/11. Come on, let's find a program."

We continued past rows of booths, some religious in nature, promoting sharia-compliant investments and VIP hajj tours and Muslim charities, others secular, the Peace Corps and Boy Scouts of America. Soon, we came upon the convention's social epicenter, a Starbucks outlet in the center of an atrium. The line for the counter was fifty deep, the surrounding tables abuzz with chatter and laughter.

"Hmmm," I said, observing the scene.

"What?" Ghaz asked.

"The women, they're in different styles of clothes and scarves, but all the young guys kind of look the same." I gestured to a large table of guys to our right. "Medium build, brown skin, black hair, some with gel, wearing button-down shirts and trousers. That basically describes every one of the guys at that table."

"Guys tend to wear the same crap anyway," Ghaz said.

"Fine, but look at their faces. They all have short beards. Okay, on that one guy it's more heavy stubble, but still. Why do they all have the same style of facial hair?"

"Prophet Muhammad had a beard," Ghaz explained. "So, I guess it's, like, a nod to the Prophet, without growing it mullah-length."

"How long do we have to stay?"

"We just got here! Are you really that uncomfortable?"

"This is normal for you, but for me . . . we're in a place where you and I can't walk around wearing what we normally wear or even act like we'd normally act, and Umar couldn't walk around holding hands with a guy. I'm not used to being anything but myself."

"You're a rare brown bird, then," Ghaz said. "Let's at least get the schedule and see if there's anything interesting. If not, we can bail."

"Hey look—there's Umar."

He was at one of the tables drinking coffee with a few other guys, all of them with the same clean-cut, trimmed-beard look. Umar, with his clean-shaven jaw and hipster clothing, stood out a little.

And so, for that matter, did Ghaz, with her doily funeral dress and striking features and statuesque figure.

"Let's go eavesdrop," Ghaz suggested.

"He's not going to like that," I protested, but she was already making her way toward him.

Umar ignored us as we approached his table, stopping within earshot and pretending to be deep in conversation. A young woman in a bright purple headscarf joined them, saying, "Salaams, everyone!" After everyone had salaamed back, she declared, "Umar, you made it! Daanish told me you were driving all the way down here."

"Yeah," Umar said.

"How was the drive?" she asked.

"Uneventful," he replied, and Ghaz stifled a laugh.

One of the guys asked the girl, "What do you think of the new Kanye drop? Right now we have four votes for awesome, two for lame, and one *meh*."

"Oh—I *love* that one track," she said, and all of them immediately started singing it, one of them adding some impressive beatbox.

After they performed a few lines, the girl said, "Did you guys hear there's going to be a protest during the keynote? The keynote is some bigwig from US Immigration and people are going to protest the government's deportation methods and policies. They're making posters after Asr prayer. I'm totally going to do it, *Insha'allah*, it's going to be great. You guys in?"

"Hell, yeah," said one guy.

"Nah, my parents are here and they'd probably be upset," said another.

"What about you, Umar?" she asked.

"Uh, maybe," Umar told her.

One of the guys said, "Hey, Umar, do you know those girls? I feel like they're staring at us."

"Umar has that effect on women," another guy said, and they laughed.

Umar turned his head, shot us a *what the hell are you doing* look.

"About that program," I said, steering Ghaz away.

You couldn't get a program without a registration badge so Ghaz stopped a white convert and asked to borrow his. He was our age, with long blond hair and a long Jesus beard, dressed in a flowing white robe and tan leather sandals, like he'd wandered off the set of *Monty Python's Life of Brian.*

"Of course, Sister," the white dude told Ghaz when she asked, putting his hand over his heart and bowing.

Trippy.

Ghaz returned with a program as thick as a magazine, listing over a hundred talks, panels, and workshops. I read over her shoulder as she turned the pages. Positive Thinking in an Age of Islamophobia. Muslim Women in Sports. Nurturing Spirituality within Marriage. How to Effectively Engage with the Media. Maintaining Your Faith and Focus in a Digital Age. Halal Capitalism. Collaborating Across Communities to Fight Racism. The Quran's Most Beautiful Lessons.

"Some of those sound pretty interesting," I commented.

Ghaz flipped to the next page. "How to Be a Zulaikha to His Yusuf," she read.

"For real?" I exclaimed.

"You are so gullible sometimes! But Mars, look! There's a panel called LGBTQ Issues and the Muslim Community. It's in twenty minutes! We have to tell Umar."

Ghaz returned to the Umar's table, standing several feet opposite and gesturing with her head for him to follow us. If Umar hadn't already been regretting that we'd come to the convention, he surely was now.

Umar excused himself and followed us to the escalator, waiting until we were all the way up before stepping on it himself. I found his theatrics a little ridiculous, but he clearly thought it was necessary.

We convened in an empty corner on the third floor.

Umar shook his head. "You guys couldn't be subtle if your lives depended on it."

"Stop complaining and look at this," Ghaz insisted, showing him the program. "A queer Muslim panel! Maybe this will give you the answers you seek."

"Wow," Umar said. "I think this is the first time they're addressing this topic."

"And maybe one of the panelists will be a hot, gay, college-bound kid who loves Allah, his lota, romantic walks, ice cream, and dancing in his bedroom with the lights turned low," Ghaz breathed.

"Um, I don't want to date myself," he objected.

"That is exactly who you want to date!" she insisted. "You, but a few inches taller."

"Can we not talk about this here?" he protested. "I'll get to the panel first, you follow. After it's over, we can meet by that big jester statue in the lobby."

No one was checking badges at the door so Ghaz and I were able to walk right in. Only a few seats remained, but we managed to find two where we could have a good view of Umar on the opposite side of the aisle, where most of the men were. He had removed his scarf and was rolling it into a rope across his lap.

I hoped this panel would help assuage his guilt.

The panelists took seats behind a long table draped in black cloth. One was a chubby-cheeked desi man with a short beard, the other a woman whose hijab extended, hoodlike, several inches past her forehead.

The moderator, a young woman in a canary-yellow hijab, began to introduce the panelists. The chubby-faced man was a sheikh, an Islamic scholar. The woman was a chaplain who advised Muslim students at one of the UC schools.

"Queer Muslims who are super religious!" I said. "Umar will definitely find this panel useful."

"They're not queer," Ghaz replied, her voice low and stiff.

"What?" I said.

"They're not queer."

"Are you serious?" That was like having a panel called Women's Issues in Islam and having no women on it. Or a panel called African American Engagement with Islam with no black people. How could everyone in this packed room sit here and act like this was actually okay? Part of me wanted to walk out in protest because this panel was already bullshit, but I wanted to be here for Umar, especially now that someone else was speaking for him.

"I should warn you," the moderator began, "that we will

be discussing some sensitive topics relating to sexuality. So, if any of you will be made uncomfortable by it, you should leave now."

No one got up, not even the parents who had brought little kids, one of whom was walking up and down the aisle like he owned it, sipping on a juice box.

"For those of you who don't know what LGBTQ stands for," the moderator continued, "it stands for Lesbian, Gay, Bisexual, Transsexual, and Queer."

Except it was transgender, not transsexual.

It was safe to say this was off to a bad start.

Ghaz sang into my ear, "I'm just a sweet transvestite, from Transsexual, Transylvania!"

"What?" I whispered.

She sighed. "*Rocky Horror Picture Show?* Probably the biggest cult film of all time?" and then shut up because the sheikh began to speak.

"*As-salaamu alaikum wa rahmat ullahi wa barakatuh,*" he greeted the audience.

When the sheikh wanted to emphasize something, he both raised and deepened his voice and brought his lips closer to the mic so the words resounded across the room.

"ISLAM," he announced, "has NEVER had a problem with homosexuality."

Well, that was rather promising.

"ISLAM has always accepted that a certain percentage of the

population will be attracted to members of the SAME SEX," he continued.

It was interesting that he referred to Islam like it was a single thing, not a diverse religion with many sects and more than one billion followers.

"There is NOTHING aberrant in this attraction! You can be attracted to members of the same sex and still be a good, OBSERVANT Muslim."

I glanced at Umar. He'd stopped rolling his scarf, was listening intently.

"BEING a homosexual," the sheikh continued, "is not a problem in Islam. We should LOVE and ACCEPT the homosexual as part of our community. However, there is a distinction between the homosexual PERSON and the homosexual ACT. According to all the Islamic scholars—and anyone who says otherwise is playing interpretative GAMES with the text that DEFY logic—what has been universally accepted by all legitimate scholars, what is stated in the Quran through the story of Prophet Lut, peace be upon him, is that to ACT upon your homosexual URGE is a sin. It is a GRAVE sin. So, homosexuals who wish to be good Muslims and avoid sin must fight the URGE to act upon their homosexuality."

It was classic love the sinner, condemn the sin rhetoric. Across the aisle, Umar had turned pale and still. Next to me, Ghaz was clenching her fists.

"Now, I have people come to me and say, 'Sheikh, gay people

are BORN that way. If ALLAH made them this way, would He not WANT them to live as homosexuals, engage in homosexual RELATIONS with another man?'"

This was similar to Umar's argument.

"To THEM I say, just because you're BORN with an urge does not make it RIGHT. Lots of people are born with innate, sinful urges that they must FIGHT against. For example, PEDOPHILIA. Some people have the innate urge to have sex with young children, but they must FIGHT THIS URGE if they want to be good people because to ACT upon the pedophilic urge would be a sin."

Ghaz gasped. "Oh, no, he didn't."

"Compare homosexuals to pedophiles? Oh, yes, he did," I muttered.

Umar was staring at his feet.

"The same goes for," the sheikh went on, "KLEPTOMA-NIA. Some people are born with the desire to steal, but they must RESIST the urge to act upon it. Now people ask me, 'But Sheikh, how does a sexual act between two CONSENTING ADULTS harm anyone?' Well, does the fact that two adults consent to SNORT COCAINE together mean it's no longer a SIN? While it is important for us to accept that there is nothing sinful about homosexual attraction, to ACT upon it is most definitely a GRAVE sin, and there are NO EXCEPTIONS."

There were so many fallacies to his arguments, I didn't know where to begin.

Ghaz was gritting her teeth, her foot shaking. A young woman walked down the aisle with slips of paper and pens to write questions on. Ghaz grabbed four slips and began scribbling furiously.

The female chaplain spoke next. She had a soothing counselor's voice, and maintained a steady, gentle tone.

"As someone who works with Muslim students, I've had several Muslim students tell me they are gay and are valiantly struggling to fight the urge to act on it. When I see the courage these students have, the love they have for Allah, their willingness to fight their own physical impulses to obey Him, it makes me humble about my own faith. And we must, must, must love and support these people, not only because they need love and support in their struggle, but also because if we don't they could turn away from Islam. I had one student who was so upset by homophobic comments he heard other Muslim students make that he decided to leave Islam, go to the Gay Pride parade, and come out to everybody."

As the audience murmured in dismay at this boy's actions, I couldn't believe how glibly the speakers were reducing queerness to an "urge"—acting like they were only denying people like Umar sex. But it wasn't only an urge, and it wasn't only sex. They were essentially telling them don't have too much pride in it, don't kiss anyone or be held by anyone or hold anyone, don't go on long walks with your lover in the moonlight, don't tempt it by dancing too close, don't mind your frustration while your heterosexual friends and family fall in love, get married, kiss, fuck, have kids. Don't find a loving partner. Resign yourself to growing old alone. They were denying Umar his dreams, dreams he deserved as much as anyone else. They were denying Umar love, companionship, intimacy.

"But *masha'allah*," the chaplain continued, "I know many homosexual Muslims who continue to fight the urge in their quest to please Allah, *subhanahu wa ta'ala*. And with our continued love and support, they will continue to choose Allah."

So, this was the message. Either live your life as a celibate, and choose Allah, or don't, and reject Him.

The audience burst into applause. Umar was looking straight ahead now, his hands folded in his lap.

"Note," Ghaz said, "they didn't even mention lesbians. Even the LGBTQ panel was patriarchal."

The moderator announced there was only a little time left for questions. "I received a lot of questions, *al-hamdu lillah*," she said, "but unfortunately we only have time for one. Here's the question: I wear hijab. What if one of my female friends comes out to me as a lesbian? Can I still hug her?"

The chaplain ceded to the sheikh who said, "You should treat her as you would a non-*mahram*, an UNRELATED male. So, don't touch her, don't hug her, don't be alone with her. However, if she is Muslim you should encourage her down the path of righteousness Allah has clearly laid out for us."

"Oh, for crying out loud," Ghaz said. "I have to get out of

here before I blow. I'll see you and Umar by the jester."

The audience broke into another round of applause. As I stood to leave, I noticed a guy in the row behind me. He had a dimpled chin and long, lush eyelashes; broad shoulders; short, wavy hair; a hint of stubble. He was wearing a light blue denim shirt that fit nicely. I'd seen enough of Umar's outfits to recognize a well-tailored shirt. He seemed dismayed, lost in thought.

He looked up, and I realized I'd been staring.

"Hi," I said.

"Hi."

"I'm Mariam. My friends call me Mars." I was about to offer him my hand, but then remembered that unrelated men and women weren't supposed to touch.

"Salaam, I'm Ali," he said.

"What did you think of the panel?" I asked.

"Uh . . ." He scratched his dimple. "It was interesting. You?"

"I found it extremely upsetting and problematic," I declared.

"Yeah," he said, but didn't elaborate.

"I'm going down to the lobby to meet my two best friends—would you like to come? You should meet them. They're really cool," I said, hoping he wouldn't think I was totally weird, especially considering my current status as fashion emergency.

Ali studied me for a moment and I smiled, hoping to convince him of my good intentions.

He smiled back and said, "Sure, why not?"

On the escalators, we fell into easy conversation. I learned he was from Charlotte, North Carolina, was starting at Duke in the fall, that he hadn't been to IANA in a while but had come this year with his family because they wanted his older sister to find a husband.

"Oh yeah," I said. "I saw a sign for a matrimonial speed dating event outside one of the rooms. Did your sister do that? How did it go?"

When Ali smiled, another dimple, small, subtle, appeared on his cheek. "She has a very sharp, dry sense of humor. A lot of people don't quite get it at first, so I don't think speed dating is the way for her to go."

"Unless she meets someone who gets it right away. That could be a sign. Ah, there are my friends."

Ghaz and Umar were standing on opposite sides of the giant statue of a Mardi Gras jester, trying to seem like they weren't talking to each other. The statue was a little obscene, the hem of the jester's shirt sticking out from between his legs like a golden phallus. Every convention center I'd ever been to had been staid and corporate, but New Orleans danced to its own rhythm.

"Ghaz, Umar, this is Ali," I said. "We met at the panel."

"Umar and Ali!" Ghaz exclaimed. "The second and third caliphs."

"Second and fourth," Umar and Ali corrected her at the same time, then looked at each other and smiled shyly.

My heart melted.

"We're going to get some coffee and beignets," Ghaz told him. "You want to come?"

Ali checked his phone. "I have to go to a panel in twenty minutes. My friend is on it and I promised him I'd be there. But I'll walk you guys out."

"Great!" I said, a little too enthusiastically, judging by Umar's deepening blush.

As we walked, I said, "Umar, Ali is also starting his freshman year this fall."

"Oh yeah? What school?" Umar asked him. As they began to chat, Ghaz and I discreetly fell behind.

"You think he's gay?" Ghaz asked me.

"Not sure. But he's so frigging cute. I know he's not a bear, but I think that's more about Umar's fantasies."

"Oh, he moved on to straight boy jock porn months ago," Ghaz said.

"What? I didn't know that."

"That's because you don't ask about his porn habits."

"Do *you* think Ali's gay?" I asked.

"He's wearing chambray," she said, like this would mean something to me.

Outside, Umar and Ali were deep in conversation. We stopped several feet away, far enough to allow them privacy but close enough to observe.

"Look at that dimple," Ghaz noted.

"I know, right?" I said. "He gets one on his cheek, too, when he smiles."

"*Yum*," she said.

They both pulled out their phones.

"They're exchanging numbers!" Ghaz exclaimed. "Well done, Mars!"

They said good-bye and Umar signaled for us to follow him. By the time we were a few blocks away, Ghaz had taken her hijab off and Umar deigned to walk alongside us.

"That whole thing with Ali was awkward," he said.

"It was," Ghaz agreed, "until it wasn't."

"Okay, he seems cool, but I need you guys to understand something. Just because another guy and I are both gay doesn't mean we'll hit it off. That's like me saying, Ghaz, you're straight, and that guy over there, he's straight, too! You two should hook up!"

"Point taken," I said. "But isn't he cute?"

"Uh, *yum*," Umar replied.

"Did he tell you he was gay?" Ghaz asked.

"No, but I got the vibe."

"And you got his number," I added.

Umar grinned, and Ghaz did a little dance that made him laugh.

Though Decatur Street in the French Quarter was lined with lovely pastel buildings with wrought iron balconies, the scene was cheesy. Tacky shops sold cheap souvenirs and gator bites. Tourists crowded the sidewalk, rode by on horse-drawn carriages. There was music in every store and on the street, and food and drink everywhere you turned: oysters and muffulettas and pralines, Bloody Marys and hurricanes, delicious smells permeating the heat. This was a city that embraced its appetites, and the sweaty mass of tourists was only too happy to oblige. When we sat down on the patio of Café Du Monde, I'd never been so grateful for a ceiling fan.

Outside, a sax player performed on the sidewalk, playing a lively rendition of "My Favorite Things." After the gluttonous brunch, I couldn't imagine eating again, but the moment the beignet coated with powdered sugar was set before me, I knew I'd have no problem. As Ghaz caught up with social media on Umar's phone, he'd been eating quietly, and I could guess the object of his contemplation.

"I'm really sorry about the panel," I said, licking sugar from my lips.

Ghaz looked up from the phone. "Me, too."

"You know what's really annoying?" he asked.

"What?"

"There's this verse in the Quran; it's really beautiful. 'Allah created for you mates among yourselves, so you may dwell in tranquility with them.' And the verse, it's gender neutral. It's like Allah is saying, 'I've put you on earth to find love'. And then you have to listen to these straight people who tell you, 'No, that doesn't include you, queer people. Allah doesn't want you people to love. He wants you to suffer gladly, even if He did make you that way.'"

"And the way everyone applauded at the end," Ghaz said, "like, 'Let them suffer and be celibate! Yay!'"

"And when he started comparing homosexuality to pedo-philia?" Umar said.

"Oh." Ghaz set her fist on the table. "I was like, 'Queer people aren't sick. You know who's sick? You, for thinking like that. Boom! Done. See you later.'"

I shook my head. "Come on, I don't know if most mainstream religions could ever fully embrace homosexuality. Will the Catholic Church ever come out and say sex between two men or two women is A-OK?"

"Maybe," Ghaz said, "when it's the future, and there are more robots than people. Robots might have more sense."

"Oh, the way mankind is going, I have no reason to doubt the future moral superiority of robots," I said. "I love America, but most of the time I feel like this country's going to shit."

"How bad do you think it's going to get?" Umar said. "I mean, they can't actually put us in internment camps. It couldn't go that far, that would be America having a total breakdown. We have good bones, right? The Constitution is strong. We have gay marriage, the Bill of Rights."

"For now," Ghaz replied darkly.

"I don't know, friends," I said. "A few years ago, I would

have agreed with Umar, but we live in strange times."

"Let's talk about something less depressing," Ghaz said. "Guess what we're doing tonight?"

"What?" we asked warily.

"Going to a drag show!"

"Ooh. Maybe Chi Chi DeVayne will be in it," Umar said.

"Who?"

"She's a drag queen from New Orleans. I'm not a huge fan, though."

"Okay, well," Ghaz said, "why don't you invite Ali?"

"To a drag show?" Umar said. "I barely know him! That could be awkward in so many ways."

"You have a point," she concurred. "Have you texted him yet?"

"No! I don't want to seem *desesperado*. It's been, like, half an hour."

"Another good point," she said. "Umar, when did you start getting so smart?"

We went back to the hotel, took a nap, had delicious po boys, got ready for the night ahead. But when Ghaz was finally dressed, Umar was still in his boxers, lying on the bed, watching a *Drag Race* marathon on TV.

"Why don't you guys go and I'll meet you there?" he said.

"Liar," Ghaz said, smacking his foot. "You'll stay here and order room service and watch *Drag Race* all night."

"Season five is one of the best," Umar agreed. "Roxxxy

Andrews takes off her wig and has one on underneath."

"Umar, we're in *New Orleans*. Are you seriously going to miss an *actual* drag show for one on TV?" Ghaz cried. "Please don't tell me you're feeling guilty."

"Why would I feel guilty?" he asked.

"Um, because today a sheikh and a chaplain told you that you should. Now do you want to get up or do you want me to *drag* you out of here?"

Umar and I groaned.

"What is with your jokes today?" I asked.

"Side effect of all the fat and sugar I've been consuming," she said.

"Fine," Umar said. "Though my cousins were thinking of visiting the French Quarter tonight. What if I run into them? I told them I felt sick and was going to stay in."

"What would they do there?" I asked. "Do they drink?"

"No, but they could walk around, find a hookah joint."

"So wear a disguise," Ghaz suggested.

Another disguise. How many disguises did this community require of its members?

"Like what?" Umar asked.

Ghaz rubbed her hands together with a wicked grin.

Thirty-two

AN HOUR LATER, we were walking down Bourbon Street. Umar was wearing his black Tabitha wig, holding a green, purple-feathered Mardi Gras mask up to his face, which would have been pretty weird had this not been New Orleans.

So far Bourbon Street was our least favorite part of the city, packed with tawdry bars offering massive to-go cups of booze and the occasional strip show. The whole scene felt like a perpetual, hormonal, misogynistic spring break. Drunk guys dangled beads over bar balconies, hoping for someone to take the bait and show them some skin in exchange for a necklace.

"No one's showing their tits," Umar observed.

"It's too early for tits. I bet if we came back at three a.m. we'd see some," Ghaz said.

"I wouldn't want any of these guys to see my tits," I said. "Would you?"

"No way. Well, maybe that one guy walking over there."

"Hey, mask boy!"

Umar looked up. A plump woman in a shiny red dress was calling out to him from a balcony above. "Take this, honey!" she exclaimed, tossing down a heavy necklace of gold and purple beads with a jester pendant.

"Wow, you just got beads for being cool," Ghaz said.

Umar put the necklace on, even humored Ghaz by posing for photos.

The gay club was on a corner of Bourbon Street populated with rainbow flags. The drag show was on the second floor, in a black box with some café tables and a small stage. Umar removed his wig, saying he'd rather die than be caught wearing such a cheap Shake-N-Go at a proper drag show, which turned out to be a celebrity impersonation starring two queens. The African American queen, with a curvaceous body and sparkling pink lips, imitated a different celebrity each time—Aretha Franklin and Diana Ross and Whitney Houston—but the white one stuck to her tried-and-true act, a trashy Britney Spears.

During the song "Toxic," Britney started dancing toward Umar, flaunting her long, leather-corseted body and gyrating her whip. Ghaz passed Umar some dollar bills under the table. Blushing, he held his Mardi Gras mask to his face.

Britney wrapped her legs around Umar's chair and ran her

cuffed hand down his chest as she leaned far back, then threw herself forward, her lips perilously close to Umar's mouth. We watched, duly impressed, as she tapped his nose with the handle of the whip while simultaneously stuffing the dollars he'd given her into her cleavage and shaking her ass. She could really multitask.

She whispered something in Umar's ear then whirled around in time with the music, snapping her whip as she pranced back onto the stage, executing a perfect split that made the audience cheer wildly and resulted in another round of dollar bills.

By the grand finale, I was pretty drunk, though I'd only had one; the vodka soda I'd ordered was basically all vodka with a splash of soda.

After the show we headed downstairs, but when Umar went for the exit Ghaz pulled him back into the club. Behind the bar were two huge screens displaying the video of whatever pop song was blaring from the speakers. The bartender was shirtless, and there were two ripped dancers standing on either leg of the U-shaped bar, one in a tighty-whities, the other in a G-string.

Ghaz immediately gravitated to Mr. G-string, waving a dollar bill. Seeing her, he bent over, his hands flat on the bar, his smooth, sculpted, and very naked buttocks gyrating madly.

"That's called serving cake," Umar told me, watching intently while maintaining a careful distance.

"What?"

"Buttocks are cakes," he reminded me.

"Oh, right."

Ghaz lightly slapped Mr. G-string's cakes, added a dollar bill to the others in his barely there waistband, and danced back to us.

"Don't touch me with that hand," Umar warned her, yelping as Ghaz proceeded to rub her hand down his shirt.

"Mars! Let's do shots!" Ghaz cried.

"I'm already drunk," I said. "I need a breather."

As Ghaz went to do a shot alone, Umar and I stood by the wall, dancing to Adele's "Send My Love." Next to us, a short muscly white guy in a baseball cap hit on a black guy dressed in a fringed vest, a tattoo of a flock of geese on his bicep. By midsong, they were grinding. By the song's end, they were making out, holding on to each other's cakes.

Umar turned toward me.

"I couldn't do that," he said apologetically, though I was the last person he needed to apologize to. "Hook up with someone I don't know. Even touching the butt of someone I don't know . . ."

"You don't have to do that," I assured him.

"I don't belong at the IANA convention," he said, "but I don't quite belong here, either."

"Didn't Ghaz tell you about some LGBTQ Muslim group that has an annual retreat?" I said.

"Yeah."

I could tell he didn't want to talk about it more, so I held his hand and got him to dance.

After the song ended, I said, "What did she whisper to you?"

"Who?"

"Britney."

"She said, you're too beautiful to keep hiding."

We heard Ghaz's raucous, drunken scream. She'd befriended a bachelorette party at the bar, hollering along with them as the bride-to-be did a body shot off Mr. G-string, licking salt from his groin.

"You think we can check out some live music?" Umar said. "I've had enough gay for the day."

I dragged Ghaz away from the bachelorettes and we took a Lyft to Frenchmen Street. To Umar's relief, the allure of Frenchmen Street was less soft porn debauchery and more music and dancing, bar after bar of live music, people spilling out onto the streets, dancing on the sidewalks. The energy was infectious, even the blues music was tinged with a certain joy. All kinds of people were out and dancing: white people, black people, brown people, old people, young people, lanky girls sporting dreamcatcher earrings and ankle boots, hipster guys with T-shirts to their knees. There was even a guy in a white horse mask and red sneakers sitting on a chair on the sidewalk rocking out on his guitar.

We were in love.

The number of bars was a little overwhelming, but we found ourselves drawn into one by the female lead singer's deep, soulful voice. It was a blues/funk band, and next to the stage danced a pasty man wearing tap shoes decorated with glow-in-the-dark skeletons, his heels clattering rhythmically, the other dancers allowing him ample room to do his thing.

Ghaz and I ordered drinks, Umar a Diet Coke.

"To NOLA! And to homosexual urges!" Ghaz proposed.

After we toasted, she declared, "I love New Orleans! This is a city that knows how to *live*. I mean, look at this street, look at how alive it is. And this is a touristy street—imagine all the cool non-touristy places you can discover! I think I'm gonna stay here."

"What?" I said.

"I can't go back home, and now that my parents won't help pay for NYU, how am I going to afford the exorbitant tuition? It's one thing to have one hundred thousand dollars in loans, but two hundred, plus like another eighty for room and board? To study acting? How will I ever pay that off?"

"Well, you could talk to the financial aid office—"

"Why bother? I won't qualify for a free ride, which is what I need. It'll take me some time to figure stuff out anyway, and what better place than here? It's such a cool city, and way cheaper than New York. I'll find a job, a place, take a few acting classes on the side. You guys will come visit me. It'll be awesome."

Before I could respond, a cute guy who'd been eyeing Ghaz since we'd walked in made his move.

"Hello, beautiful," he said in a Scottish accent, which meant he had her at hello, "would you like to dance?"

"Certainly," she said, giving me her drink and accepting his hand.

"Do you think it's a good idea for her to stay here?" I asked Umar.

"Honestly, I don't know," he said. "She can't go home. But she has no support network here. Should we go keep an eye on her? She's pretty drunk."

Ghaz and the Scot were alternating between wild dancing and making out. At one point, they started spinning each other around, succeeding in knocking over the merch table, the skeleton-shoed tap dancer nearly crushing a few CDs as they slid beneath his feet. As the band looked on in dismay, a bouncer came over to kick Ghaz and the Scot out. Ghaz dashed over to us, grabbed our hands, and said "Run!"

"What happened?" Umar said as we ducked into another bar. "He was hot."

"Rodent breath, alas," Ghaz said, but we didn't hear more because the band began a pumped-up rendition of Stevie Wonder's "Superstition," to which you had no choice but to dance. After a few songs, we left, thinking we'd go home, but as we passed the next bar, the music beckoned yet again, and we danced for a song, and then we said we were definitely going home, but as we walked by the next bar the same thing happened. When we ran out of bars there was the brass band of teenage boys who'd started playing in the street, and as exhausted as we were we couldn't stop moving. With all this eating and drinking and dancing it was a wonder people in New Orleans got anything done.

By the time we finally called it, Ghaz's feet ached so much she was hobbling down the sidewalk barefoot, heels in hand, taking drunken swigs of toxic green Gatorade, while insisting we walk for a bit. We wandered away from the revelry of Frenchmen Street, stopping to give a few bucks to two homeless teens with a mangy dog. When we passed a side street lined with elegant, lamp-lit houses, Ghaz pointed at a stoop.

"Sit," she said.

The stone steps were just big enough to fit the three of us across. We let out a collective moan as our bums hit something solid. It had been hours since we'd been still.

There was a party at the other end of the block, in a redbrick house with lovely arched doors that opened onto an ornate balcony, funky soul music and peals of laughter floating downwind toward us.

"The city is so full of mirth!" Ghaz exclaimed. "Do you think it has a dark side?"

"Voodoo," Umar said.

"Katrina," I said.

"Poverty," Umar added.

"Endemic racism," I said.

"Of course. Everything has a dark side, doesn't it?" Ghaz gulped the rest of the Gatorade then set down the empty bottle. I made a mental note to make sure it was recycled.

"So you guys," I said. "I think I want to visit India."

"What will you do there?" Ghaz asked.

"I don't know—travel. This trip has been intense in so many ways, but it made me realize, sometimes it's good to get out of your comfort zone. India is completely foreign, but I also have roots there. I think it would be interesting to see what I'd discover."

"It'll be your *Eat, Pray, Love*," she pronounced.

"Um, no. More like . . . Explore. Wander. Ruminate," I said.

"Ruminate on Rumi," Ghaz said.

"That's terrible," Umar told her. "Plus, isn't Rumi from Iran?"

"It's a pun pun pun," Ghaz sang, and nudged him. "What would our Umar darling do if he went to India?"

"I know," I said. "Sigh. Shop. Dance."

"Sign me up," Umar said. "But I've decided to do something, too. When we get home, I'm going to get in touch with the people who run that queer Muslim retreat."

"Awesome!" Ghaz declared. "So, this time next year, Mars will be in India, Umar at gay Muslim camp, and I'll be living in one of these lovely apartments with French doors that open onto a moonlit balcony."

"Ghaz," I said, "are you sure about this plan of yours?"

"Why wouldn't I be?" she said, and slung her arm around me. "So, if you do go to India, will you get in touch with your dad's relatives?"

"I don't know," I replied. "Maybe. But what if they're all like my uncle?"

"You ever hear from Uncle Sanjeev Sharma?" Umar asked.

"Nope. Probably better that way."

Ghaz shook her head. "Your father's younger brother is supposed to be the cool relative, but mine's a dick, too. Ugh. Even mentioning him makes me sick."

Sanjeev Uncle was actually my father's older brother, but I didn't bother correcting her; she'd adopted a protective posture, legs into chest, chin resting on her knees, her eyes, distant and contemplative and sad, offering a rare window into the closely guarded secrets of her heart.

"Ghaz," I said. "What is it? What happened with your uncle?"

She didn't respond. Umar and I glanced at each other.

"Did your *chachu* do something to you?" Umar asked gently.

"You wanna know what my *chachu* did?" she said, and let out a laugh. "Of course you do. You want me to spill my tea, the real tea, the kind that burns your throat to say it? Fine. I'll tell you guys, but only if Mars does something."

"What?" I asked.

"Call Doug."

"Seriously? And say what?"

"That you're sorry, and you loooooooove him."

"I actually was going to tell him I'm sorry, but I was thinking I'd email him after we got back."

"Lame."

"Ghaz—"

"Lame."

"But—"

"Deal or no deal? Plus, considering the situation, don't you think an email apology would be a cop-out?"

Her secret would probably depress and worry me, but it would be one less secret that she had to carry alone. And she was right—an email apology was a cop-out. After ghosting as I had, a phone call was the least I could do.

"Fine," I said, marveling at how even the possibility of hearing Doug's voice made my heart beat faster. "I'll call him."

Ghaz clapped her hands. "All right! Mars and Doug, sitting in a tree! Mars and Doug, in sweet *Monty Python* love again!"

She reached for the Gatorade bottle. Realizing it was empty, she threw it aside. I leapt up and retrieved it, placing it safely between my feet.

Ghaz smiled. "I did that to make you jump."

"Ha-ha," I said.

She shook her head. "How are you going to handle India? In South Asia people have no qualms about throwing trash out their car windows."

"You had something you wanted to tell us?" I reminded her.

"What? Oh, yes. God, you guys are suckers for sob stories."

"Your *chachu*," I prompted.

"Oh, my *chachu*. He was my favorite relative. He'd always play with me when I was a kid, say the nice things my momma never did. *You know why they named you Ghazala? Because a gazelle has the most beautiful eyes.* When he told me that, I coasted on it for weeks. He'd always bring me Starburst because I loved them. He'd ask me trivia, usually things I ought to know, and if I was right I got a Starburst. And he'd read me and my sister stories, and he'd be all dramatic, like if he was reading about a lion he'd get down on the floor and roar. Not many desi uncles will get on the floor and be silly with the kids, you know?"

My stomach was already twisting into a knot. This did not sound like it would end well. By the end, Ghaz would surely be hurt.

"He didn't visit for a while, and when he came back I was eleven. I already had my period, and I had tits." She cupped her breasts, lifting them slightly. "My mom took me to Target to buy bras and she was so pissed the whole time, like it was my fault that I had boobs so early, and nice ones, too.

"Anyway, he's visiting, he's married now, his wife is super pregnant. She was nice to my brother and sister but cold to me. And my mom was watching us carefully. She wanted to make sure I wasn't familiar with my uncle like I used to be, now that I had tits. But I felt different, too. I wasn't about to sit next to him on the couch and ask him to read a story. And I'd seen him stealing a glance at my chest at the dinner table, when my *dupatta* fell to my waist. A few minutes later, my mother called me to the kitchen and yelled at me for not keeping it up.

"She was like, 'Do you want people to think you're a slut who likes to show off her chest?'

"And I didn't, but the truth was, I kind of liked it when he looked."

She stopped there, glancing up at the redbrick house. The party had diminished to a few lingerers in the corners of the balcony, conversing softly to a soundtrack of mellow jazz.

"Harry Potter," she said. "The third one, the best one. I couldn't put it down, so I stayed up late, reading it under the covers with a flashlight. When I heard my door open, I thought my mom had come to yell at me, so I turned off the flashlight and hid under the covers, hoping she'd think I was asleep. But it wasn't my mother; I could tell by the way the person was breathing, by the heaviness of the footsteps. He didn't come all the way to the bed, but I could smell his sandalwood perfume. He wore it every day—his clothes smelled like it. I tried to stay really still, pretend to be asleep, but oh my God, my heart. I thought it would leap out of my chest and hit him in the face. There was this weird sound, like slapping. It didn't last long, a few minutes. One of my feet was sticking out of the blanket and it twitched and I was so nervous he'd know I was awake. I heard him suck in his breath, and then I heard him leave and shut the door.

"When my mom came to wake me up in the morning, she freaked out; she grabbed me and started shaking me, saying, 'What did you do what did you do?' I kept saying *nothing*, and she slapped me and pulled my hair and said, 'Don't lie, I can smell him in your room.'

"I don't know why I felt like I had to protect him, but I said he came in to give me a book, but I'd already read it. But I also said it to protect me, you know, because I didn't think my mother would ever believe me."

Ghaz paused. Umar had been squeezing my arm ever since her *chachu* had entered the bedroom, hard enough for me to know it was time to trim his fingernails.

"My mom never brought it up again. My *chachu* moved to the West Coast, so I didn't see him for a long time. Then, when I was fifteen, I hooked up with this guy and he told me to go down on him and I said no because I'd already decided I didn't like how pushy he was. So, he started jerking off, and I thought, I know that sound, that's the same sound my *chachu* was making that night. He was watching me, I mean, not even me, the outline of my body as I lay under the covers in the dark, and jerking off."

"Have you seen him since?" I asked.

"I saw him at a wedding a few years ago and it was all I could do not to spit in his face, because apparently, the desire to spit in other's people faces runs in my family. And there you have it. My *chachu*'s secret. My secret." She leaned back on her elbows. "In vino veritas."

"Oh, Ghaz," I said. "I'm sorry."

"Yeah," Umar said. "Me, too."

"Is that the piece of the puzzle you wanted?" she asked.

"What?" we said.

"Is that the clue that explains my sexual promiscuity, which, by the way, is partly a figment of your imagination because I haven't had sex in months. Does it explain my desire not to have serious relationships? Listen, I know that I have had fucked-up things happen to me, but I'm not going to let it define who I am. I won't let it. And if there's anything that's messed me up, it's my mother. All I've ever wanted in my entire life is for her to say, 'Ghazala, I love you, Ghazala, you make me proud, Ghazala, you have nothing to be ashamed of, Ghazala, I'm sorry I hit you and called you all those terrible things'. I got an email from my friend today; she said the billboard's gone, there's some Swatch ad there now. It wasn't even up a month, and I thought, was it worth losing my family? But then I thought, I never really had one, not in the way I wanted. My father has never once stuck up for me in front of my mother. Even when he thought she was being too harsh. The bitter irony of my life is that it's when I'm with my family that I feel the most alone."

Before we could respond, she jumped up, stretched her arms toward the sky. "I'm done," she said. "No more depressing talk. And I'm hungry! Come on, get up! Let's find some Cajun nachos, stat."

Thirty-three

WHEN WE GOT BACK to the hotel, I stayed down in the courtyard to call Doug. It was four thirty a.m., and I figured he wouldn't answer, that it would go to voice mail, I'd leave a heartfelt message of apology, the ball would be in his court.

Except he answered on the fifth ring, the last ring, the one where you're convinced it'll be a missed connection.

"Hello."

"Doug? It's Mariam."

"Mariam. Hey. This is a surprise."

"Did I wake you?"

"No, I was up. Drove out to the mesa to stargaze. Just got back a little while ago."

"Must have been beautiful."

"It was."

"Any shooting stars? Comets?"

"Two shooting stars."

"Wow."

"Where are you?"

"In New Orleans, on a road trip."

"Ah," he yawned. "Now I know why you're up so late."

"I came with Ghaz and Umar."

"How are they?"

"Okay. I mean, things are . . . so complicated I don't even know where I'd begin."

A pause, then "Mariam? Did you call to talk about something specific? It's pretty late."

"I know. I'm sorry. Which is also what I called to say."

"What?"

"Sorry. What I mean to say is that I called you because I want to apologize."

"Okay."

"The way I treated you was cruel. I was falling in love with you and I completely freaked out. I guess I was thinking of how my father left us, how love means you're going to end up hurt one day."

"You could have talked to me about it. We could have slowed down."

"But I was already in too deep to slow down. And I was

worried—no, I knew you'd convince me to stay with you if we talked, because it's what I really wanted. So, I cut you out of my life, I ghosted, except I haven't been at peace since. I was unkind to the kindest person I know. Can you forgive me?"

"Nah, I'll be angry at you for the rest of my life."

I swallowed. "Really?"

"I'm kidding."

"Oh."

"That would hurt me as much as you. Honestly, I was upset, and sad, and confused. But you seemed so adamant, after a few tries I thought I should respect your desire for space. And yeah, my heart broke a little. I'd talk to Ellie about what you did, and one day she said to me, 'Imagine life as journey, and you're only allowed so many things in your backpack. What are you going to carry with you? Do the things you carry sustain you in some way?' It made me think. Carrying around resentment was only sustaining more resentment. That's not who I am—who I want to be. Like you don't want to be unkind."

"Who's Ellie?" I asked.

"My girlfriend."

The G bomb. Of course. How could I not have guessed? A guy like Doug wouldn't stay single for long. "You have a girl-friend?"

"She's interning at the museum with me. She's great. You'd like her."

Oh, we'd be best friends, me and Ellie of the wise aphorisms.

"I miss you," I said. "I'm not sure if I'm allowed to say that, but I do."

"I miss you, too. Well, the pre-April you."

"Do you remember when you used to invent silly dances to make me laugh?"

"How could I forget? I think my favorite remains stampeding elephant caught in revolving door."

I laughed, and so did he. It felt nice, to be laughing together over a shared memory.

"I blew it, right?" I said. "You and me?"

He hesitated. "Are you asking me if we could get back together?"

"No. Yes. Maybe?"

"If you'd asked me before the semester ended, I might have said yes, that maybe we could move past what happened, maybe it could even make us closer, but I'm in a different space now, literally and figuratively. It's going really well with Ellie."

Damn Ellie. But Doug deserved someone who made him feel good. "Well, I'm happy for you," I said. It wasn't really a lie, because I *was* happy for him. In theory.

"Thanks. And thanks for calling. I was hoping we'd get some closure."

Closure. More like having the door slammed in my face.

"Yeah, me, too."

"Sleep well. Sink into some beautiful dream."

"You too."

It would have been worse, I consoled myself, if he had been angry or bitter. The good place he was in had helped him forgive me, and, even if I'd ruined us, at least I hadn't ruined his prospects for happiness. But I hadn't ruined mine, either. I didn't believe there was only one person you were meant to be with. I didn't doubt I'd fall in love again one day. But if Doug wasn't the only, what if he was the best? What if, for the rest of my life, none of my other loves ever quite measured up?

When I returned to the room, Ghaz was sleeping with one leg off the bed. As I gently settled her back onto the mattress, I thought, *I'm going to be okay*. Even if I did inherit a flight response from my father, I also had some of my mother's steely core. And, I had my mother. But what about Ghaz? How could I make sure she was okay? What did you do when your family was not the solution but part of the problem?

But we were her family, too, Umar and me. And it was time for us to step up.

I tiptoed out of the room, returned to the courtyard, and called my mother. It was six a.m. in New Jersey but she was already up, making her morning smoothie.

"I need your help," I said, and she listened.

Back upstairs, I poked Umar's side till he woke up. In a series of whispers under the covers, I told him of the plan my mother and I had come up with.

"You have to try to convince her," I said. "I think she'll listen if it comes from both of us."

"What if she gets upset?" he asked.

"If she's upset, she's upset. She knows we love her and we only want to help. She won't be upset forever. Come on, Umar. We can't keep ignoring this. What she's been through, it can't be laughed off, or danced away."

"Yeah, I know. Okay. You bring it up, I'll back you up."

"Deal."

Umar rubbed his eyes. "What time is it? I might as well pray Fajr."

Ghaz woke me at noon, her self-proclaimed hangover from hell having no effect on her energy level. "Another beautiful, sweltering day in the city of sin!" she cried. "Let's go eat!"

I muttered my assent and she moved on to Umar. As I walked to the bathroom, I saw Umar's prayer rug was still spread out on the floor, one corner folded over. I hoped he had asked Allah for Ghaz to say yes to my plan.

"So," I said as we were walking to the French Quarter. "I called Doug last night."

"Shut up!" Ghaz said.

"And?" Umar said.

"I apologized. He said he'd already forgiven me. He has a wonderful girlfriend named Ellie. He's happy."

"Stupid Ellie," Ghaz said.

"Oh, man," Umar said. "Sorry."

"It's all right. I mean, what did I expect? Stuff like that only happens in the movies."

"You mean, you'd call him," Ghaz said, "and he'd be, like, 'I haven't stopped thinking about you either', and then the next morning there'd be a knock on your hotel room and he'd be standing at the door, with a single red rose and a vegetarian breakfast burrito."

Umar sighed. "Wouldn't that be nice."

"If it'll happen to any of us, it's going to be you," Ghaz assured him. "Ali seems like the red rose type."

"He hasn't texted me."

"Have you texted him?" I asked.

"I only met him yesterday!"

"Well, he's probably thinking the same thing," Ghaz argued. "Oh—this is it!"

The hole-in-the-wall Cajun joint Ghaz had chosen had a line outside. I thought about broaching the subject of Ghaz's future as we waited, but figured these conversations always went better with some food in the belly.

After we were seated, Ghaz ordered a shrimp po boy and a Bloody Mary.

"Drinking so early?" Umar said.

"Uh, it's the afternoon. And a Bloody Mary's not a real drink. It's, like, vitamins with a little vodka. Look, it even comes with celery."

"Nothing about New Orleans involves a *little* vodka," I corrected her.

"Mmmmm . . . ," she said, taking a sip. "I should really learn to make these now that I'm going to live here."

Umar raised his eyebrows at me. I nodded to assure him I had a plan. If Ghaz noticed the tension, she didn't mention it. Once we were halfway through our meal, I said, "So, about you moving here. I—we don't think that's a good idea."

She narrowed her eyes, picking out celery from between her teeth with her pinky nail. "Why?"

"You need a support network right now," I said.

"Yeah," Umar chimed in. "You don't know anyone here."

"I never have a problem making friends," she countered. "Did I not bring the three of us together?"

"I'm not saying you shouldn't move here at all," I said. "I have a proposal."

"This is because I told you about my *chachu*, isn't it? I freaked you guys out! See, this is why I keep some things private, because you tell people something and they think you must be all damaged. Listen, it's cool. Seriously. I'm not, like, secretly cutting myself because my uncle jacked off in front of me when I was young."

She smiled, elbowing Umar as if he were in on the joke, as if it were a joke at all, but he shook his head. "At least listen to Mars's plan," he told her.

"What is this, an intervention?" she groaned. "Fine. I'm listening."

"I talked to my mom," I told her. "She said you could come stay with us for the rest of the summer, longer if you needed to. We can go to the NYU financial aid office together, see what the possibilities are. Maybe you could stay at NYU, or maybe you can transfer to a cheaper school. But come to my house, and let's at least figure out what all your options are."

"So, rather than live in this vibrant city with no last call, where I guarantee you I will meet all kinds of people and have insane adventures, you want me to go back to New Jersey and crash with you and your mom and your brother, who refers to me as Hot but Batshit Crazy?"

"I told you that?" I said, surprised. "He doesn't really mean it, the batshit part. And it will be good for him to have more strong women around. Listen, we explore your options this summer, you can work, save some money, and if, at the end of the summer, you still think moving to New Orleans is the best plan, then that's what you should do. I'll even help you pack, I promise. And believe me, I also have a lot of stuff I need to process when we get home."

"Like what?" she said.

"My dad, Doug, the state of America. But let me finish my proposal. You come stay with me, explore your options. There's only one condition."

"Here we go. Spill it—no wait." She picked up her drink, tossed the straw aside, brought the plastic rim to her lips, drank every last bloodred drop, set the cup down, and burped. "Now spill it."

"My mother wants you to see a therapist. We both do."

"Are you serious? Don't therapists cost money?"

"We'll figure it out," I assured her.

"It's a good idea, Ghaz," Umar said.

"Says the guy who's still in the closet!" She shook her head. "I need some air."

"Wait—where are you going?" I called out, but she didn't stop.

"I'll get the check," Umar said. "You go after her."

But when I stepped outside, she'd disappeared. We were at the edge of the French Quarter, so she'd either headed deeper into the neighborhood, or one block down to the Mississippi River. I guessed she'd headed for water, and ran down Decatur, over the railroad track, up a set of stairs to the boardwalk. I didn't have to walk far to find her, sitting cross-legged on a green mesh bench facing the water.

"Hey," I said, pausing a few feet away. "Okay if I join you?"

"If I say no will you go away?" she replied.

"Probably not."

She smiled. "Have a seat."

I texted Umar our location, and we watched the parade of perspiring tourists, more than a few drinking from giant cups that said *Huge Ass Beer*. A musician wearing only striped bike shorts and a baseball hat stood at the edge of the boardwalk, playing a mournful tune on his trumpet. The river itself was murky and busy with ships of industry, barges and tugboats and tankers. It wasn't exactly beautiful, but the breeze was nice.

I was relieved when Ghaz finally spoke. "Look, it's not that I don't know I have lots to process. And I'm not actually opposed to therapy. I even thought about going to student counseling at NYU. But for someone to really understand, I'd have to tell my whole story, you know, from the beginning, all the things my mother has done, the things I did back, all the other crap that I've had to deal with. Plus, in spite of everything, most of the time, I really am pretty happy. And the idea of rehashing it all to a therapist, it seems so painful, and exhausting. I don't know if I'm strong enough to do it."

"Are you kidding?" I said. "You're one of the strongest people I know. Someone like your mother would have broken another person, made them angry and resentful, but you, you are so giving. It's not only that you're happy—you want others to be happy, too, you try to help people be happy. But I do feel like, the things you've gone through, it would be good to talk about it with someone, a professional. I'm not saying therapy would be a walk in the park, but you're way stronger than you give yourself credit for."

"One sec." Ghaz stood up, walked over to the trumpet player, dropped a dollar into his case.

"Your mother wouldn't force me to see my parents?" she asked when she returned.

"Of course not. You won't see them unless you want to."

"Are you sure your mom is okay with this?"

"You know my mom. She wouldn't have agreed to it if she wasn't."

Umar ran toward us, breathless and the sweatiest I'd ever seen him. He collapsed next to Ghaz, dabbing at his forehead with his scarf. "Sorry, went the wrong way. And now my ass is so sweaty my pants are stuck to it. What did I miss?"

"Ghaz hasn't said yes to my proposal, but she hasn't said no either."

"I'm considering it," she clarified. "I know you want the best for me, and I do see your point, but I'm not ready to make a decision right now. Can I think on it and give you an answer tomorrow?"

It was only fair.

"Sure," I said. "At the end of the day, we want you to be happy, and do what's right for you."

She nodded. "I'm sorry I got huffy back there. You both mean so much to me. If I didn't have you losers as friends . . ."

"Ah, look who's getting all sentimental," Umar teased.

"You should try it sometime," she teased back.

"Well, now that Ghaz has agreed to think it over, let's talk about me," he announced. "One, I have to hit the hotel because I desperately need a shower. Two, guess who I got a text from?"

"Ali!" I said.

Umar blushed. "I mean, nothing crazy, 'hi, how are you?'"

"That's amazing!" Ghaz exclaimed. "Do you want to invite him out tonight?"

"No, he's already left town. But I think we'll keep in touch."

I expected Ghaz to make some lewd riff on them touching, but she put her arms around Umar and me, drawing us close, then made a gagging sound. "Oh, Umar, you really do stink."

"Told you."

"Okay," she said. "Seeing as this potentially might be our last night here, and seeing how, no matter what, there's always something to celebrate, will you two promise me something?"

"What?" Umar and I asked in unison.

"That tonight, we don't stop dancing until the sun comes up."

And that was exactly what we did.

ACKNOWLEDGMENTS

This book would not have been possible without the guidance and support of my agent, Ayesha Pande; the wisdom and enthusiasm of my editor, Rosemary Brosnan; and the talented team at HarperTeen: Jessica Berg, Bess Braswell, Audrey Diestelkamp, Kristen Eckhardt, Erin Fitzsimmons, Olivia Russo, Cat San Juan, and Courtney Stevenson.

My deepest gratitude to Hamzah Raza for being resourceful as always, and to Afsana Ahmed and Ameer Khan for sharing their personal experiences and insights with me; it was a privilege to hear their stories.

A big thank you to:

Courtney Stevens and Ashley Herring Blake, for their warm Nashville welcome, advice, and generosity.

Christine Rogers, for helping make Nashville feel like home.

My sister, Mona Karim, who shared the back seat with me on all those family road trips to Toronto and Niagara Falls, and to my parents for introducing us to the joys of travel near and far. Saba and Arsal Ahmad, for making New Jersey one of my favorite childhood destinations.

Dipali Taneja, for keeping a sleep-deprived mother well fed as I worked on the proofs of this book.

Anand, Lillah, and Inaya, my three fellow travelers, *Na manzilon ko na hum rahguzar ko dekhte hain / Ajab safar hai ke bas humsafar ko dekhte hain.*

And to you, reader—thank you for including my book in your journey. Whoever, wherever, you are, may your travels begin and end with the fundamental human right called love.